# The World Beneath

The Mila Brand Adventures,
Book 1

Robert J. Crane

**The World Beneath**
The Mira Brand Adventures, Book 1
Robert J. Crane
Copyright © 2017 Ostiagard Press
All Rights Reserved.

1st Edition

# 1.

When I ran away, aged seventeen, I didn't do it for the usual reasons. There was no drug problem. No trouble with the law. I wasn't screwing up at school. And I didn't hate my family either, although I'd be lying if I said we got on well. No, when I ran away from home, I did it because I was looking for adventure.

I did it because I was looking for glory.

London; the Underground. Piccadilly Circus.

Back to the wall, I poked my head around to look out. I'd ducked into the short gap between opposite platforms. Easier not to be seen that way. Plus the wall was flat. None of the slightly awkward curves of the platform itself, like everyone within it was packed into an oversized Pringles tube.

Man. Pringles. My stomach whined.

"Shut it," I whispered.

It didn't last long. A train pulled in, regular like clockwork. As a blast of air was dragged alongside it from the tunnel, the smell became almost suffocating—stale and warm and filled with about a million lingering coughs.

The train slowed. On the platform, men and women clustered, guessing at where the doors were going to be. All the attention was on it, those within hurrying to get out, all without scrambling to get in.

Time to move.

I reached for my talisman. Strung up on a chain around my neck, it was teardrop-shaped, just a bit bigger than a pound coin.

I squeezed it. Gentle heat emanated into my palm. My fingertips pressed against an indented pattern, all swirls and crazy lines.

After shooting one last glance in both directions—the train came to a stop on my right, doors opening as it unloaded and filled up again, and the left-hand platform was near-empty—I raised my free hand, pointed at the wall, and swiped down.

A shimmering white hole opened in the wall. Edges weren't perfect; hunger had set me off at a bit of a shake—but the maw widened, pulsing with lights.

"You ain't got nothing on me, Harry Potter," I muttered, and stepped through.

The lightshow went into overload. For a moment, between places, I was almost blinded. Colors spun and flashed in a kaleidoscope, turning, turning, explosions going off with bright flashes, firework trails drawn across my eyes as white turned into yellow into red and then purple, going blue—

Then, as if some unfelt gelatinous membrane had finally given, I fell out.

I stumbled, caught myself one-handed before going down completely, skin dark against sand-colored rock beneath. My brown hair swum into view, jerked down by gravity.

I pushed up and—

The gateway had deposited me into a temple. Only this was nothing like any temple I'd ever seen, either on old documentaries or recreated in adventure games or breathed through words in adventure books. I mean, all right, there were a handful of passing resemblances—it was stone, for one, and yellow spiraled throughout as vines had crept in to reclaim this rock.

But the *angles* were wrong. No squares, no curving

statues. The walls were a hodge-podge of jagged bits, jutting forward and then jerking back, up and down, up and down into sharp points. Like the inside of a geode, I thought, blown up and stretched.

Or the mouth of a shark.

I reached to touch for the nearest jag. Its edges were captured in soft white light.

I ran fingers across. The edges were still sharp. And the points ... I prodded, and consulted my fingertip. It hadn't broken flesh, but I didn't doubt that it could given the chance. Tripping into the wall, for example ... that made me cringe. Raked by a thousand little knives on the way down.

I'd fallen into a hall, ceiling high above. Flat metal bowls hung from cords of rope; I assumed they were meant for wood to be burned for light.

Behind me, the hallway descended into gloom. But ahead: light. Soft, like the glow of a sun.

I safely stowed my talisman under my shirt after a quick check to make sure I hadn't shattered it on the floor when I'd almost brained myself, and trekked toward the hallway's end. My fingertips lightly trailed the jagged zigzagging to my left.

A tiny slice of this room had been visible from where I'd first landed. Now, though, its full majesty revealed, I gasped. Cool air filled my lungs, a subtle mossy taste on the back of my tongue. Fresh; none of the dead man's breath that was the Underground.

The room was huge, hundreds of meters across. Sure enough, a divot had been torn in the ceiling, a long gash, like a giant bear's claw had ripped through. Sunlight spilled through it. Roots crept around the edges, wide as my waist or even wider, but practically spindly lines from my vantage point. This was where the yellow ivy had come in, creeping down instead of up.

Walkways like shelves crisscrossed the walls, and holes whose openings gave way to deeper darkness beckoned.

From afar, these doorways were wrong too: all spiky angles, some *almost* square but not quite, most looking as if they'd been drawn by a child who could only produce short, sharp lines.

I'd been deposited on one of these—midway up, it looked like, based on the walkways on the adjoining walls.

Not, of course, that mine attached to either. That would be far too simple.

I shuffled to the edge, looked down.

The drop was long. Even surviving to the next ledge down was unlikely.

I scanned for a chip of rock that might have come loose, mostly out of curiosity. But there were none; this material was apparently immune to weathering. At least by time, anyway, I amended as I glanced at the gash in the ceiling. A real number had been done there.

The temple's midsection was filled with platforms. All were held in place by lonely struts—and like the walls, the doorways, even the platforms themselves, the struts, too, were oddly misshapen,. What should have been a straight line from floor to platform was a flattened zigzag, shifting jerkily back and forth without rhyme or reason. One that was particularly ridiculous caught my eye: so stupid were the jags that the platform it held was not even an inch above the point where the strut reared from the floor.

But there in the center—that was the most exciting, most breathtaking, of all. Not at all jagged, a rocky spine lifted skyward. Almost *literally* a spine: the rocks that comprised it looked like vertebrae. Floating and detached, they softly undulated up and down.

A ribcage surrounded it at the very top, the last twenty meters or so. Contained within was a cache, though impossible to see from my vantage point. And if I were right about where I'd been deposited …

"Decidian's Spear," I whispered. Could it really be here?

I glanced beneath me again. The nearest platform, kite-shaped (ish), was maybe midway between levels, just a tad closer to mine. I could make the jump, but I'd need to roll, unless I wanted to break my ankles. And though I could open a gateway beneath me if the worst happened, there was no telling where I'd end up—such as falling into the path of an oncoming train. Not ideal.

I took a breath, four steps back into the corridor from which I'd come ... then ran, and leapt—

Arms pinwheeling, I flew—

Feet touched the platform's edge.

I threw myself into an instinctive roll—

The platform lurched underneath—and I hit the edge as it shifted. Collapsing?

I jerked my hands out as half of me felt empty air. Scrabbled—

Caught.

I grunted. Dangling, and held only by my hands. By my *fingernails*, it felt like; they had caught an edge, and *damn* did they hurt.

*Do not snap,* I told them. *Don't you dare snap.*

I pulled. No hunger pangs now, but I felt my emptiness even over the surge of adrenaline, and so although fairly light, I struggled to drag myself back over the edge. That the thing kept up its incessant *shifting* wasn't helping ...!

"Work with me here!" I bleated stupidly.

Stomach cresting the edge, it was easier. I dragged my feet up and over, and receded from the platform's terminus.

Long breath loosed. "Spear. Think of the spear."

I shot another look in its direction—and gawped. The entire room was *moving*, platforms shifting, coming close enough to neighbors to practically kiss and then descending or creeping away again.

Forming a path?

I watched as the kite-shaped rock I'd landed on drew up, up ... and finally ceased, four or five feet from its nearest friend. They hung for just a moment—

Time to get off.

I pushed onto my feet, rushed for the edge again, leapt—

Landed, no roll this time. Almost as soon as I had, my new platform began its shift, turning uncomfortably underfoot. Like a tour guide, almost: *And here are the walls with the doors to ancient wonders ... and here we come around now to another little square for you to drop onto; and it is a bit of a drop this time, mind that gap, just like the Underground—only you won't land on tracks and be pulverized by the departing train, you'll drop some eighty meters to your death against rock and dank pooled water. Oh, and here we see ...*

I hit the next, bending legs to take the impact. Rising immediately, I scoured for the next place.

"Useless security system," I complained to any builder spirits who might be listening. "You're just taking me right to it!"

On I went, coming closer, closer, in an awkward dance that took me in every direction it could think of.

Nearer the central spine, I was close enough to see its vertebrae moving up and down. They were rocks, surely, not bones. They *had* to be.

The ridiculously off-center platform took me on a curving path around, close to the temple's floor. ('Close' being the operative word; still some thirty meters above, I could make out the detail now, see a crack in the floor, and water come in from thousands of years of rain—and skeletons and decayed clothing and rusty armor—but a drop would still pretty much gimp me.)

I swung around the spine, so close I could reach for it.

Yellow vines hung down, the shade of a ripe banana.

I stared up.

"Don't tell me I'm climbing. Do not—"

But I wasn't; not here, anyway. A last platform rose from beneath, not pausing, so I caught sight of it almost too late to *jump*—and then I was on it, rising beside the hundreds of stacked vertebrae, each almost as tall as me.

I stared as they passed. Reached out ...

My fingers met an invisible wall. Not totally inelastic; I suspected I could make it yield if I pushed just hard enough … but what would happen then? I pictured one of the vertebrae going with it, the entire length of the spine collapsing—on me.

The ribcage drew near …

My eyes lit. A room was enclosed, and I could see its floor, a minute shaft of light breathed out of a single crack.

And then the platform ceased moving.

I swayed in surprise, carried by momentum for a moment longer.

"Oh, no way."

It didn't recede. Just waited … two feet below the bottommost rib.

Teeth gritted, I belted, "You couldn't just make it *simple*, could you?" Shaking my head, I steeled myself. "All right. I'm going." A last aside to any lingering phantoms: "Spear better be damn well worth it."

If it was even here, of course.

It had to be. *Had to.*

Eyes on the rib—just the rung of a ladder; a bloody big ladder—I crouched low, and jumped.

The first time my hands slid off, and I landed heavily on my backside. A jolt of panic filled me at the thought of meeting my platform's edge—but I shoved up, checked it remained stationary, and leapt a second time.

I caught it, and hung.

"Monkey bars," I told myself. "Just, like … up."

The ribs were small, almost like those of a human, but not nearly as close together as ours. I needed to push myself to inject the force needed to reach the second— but I had it, and then the third.

When I was high enough to plant my feet, something gave a stony rumble beneath.

I glanced down.

The final platform was descending.

"Thanks for waiting," I told it. Then, to myself: "All right. Don't screw up now."

That would be just my luck. All this searching, jumping through gateways into the wrong worlds, finally landing in the right one, even finishing this stupid game of parkour the builders had set up as one last hurdle ... and then I'd slip and fall to my death with Decidian's Spear just meters from my fingertips.

What a positively pleasant thought.

With my feet on, I was able to climb much easier. It was just like a ladder, albeit the sort built into a wall: perfectly vertical, no angles.

Up I went, past vines snaking down. The gash did not run directly overhead, but angled rain could have easily come in this way and made my handholds slick. I was thankful it hadn't.

I rose, rose ... sweat burst on my forehead, licked by a gentle, cool breeze breathed in from above ... and then, at last—*at last!*—an opening rose to meet me. Carved between the ribs where the bottom of the sternum would have been, it led into a small cavity. And in the center ...

I pushed myself up, heart thudding madly in my chest.

"*Yes*," I breathed, stepping for it.

Atop a wide podium, it sat: Decidian's Spear, long and shined to a sheen, its pointed tip silver, as though it was new, not a thousand years old or more. Strange energy clung to it, infusing the air, making my skin break into gooseflesh—

"Search the chamber!"

I froze. Spun.

Along the nearest, topmost walkway, was a man. My age, maybe a couple of years older, he was dark-haired—and maybe handsome; even from here, the set of his jaw was so clear, square and sharp and perfect. A tight-fitting jacket betrayed the V of his chest.

He strode, every step rigid. But not awkward; this was a practiced gait.

"Who …?" I started whispering—and my breath caught.

The stranger must have come from one of the angular doorways—because from behind him, flooding out onto the walkway in droves, were an army of bulky, armored, green-skinned, ugly trolls.

No, not trolls.

Orcs.

# 2

I ducked back into the cavity, spear—okay, not *forgotten*, but for a moment out of mind.

Was this a guard outfit?

No. They were Seekers, too—or at least I guessed the man leading them was.

*Damn it!* Why couldn't I have beaten them here by a slightly wider window? Twenty more minutes to get in and out, that was all. Tiny, on the scale of time Decidian's Spear had been lost.

I crouched low, listening. Walkway to the left of this opening, there was no way the orcs or their commander would see me. But if any should flow out of the doors *opposite* in their search …

I grimaced. Television, movies, and books had decided for decades to write orcs off as unintelligent, practically useless creatures, threatening only due to their numbers.

I, on the other hand, knew better. Though neither smart nor stupid, their eyesight was solid.

Also the numbers thing. Did I mention the numbers thing? Because as far as I could count, this was one Mira Brand, against … at least a couple dozen orcs, easy.

"Mr. Borrick!" came a low voice across the expanse. "Something has activated the security system!"

A noise like a slap against metal echoed across to me.

"I'm not blind, Murshan. Search for intruders!"

The clunking sounds of armor echoed through the chamber as the orcs fanned out.

I pressed lower, cursing. Would they clamber onto the platforms and mimic my path out to the spear, to claim it for their leader? I couldn't see that. They were too bulky, even without the armor. The extra weight meant extra momentum—which meant a lot of overshooting.

But what if they could bypass it altogether? Whoever built this place couldn't have been stupid enough to have made the only way up here a game of stepping stones.

Didn't matter. The orcs might not be able to climb the moving platforms—but they weren't all orcs, were they? This Borrick fellow, he was as outwardly human as me. I didn't doubt that he'd be able to make his way across. Perhaps even more deftly than I had.

But that didn't matter either. The only important thing now was my exit. My *safe* exit.

Simple. I'd just open a gateway and pass through.

I frittered at my belt. Detaching my compass, I lifted it, held it beneath the light streaming in from above.

The worlds beneath connected haphazardly. It was true that you'd never know where you were going when opening a gateway—at least, if you were cutting in blindly. With a compass like this, though, I could see the points of connection. Could see if I were cutting through to some alien location like this temple … or was in danger of opening a hole to the bottom of an ocean.

I flexed it back and forth, willing it to yield …

A moor, enshrouded in mist, appeared across the compass's face.

My lips pursed. Not London.

I dared another look out of the opening to the spear's hideaway. No orcs this way, and none climbing the platforms ahead of me.

I could just cut through and hope for the best; make a blind trek back between worlds, back and forth until I found my way to London once more.

For a moment I debated it … then cursed, snatched up the spear, and leapt onto a platform as it drifted by.

"Mr. Alain, sir!" an orc roared. "Intruder!"

The entire mass swiveled as one. Thirty or forty of them, easily, spread across the closest walkway.

Closest to the front, Alain Borrick. Now I saw him clearly, and the handsome fellow was, indeed, my age. His eyes flashed at me.

"She has the spear!" a nearer orc cried. He—or she; never could tell, and it'd be rude to presume—reached over a shoulder, and withdrew a club, end covered in bony barbs.

All along the edge, others followed suit; I saw swords, knives … a whole bevy of implements I didn't want to meet the business end of.

"You want this?" I called, holding the spear overhead. "Gotta catch me first!"

I leapt onto the next platform as it passed, rolled, righted, and then immediately threw myself onto another.

What a terrible security system. Awkward to get to the spear, and impossible to appre*heeeend*—

I shrieked. The platform beneath me had abruptly changed direction. So close to the edge, my body arched almost comically as my middle tried to carry me forward but my head and feet pulled back.

The temple rumbled.

Disbelief filled me.

Every platform, as one, was moving in the same westerly direction—to the walkway covered in orcs.

Borrick's face brightened. He really was handsome, devilishly so, I saw as I was drawn across the shrinking distance between us. Chiseled, and yet smarmy. The kind of person, in a movie, some starlet would both yearn for and hate in equal measure.

No yearning from me. Nothing good waited for me over there, that much was clear by the hungry look on his face.

The platforms condensed into a line. Twenty meters

clear …

I glanced at the compass. Now I caught a glimpse of forest—green, not the yellow of the ivy, and pouring with rain.

"Give me the spear," said Borrick, "and you can leave. No harm will come to you."

I considered, just for a moment, eyeing it.

Freedom or glory. Freedom or glory.

Tough choice, at least for me.

"Nah."

And I broke into a sprint.

The line was not flat, each platform rising and falling six or eight inches as they finished coalescing. But they drew a straight path back to the doorway I was pretty certain I'd come from—and with it, the London Underground.

"GET HER!" Borrick barked. "But don't hurt her!"

"Mr. Borrick, sir, the gap—"

"JUMP IT!"

Clanking, the orcs leapt. A couple of cries signaled misses—but heavier noises overpowered them. Right behind me.

Platforms and walkway almost touching now, I sprinted. Borrick was just up ahead, and in a moment I'd be past—

I had a flash of him leaping, pushing me over the side, grabbing the spear from my hands before it went with me—

Not on my watch.

I swung the spear round at him. Not close enough to thrust. Enough to deter, though, the wide spearhead slicing through the air with a whistling sound.

He didn't move.

I screwed my face up at him. He smiled back—"You can't outrun them. Not on those little legs."—and then disappeared into an angular doorway to darkness at his right.

I hurtled down the line. It clunked into place at last. I wobbled, then caught myself, powered on.

The ledge I'd first looked out on was within spitting distance. A vine, caught from the ceiling, was trapped between it and the closest slab of kite-shaped rock; my first stepping stone. It was pinned in a U shape, rising above the platform again and snaking over the edge.

Borrick was right. I wasn't going to make it.

Another glance at the compass. A flash of orange: sand. Desert, maybe. Sahara?

A bellow went up from behind.

They were almost on me …!

The vine!

I wasn't seriously considering …?

Yes, I was!

Just as something behind me swung—I felt a breath of air against the back of my neck—I put on a desperate burst of speed, and leapt—*sideways!*

The platform disappeared, past my head—

I had one terrifyingly endless second to scream as I sailed—

Then I clutched at yellow as I slammed into the vine. It arced backward with me—*Please don't snap!*—

My hands barely found purchase—*Please don't drop the spear!*

And then I was sliding down, riding it until I released, praying neither my ankles nor Decidian's Spear snapped on impact, and crash-landed in a heap on the level below.

"Oww," I moaned.

"She's on the lower platform!"

"This way!"

They hurtled off, armor clanking above me, its volume barely diminished by the rock separating us.

I dragged myself up. I didn't know the layout of this place, but it would be just my luck that one of the corridors led to a staircase directly down here. I might have only minutes to drag my bruised butt out of here.

I lifted the compass, praying it was not broken.

It wasn't, thank goodness.

Better, it teetered. One half of the image looked like idyllic Scotland, with beautiful rises over a loch. The other half bore the unmistakable sign of an Underground station.

"Yes!" I whispered.

I moved down the nearest doorway. There was less light here. I hoped the border would vanish soon enough to give me a guaranteed gateway before I descended too far into its gloom, and would need to rely on my dim flashlight.

When the boundary was a quarter of the way across the compass face, London Underground sign dominating— Piccadilly Circus again!—a crash sounded from behind me.

I spun.

Still gripping the vine I'd descended on, a squat, dazed-looking orc blinked. He grunted—

I froze—

And then the cloud over his eyes passed. They set on me.

"Thief!" he bellowed—and charged.

# 3

I threw the spearpoint up in front of me, thrusting it toward him like a shield between us.

"Stop right there!" I cried.

The rage on his face dissolved, replaced with an expression of perplexity.

"That's right," I breathed. I jabbed, just to make sure. Then, one eye on the compass—still not a guaranteed path between worlds—I took a half-step backward.

"*No!* You are the one who has need to do the stopping!" the orc roared.

I paused, taking him—and that sentence—in. He was short compared to the rest of Alain Borrick's little army. The ruby red of his armor was grimy, boney barbs jutting in all directions from the pauldrons, gauntlets, and vambraces. One of the barbs, reaching skyward from a shoulder, was broken. Black had crept inside, like a fractured tooth had given up and gone bad.

A mop of messy black hair stuck out in all directions at the top, almost comically small against his oversized head.

"You didn't say 'Simon Says'," I muttered, backtracking yet farther.

"Stop your walking!"

I paused.

The orc grunted heavy breaths.

I dreaded him drawing close enough for me to smell.

"Listen, orc," I started. "I'm not—"

"Burbondrer!"

Another hesitation. "Huh?"

"I am Burbondrer of Ocklatojsh!" He hammered a fist as big as my head against his chest. Human armor would have buckled, irreparable, under the blow. The dully gleaming orc armor just vibrated. "And *you* are a thief!"

"Mira Brand, actually," I said, backing up another step. "And I'm no more a thief than you are." I hefted the spear. "Didn't see your name on this. Or Mr. Borrick's, for that matter."

"I said stop!"

"Yeah, well, I said it first."

"I challenge you!" Mop-head sucked in a deep, rattling breath. Inflating his chest, he said, in what I imagined was his most proper, officious voice, "Burbondrer of Ocklatojsh challenges the thief to fight *with honor*!"

"First, I told you already; it's Mira Brand. And second … yeah, no. I'm afraid I'm going to have to decline your challenge in favor of a subsequent engagement. And unfortunately for you …" I glanced up, stepping backward again. "It ain't fancy dress."

Burbondrer's face contorted in rage. Then he loosed a roar, magnified in the corridor. Gripping his club and bringing it around, he charged.

I jabbed—he didn't stop—and so I swiveled, hurtling down the hallway full of sharp edges with one eye on the compass, one on the floor so I didn't go sprawling. Shame I didn't have a third, on the base of my skull; I could use it to see how close he was to stomping my head like a bug.

The compass flashed as the sign for Piccadilly Circus overtook its face. I spun, eyes on the mop-haired orc, needing just seconds—

I didn't have them. He was almost on me.

I swung the spear up again, face height—

Burbondrer slammed to a stop. The sharp silver end of Decidian's Spear hovered mere inches from his bulbous nose.

"I'm not fighting you," I breathed. "So let's do us both a favor, and get to walk out of here without any new *holes*, shall we?"

Burbondrer considered, wheels turning behind his face. Then ...

"NO!"

He swung.

I dodged back.

Forgot their reach—!

Spines from the club's end sailed past, just an inch away from dragging across my stomach and sending my guts all over the floor.

I planted my feet again, and jabbed at Mop-head.

"I will use this!" I belted.

"Then do it! DEATH BEFORE DISHONOR!"

"I'd really prefer neither," I muttered as another swing went over my head. I ducked, and the club clattered into the wall. Chips of bone rained down over me—then I was scrabbling back, darting out from under Burbondrer's next swing, and bringing Decidian's Spear up to bear.

"I don't want to fight!"

"Nor do I!" he yelled, and swung—I yelped, dodging back. "But you cannot leave with Decidian's Spear." Another swing, at my legs. "The shame upon myself—my family, my name—I could not live with it!"

"You think that's hard to live through? Try catching a spear to the heart."

I stabbed at him. It drove into the space between his breastplate and pauldron. Tension pushed back for a fraction of an instant, then dissipated.

Mop-head screamed, high and ear-burstingly loud.

And then *I* was joining him, as he flailed in shock and a spiny barb from the club traced a long line up my forearm.

I stared at it in shock.

A deep crimson streak, softly widening as blood oozed

...

I yanked back Decidian's Spear. Deep purple liquid, thick like syrup, coated the point at its end.

I readied my feet for another swing ... but Burbondrer backpedaled. Clutching the wound with an oversized hand, he let the club drop. He followed, landing on his knees just short of me, hand extended upward, shaking, as though he were waiting for me to hand him the spear.

"I've failed," he said, ghostly quiet. "I ..." He lifted the hand from his wound. Dark liquid coated it. Not a lot, and even less considering the sheer size of him ... but his lips quivered.

I backed away, not entirely believing my eyes. He was kneeling there, useless, over just one jab? Orcs were supposed to be tanky, strong-willed, ready to sustain a thousand wounds and keep on fighting. And yet this one, daring enough to descend after me and challenge me to a fight I didn't want, had traded a battle-cry for a baleful look up at me.

Maybe he really was an adolescent.

He peered at me. Red rims outlined yellow eyes.

"Please." He hiccuped. "This is a task set by my elders." A sniffle snuck its way out. "I'll be made to look a fool. Again," he added, piteously. He was plainly holding back tears, his lip quivering as he awaited my response.

I felt ... pity. For an *orc*. What world *was* this?

"Yeah ..." I finally said, slow. Gathering myself together, I consulted the compass one last time. Definitely Piccadilly Circus.

"Look, I'm, uh ... sorry, or whatever, about this." And I meant it, kind of—which flooded me with another alien feeling. Almost as though I wanted to throw the spear down at his feet; give it to him, rejuvenate some of his wounded pride, and just escape from here empty-handed.

But I couldn't.

"I'm sorry," I muttered. "I just ... I need this more than you."

Reattaching my compass to its resting place, I gripped the talisman in one hand. Leaning the spear carefully against the wall, far enough that if this were a feint Burbondrer could not get to it in time, I swiped down.

The gateway opened, white and sizzling with frantic explosions of color.

Burbondrer stared—at it, as it widened, then me.

I collected the spear, held firm.

"Sorry," I said again, stupidly.

And as his head sank and his eyes closed, tears of utter defeat starting to stream down his face, I turned my back on the spectacle and stepped back through to my world.

# 4

Back into the Underground. In fact, except for being on the opposite side, I'd managed to re-enter in the same cut-through between platforms. Which was good, because except for a young man who smiled at me as he passed, no one had seen me.

Then I realized it was not my sudden appearance that had caught his eye, but the spear in my right hand—although now it was not a spear. It had shrunk, glamour over the top, so that it became … an umbrella.

An *open* umbrella.

How utterly innocuous.

"That's a bit of bad luck," he said. He was young, handsome, a blond-haired Adonis—and looking right at me as I held an open umbrella in the underground.

"I've done worse," I said. "Broke a mirror once a few years ago. Still working through the seven, but everything seems to be coming out all right." I held up the spear-turned-umbrella. "Guess I like to tempt fate."

"I'd say so. All the same, though, try not to run under a ladder when you go scrambling from the black cloaks in a few minutes, okay?" he asked, giving me a wink. "You seem a resourceful girl; I'm sure it'll all come out all right. Best of luck."

I pulled an uncomfortable smile at the departing man's back, wondering what the hell that was supposed to mean, and folded the umbrella shut, hoping it had started raining outside and I didn't look like a loon.

Given that there had been clear skies earlier, I probably looked like a loon. But he sounded like one. Black cloaks? What was that all about?

Never mind. I turned my eyes back to the umbrella; it could be a crossing guard's sign for all I cared, with a great big *STOP* written in blaring bold letters. Passers-by might think I was a mental, scruffy runaway who believed her calling was to help kids cross roads. And that was fine by me. Because *I had it.* After all this searching, all this *hoping*—I had found Decidian's Spear. Step one of my quest.

At long, long last.

After affixing the umbrella to my belt via a small metal loop on its base, I slumped against the wall, sighing. I'd be hungry again soon, and I'd have to find something to eat. Not a whole lot at my new digs. The adrenaline had kept me going, but now I'd stepped back into the stale embrace of the Underground, it fled all in one fell swoop, as though someone had opened a valve for it to run out of my feet and into a bucket.

Like bloodletting. Which I was doing a bit of, I noted, checking the scratch up my forearm.

That thought brought back the image of Burbondrer, kneeling on the floor of a temple he was sworn to protect.

A pang of sorrow filled my gut.

I fought to dismiss it. Why should I feel sorry for an orc? This one was in an army; he was supposed to be tough. It wasn't my fault that he found out too late he didn't make the grade.

It wasn't that, though..

*"I've failed."*

The words echoed.

I shut the door on them. Didn't matter. I needed the spear far more than some stupid orc did.

A train pulled into the station at my left. I eyed it with

distaste. I'd heard they whipped hair and dust and other grime down the tubes as they came and went.

People clustered in their usual way. The doors opened, and passengers clambered on while others departed, neither pausing to permit one flow to conclude before beginning their own.

Then they were bustling by, passing me as they joined the opposite platform, yet more streaming for the stairs.

Okay. This pause was enough. Breath caught, legs gone to jelly just a little bit, it was time to get going again.

I joined the queue filtering onto the stairs.

My fingers trailed the rail. The paint was red, but had gone dull, and was full of chips.

Again, I thought of Burbondrer.

Midway up, the lad beside me cleared his throat. "Anywhere you can, err, recommend?" His accent was American, although I couldn't pinpoint where; east coast, west, it was all the same to me. Only the south I recognized, for that stereotypical Texan twang, and I doubted that was remotely as pronounced among its peoples as TV and movies had led me to believe.

I glanced across, eyebrows knitting. "Me?"

He nodded, adjusting a thin pair of spectacles that were *way* out of style; the sort I'd expect to see on someone's grandparents, *maybe* parents, but only if they were on the older side.

"To visit," he clarified nervously.

"Uh … it's London."

"Well sure, I know *that*. Anywhere in particular?"

I blanched. Eyed the woman in front of me as though she might help out. Just the back of her head answered.

"Me?" I repeated.

He laughed, but there wasn't much humor in it. It was awkward—like he'd realized what a social klutz he'd lumbered himself with for travel advice.

"Err … well, I guess there's the London Eye …" We reached the top of the staircase. Light came from the end of a short walk that rose to another wide set of steps, then exited on the street. I ambled slowly, racking my brains, and finding they didn't particularly want to be racked. "Tower of London … um … oh, Buckingham Palace, I guess that if you want to see where the Queen lives, or whatever …the British Museum … uh … ."

Damn it. Why had every place in London utterly deserted me? All I had were a list of clichés—which were probably exactly the same as his own, whoever he was.

Up the steps, and on the street. Sure enough, clear skies, save the odd streak of cloud. As ever, London was positively heaving with people—most of them coming this way, making for the very station we now stood obstructing.

"Sorry," I muttered, edging aside.

I hoped my friend took it upon himself to make leave … but he came with me, dawdling awkwardly by my side.

Without stairs or passers-by to contend with, I could take him in fully.

He was tall-ish, or at least taller than me; maybe an inch shy of six feet, I reckoned. Brown hair, blue eyes—those ghastly frames!—and a round face. His skin was white, maybe a bit paler than most, which meant he fit right into 'sunny' England.

He had a sweater on, this deep green, almost brown number, like the skin of an avocado. A shirt collar stuck out around his neck, perfectly white, folded so tight that he could probably shave with it. Khaki trousers, and at the bottom, a pair of … were those *loafers*? I thought it was illegal for anyone under forty to chuck a pair of those on in the mornings.

He also sported a rather unattractive manbag, strap slung over his shoulder, clutched tight and close to his chest.

*Dork*. That was the word for him. I bet if he were visiting in winter, he'd have one of those ridiculous Doctor Who scarves—the sort you actually *needed* a Tardis to store, 'cos they were about seventy feet long.

Seriously though, who needs that much scarf?

Searching again for places, I ran a hand along my left arm—and hissed.

"Are you—" Then his eyes were on the long red line drawn up my forearm. They bulged, and he took a step back, hands out in front of him like I might try pressing it against his face. "Geez! How—when did you—"

"It's nothing."

"It's—*geez*, that isn't 'nothing'!"

"It's just a cut."

He closed his eyes, and then for good measure turned his entire head. Just in case somehow his eyelids dissolved, I guess. "I think I can see bone."

My eyebrows knitted. Bone? Drama queen much? All right, Burbondrer had sliced me pretty much from wrist to elbow, but it wasn't *open* or anything. If not for the length, it might be a cat scratch.

"It's not *that* bad."

He made a queasy sort of noise. "It's pretty bad."

I huffed. But figuring I'd do him a favor, for no reason other than I was worried he'd faint, head landing right in the path of an oncoming cab, I tugged at my shirtsleeves. The material was way more flexible than I figured this guy's shirt must be, and they unfurled with little more than a soft tug.

Buttoning the cuffs, I said, "There. Can't see it now. Happy?"

The guy dared a one-eyed look.

"Better," he said shakily. He cleared his throat. His glasses had slipped down a fraction, and he pushed them back up with a thumb. "Geez. Didn't expect to see …"

"How did you miss it? You were stood right next to it."

He looked like I'd just told him I could see some of *his* bones popping out; his face fell, ashen. "I was?"

"On the stairs. And up here—"

He shook his head, held up a hand. "Please. I don't want

to think about it."

"It's just a scratch."

"A scratch!" he cried.

"All right, calm down. No need to get hysterical over this." I waved my left arm. Thanks to the dark grey of my shirt, he was spared of any growing splotches of blood where fabric and flesh connected. Which hurt, by the way.

Sweater-geek took a calming breath. Another. A half-dozen, maybe.

I watched with a lifted eyebrow.

I *could* just leave … but this was kind of an experience.

Finally, steeled, he opened his eyes. Flashing an uncomfortable grin, he bustled aside for passers-by as a new flood poured from the Underground tunnel beside us.

He cleared his throat. "Sorry about that. Uh, I'm Carson." And he stuck out a hand.

"Um. Right. Mira—Mira Brand." I took his hand and gave a short shake. Weak, both of us. I guess neither of us expected to be shaking.

"Like James Bond!"

"Huh?"

"'Mira—Mira Brand,'" Carson parroted. He coughed. "Like the way Bond does it."

"Err … Bond starts with his surname."

"Well, sure, but it's close."

"I don't think it has anywhere near the same *punch* if he starts off with 'James.'" I pictured Daniel Craig introducing himself to some blonde stunner. *The name's James. James Bond.*

Eh. Not sold.

Anyway. What was I doing here? I'd got swept up with the nerd from out west, and started thinking of all the pop culture I hadn't missed these few months. Not ten minutes ago, I'd fallen back into the Underground with *Decidian's bloody Spear*, damn it. I needed to get back to my hideout with the thing.

"Right. I hope you have a pleasant trip. Maybe someone else can give you better travel recommendations while you're here. Or a tourist information board?" I was stepping away already, glancing around vaguely as if one might materialize. Then, back to Carson, widening the gap: "Maybe stop in a pub. You're over eighteen, right?"

A befuddled look overtook him. "Nineteen."

"Sorted. Bartenders probably get asked places to go by tourists all the time. And speaking of places to go …"

"Oh, *geez*."

White-faced, Carson lifted his right hand. He stared, horrorstruck—then turned it toward me.

A thin line of crimson stained his palm.

I paused. Consulted mine. Darker.

Then it dawned on me. "Oh yeah …" I'd patted my arm, hadn't I? D'oh. That was the whole reason he'd almost slammed face-first into pavement, and I'd been distracted enough to get caught here.

"Sorry," I said, kicking legs into motion again. "It'll wash right off. And, uh, I don't have any blood-borne parasites or infections, or I guess I didn't last I checked, but … I mean, we've got the NHS here, so if I've given you something, they'll treat you." Ten meters down the street now, almost free—and I still couldn't turn myself around.

Carson passed a baffled look back and forth between me and his palm.

Then he stepped forward.

"Hey—hey, wait up, would you?"

Damn it. Probably the first time Sweater-geek had been given the time of day by a girl. And okay, maybe that girl was bleeding, even shared a bit with him, but it probably didn't take much for dorks to fall in love. I remembered well enough at secondary school, spotty pox-faced Mira said hello to chubby little Eddie Monkhouse, *thinking he was someone else*, and he'd dogged me for a year.

Plus, this whole blood thing. Carson probably figured

27

I'd marked my territory.

"Look, I'm sorry, I don't know what you want—"

Carson was taller, half-jogging, and not walking backward. Distance halved, he opened his mouth to cut over me—then his gaze drifted past my shoulder. His mouth hung, eyebrows sinking low over those dangerously thin little glasses balanced on his nose.

"What are *they* doing?"

I followed his glance.

Men in black cloaks stormed up the street. There were three of them, tall and imposing, faces masked.

Like Moses parting the Red Sea, the crowd shifted aside for them.

My mouth dropped to match Carson's.

"Who—?"

As the distance closed, one of the men's cloaks shifted. Sunlight glinted—

My breath caught, chest constricted.

A dagger. And not one like any I'd ever seen. Eighteen inches long or thereabouts, it was wide at the hilt and narrowed to a slightly rounded point. Fullers were carved in its concave surface, troughs that made it looks as if long metal fingers extended along the blade.

"What are—?"

"Cinquedeas," Carson muttered. "They're, um, Italian, and, uh …"

The cloaked men stopped—right in front of us.

I gawped. They were so tall!

Carson began, "Um … can we help y—?"

Metal flashed again, from the man on the right—Carson's side. He raised the blade over his head, quick as a flash—

Carson flinched, nowhere near fast enough—

I sprang. Hands tight around his sweater, I *shoved*—

A strangled noise burst from Carson's mouth. He stumbled—

The blade sailed down—

I ducked low—still carried by momentum—I felt a whoosh behind my neck, and twisted away from it—

"RUN!" I bellowed at Carson.

And I dragged, pulling him into motion—he locked up for just a moment before following—and together we sprinted down the street.

Behind us, heavy footfalls followed, matching pace. Cries from people came, most from behind as the cloaked men shoved through in their pursuit. But there were others around us too, as I pushed, carving an opening of my own, Carson sprinting along behind—

"Oh *geez!*" he cried. "*Oh geez!*"

"Move those feet! They're gaining!"

Just ahead, another flood of people came from the entrance to the Underground. And beyond—

"I've got an idea!" I tossed at Carson, who seemed dragged along with me like debris to a gravity well.

"*Who were those people?*"

I pushed through the throng heaving onto the street, ignoring the inconvenient question as my mind raced to deal with the problem at hand. Someone yelled a particularly offensive string of words, but I was past, Carson alongside me—and the crowd reformed, like sponges coming back together.

Blocked from sight—for a moment. But how long that would last, I didn't know.

At the corner, a building was decked in scaffolding. Had been for an age, and I didn't often see builders climbing it. Which was good, because I needed to borrow their construction project for a little while.

I ducked into the scaffold.

Open windows, masked by plastic.

Good enough.

"In here," I breathed.

"What if it's not safe?" Carson grunted through gasps for air. "The structure might not be sound—"

"I like our chances better here than on the street, against

the cloaked men with the knives."

"Cinquedeas," he corrected me. The git.

Taking a glance backward—no sign of the cloaked men yet—I pushed against the plastic sheeting with all my might. It gave, but only a little, and for a moment I had the panicked thought that it had been stapled or nailed in—then something ripped—*tape*—and I fell inside.

"In!" I whispered to Carson.

He followed, ducking below the ledge.

"Help me with this."

Together we pushed the plastic back against the window. The tape remained stuck to three of its edges. With it aligned, I rubbed the tape against the wall on the left side of the empty window, hoping it would hold.

Carson, above me, gasped, "It's not sticking!"

"Well, make it!"

"I—I *can't*! It's just—"

He let go, and the weight of it sent the entire square to the floor, undoing my work—and opening a perfect hole.

Carson squawked, *"They're coming!"*

I lifted my head just over the sill—and sure enough, they there were, three men in cloaks and cowls, cinquedeas drawn as they hurtled down the street, to this building—and us.

# 5

"You idiot!" I shouted.

"I didn't mean to!"

No. But he could be at least a little more useful when men with knives were coming for me—well, us, now, apparently.

Although, maybe it was a little my fault too. Whoever these blokes were, whatever they wanted—although I had a good idea the *what* was presently attached to my belt, pretending to await rain—how likely was it *really* that they knew London? One open window in a building under construction wouldn't scream, *Hiding place!* It would just say, *Sloppy builders.* And how far out of the bounds of reality was that? Not remotely.

I gripped Carson's arm. No time to shout at him for screwing up the tape. We needed to move—and *now*.

"Get away from the window. Come on."

He moved, footsteps stumbling. "Where—?"

The room was large. I figured that maybe this was going to be a pub; it was so open and awkwardly shaped. The bar wasn't in yet, but it was marked out, a squashed but exceptionally wide U. The floor wasn't stained either. A snow of dust had fallen from sanding, I guessed, gone everywhere.

I glanced behind. Footprints?

Not that I could see; the dusty coating wasn't thick

enough for imprints to be obvious, and the off-white of the floorboards underneath matched it.

If someone cared to take the time, though …

I stepped over a discarded pile of tools set up beside a makeshift table. A doorway in the back—maybe to kitchens, or the staff room if this place was finished before the universe succumbed to heat death.

I prayed for stairs.

"This way. Quick. Move!"

Carson obeyed.

A normal square room, this, and no windows to duck out. Damn it.

From where we'd come in drifted the sound of a heavy body landing on plastic. A momentary scuffle—he'd stumbled, I guessed—and another thump; a hand landing on the sill to steady himself?

"Move!" I whispered.

We jogged through to the next room. Footsteps echoed on the floor—so much for a silent escape.

Three pairs came from behind us, loud and stomping.

"They're coming!" Carson cried.

"You don't say. Move it!"

Into the next—

There were stairs.

I dragged Carson to them.

Dusty, like the rest, a barricade was erected partway up. I could see, in my mind's eye, Carson panicking—*It could mean the floor isn't safe!*—but I'd underestimated him, because he shoved it aside.

It clattered into my knee. Jarring pain shot through me, hot and white.

"Hey!"

"Sorry!" he called, already close to the top.

I grunted.

Behind me, the three cloaked men had caught up.

I twisted, panicked.

"I don't want to fight," I called as the first hit the

stairs—

I gripped the barricade Carson had shoved so unceremoniously into me. Lifted it—

"—but I can *Home Alone* this thing!"

I lobbed the barricade down—

*CRACK!*

It slammed the first cloaked man in the face. He grunted, flailed backward, like the first domino in a chain—

I didn't hang around. Sprinting up the stairs, I crested the top—damn, this knee!—and hurtled through the next doorway.

"Carson!" I called.

From the next room: "There are more stairs!"

To his credit, he'd stopped at the bottom.

To rescind it, it didn't look as though he'd stopped for me. He gripped the banister, sucking in breaths like he'd run a marathon without preparing for it. His shirt collar had gone askew, one side sticking up by his ear. He retained his grip on his manbag strap, one-handed, knuckles white.

I moved past, grabbing him by the shoulder. "Up."

"To where? How long do we run?"

"Until we're not in imminent danger of being skewered."

"To the roof?"

"If we have to!"

"And then where do we go?!"

"I don't know! Down the scaffolding, maybe?"

"It's not all the way up!"

"Well, there must be a fire escape!"

"I thought we'd just go out a window into a back alley!" Carson heaved—and like Burbondrer before him, was he *sobbing*?

Well, of course he'd be sobbing. He shows up in London to sightsee, and ends up getting a knife pulled on him by some guys out of *Zorro*.

Third floor now. We could pluck another window covering clear and duck out onto the scaffold, make our way back to the street that way. But what then? Even supposing we made good time down the game of Jenga that the scaffolding undoubtedly presented, what would we do? Run forever? I didn't have the energy in me, not after Lara Crofting my way to Decidian's Spear and back. And the way Carson was going, he'd collapse of a coronary before we got back to the Underground.

"Right," I said, making a decision. "Okay. We get to the next set of stairs. Come on, quickly now."

"What are you going to do?"

"Make them go away. Come on, up!"

Carson booked it, pausing three-quarters of the way up.

"Higher. Right to the top."

He obeyed.

I'd stopped midway; high enough that a knife couldn't come through the banister and slice my Achilles, not so high that Carson would be in danger should things go south.

Heavy footfalls came from just around the corner. Five seconds 'til they were on me, ten tops.

I fumbled at my belt, unclipping—

"An umbrella?" Carson wasn't too exhausted to muster a tone of incredulity: "You know it's bad luck to open those indoors, right?"

"It's not an umbrella, and I don't see how our luck can get any worse at the moment, frankly."

The cloaked pursuers rounded the corner. Saw me on the stairs.

The lead—the one I must've spanged in the face, because his cowl bore a diagonal line of off-white dust—gritted his teeth and jutted out his chin, the only visible portion of his face. Cinquedea brandished, his foot met the first step—

I flung open the umbrella—

The glamour dissolved. The canopy, bright yellow and

red in alternating octants, disappeared. The metal rod lengthened, widening in my hand, stretching and stretching until it became—

Decidian's Spear, brandished right at them.

Behind, from Carson: "What the hell?" He sucked in a sharp breath. "Wait. Are you the Penguin's daughter?"

The lead, stopped in his tracks, gritted teeth, jaw flexing beneath the shadow of his cowl. He reached out his empty hand and flexed his first two fingers back and forth: *Hand it over.*

"No." I tightened my grip, two-handed, jabbing at the air.

He gestured again, more animated now.

Didn't these guys talk?

Ignoring the sense of unease creeping up my spine, I said, "You not hear me, mate? I said *no*. You know how much trouble I went through to get this thing? The spear's mine." I filled my chest. "And I will use it if that's what it takes."

The corner of his lip crooked up. He shook his head, slow.

"You don't believe me? What's that smear on the end, then? *Orc blood*, mate."

Carson, sounding as though he was on the verge of fainting: "*Orc blood?*"

"I'll use it again," I said. "I swear to you, I will use—"

Then there were sirens. Carried from the street, they blared, warbling as they came closer and closer.

"Police," I whispered. Someone had called them!

The cloaked men exchanged looks.

The lead jabbed a finger at me. All trace of the smile had gone now. His jaw was set—and for the third time, he gestured for me to hand the spear over.

Freedom or glory, for the second time today. Were these men sent by Alain Borrick, with talismans and compasses of their own to cut through to London, the way I'd found the temple and stolen the spear?

"I said no," I said one last time.

The man's jaw flexed. I thought he might bolt for me, take the chance—still three against one, spear or not—but the sirens reached apex. There were a trio, it sounded like, all just slightly out of step—and all coming from the foot of this building.

A moment later, a bang.

Echoing up the stairs: "*POLICE! LET'S MAKE THIS EASY, WHY DON'T WE?*"

Relief threatened to flood me. But the impasse had not ended. Until the police had us, and taken these men into custody, I could not relinquish my hold on Decidian's Spear. Even one second of hesitation would be enough for me to lose it, and everything I was working so hard for.

Another shout, closer: "WE KNOW YOU'RE UP THERE!"

The lead cloaked figure stepped back. He jerked his shoulders, twisted his neck. It cracked, low and unpleasant.

The cinquedea was stowed. His compatriots did the same.

Backtracking, they made for the nearest door.

Just before passing it, he looked back at me, eyes hidden by his cowl, mouth a thin line. Again, he said no words—but the meaning in the look was clear. This wasn't over.

Then they were gone.

I didn't release my hold on the spear.

"They'll run into the police," Carson whispered.

I shook my head. "They won't."

"But how—?"

There were new footsteps now, clomps echoing around this sanded wooden chamber.

If they hadn't shown up, this place might've been our tomb.

Wasn't, though, was it?

When the steps were close enough, I let the spear's

glamour descend. It shrank, canopy sprouting again, each section filling brightly.

The hitch in Carson's breath as he watched was audible. I should've glanced back to see how large his eyes bulged, how close they came to bursting out of his head like a pair of ping pong balls. Heavens knew I could do with the laugh after today—and after what was about to happen.

The first officer, a middle-aged man with receding dirty blonde hair, rounded the corner just as I was folding the umbrella closed. His eyes fell to it first, flashing with confusion. Then he was at the bottom of the stairs, one hand extended.

"Afternoon, kids. Want to tell me what you're doing in here?"

"We had to run," Carson blurted. "There were men with cinquedeas—"

"Cin-what?"

"Knives," I said. Sinking onto the step, I held my head in my hands. Exhaustion had come at last, and I had no choice but to fall into its embrace. "Blokes in cloaks with knives came after us. That's why you're here, right?"

"We had reports of an altercation," the officer said. "Anyone else in here besides you two?"

I shook my head. "No."

"There were!" Carson said at the same moment. "But they've gone—"

"All right." I guessed the officer saw babbling like this a lot. Not the time for it now, especially with floors above us still to check. "Why don't you come down with us?"

"You're—you're letting us go?"

"Well, I'd prefer if you came to the station."

*"The station?"*

Poor Carson. His sightseeing plans had been well and truly demolished.

If only he hadn't followed. All of this could be avoided. For him, anyway.

"Just to answer a few questions," the officer said. "What

do you say?"

Carson didn't respond. I didn't need to glance back; I could imagine his face well enough, his mouth hanging, opening and closing like a goldfish in a tank.

"Fine," I conceded with a sigh. "We'll come."

I rose, eased down the stairs. Every step was heavy—defeated.

Carson took a moment to move. But I glanced back, and jerked my head. Obediently, like a child, or maybe a puppy, he followed. Like mine, his legs didn't seem to want to work. He reached over himself to clutch the banister with both hands.

By the time Carson had caught up, the officer had called for backup. His partner arrived, a stern-looking overweight man with a greying mustache and a shaved head. He conducted a pat-down, and ordered me to turn out my pockets. Checking the miniature flashlight, he popped the batteries and pocketed them, then handed it back, plus my Railcard. He gave the objects on my belt a particularly scrutinizing eye, umbrella especially.

"Supposed to rain today, is it?"

"Well, it is London," I offered in return.

The stern-looking officer walked us down to the building's ground floor.

Police cars were pulled up outside. A pair of coppers stood alongside one, chatting.

They raised eyebrows as Carson and I were led outside.

"Trespassers," our escort muttered. "Brady caught them."

"All right. In the car, mate," said one. To me: "You, the other."

I obeyed. No choice. And though I figured I could maybe put on a burst of speed and find myself a quiet corner for just long enough to cut through, what would the point be? I'd run away, but London was still my home. I couldn't leave it entirely—especially when my work here wasn't done. Better to go along with this and answer their questions rather than duck away and end up on some wanted list. That was the last thing I needed—especially given the skulking necessary to find places to cut through.

So, with a crowd meandering but watching what all the fuss was about, I climbed into the back of the police car.

I looked back. Carson had obeyed too. Through the window, he stared at me, somewhere between baffled and broken.

For all the good it did, I muttered, "Sorry"—for the second time today.

# 6

I'd seen interrogation rooms on TV and in movies before.

The one I found myself in was dead on. No windows; nothing remotely interesting or exciting whatsoever. Plain floor, utterly bland table, camera in the corner pointed at it—at me, on one side.

On the other paced Constable Lawrence Heyman. He was not totally dissimilar from the bobbies who'd apprehended me and Carson. Shirt, jacket, number printed on the shoulder. No hat. And no stab vest either—no need, in here; I'd been patted down enough times. Just the once was enough; I'd had damn near everything taken from me. Only my talisman remained, dangling as it was now from Heyman's fist, plus the flashlight in my pocket, sans batteries. Oh, and my Railcard. Couldn't lose that.

Heyman was an imposing sort of man, I supposed. Less bulky without the stab vest, to be sure, but still threatening enough. Or maybe that was just the uniform doing its thing.

He frowned. Well into middle-aged, he was fighting off the jowly look, but I reckoned another can of lager or two each week and it would have him. No facial hair, but his eyebrows made up for it: the same salt-and-pepper as the hair on his head (and it was mostly salt), they were bushy great things. I wondered if he had to comb them down to get his helmet on.

"Where'd you get this?" He lifted the talisman. Its pendant swung like a pendulum.

"Family heirloom. I didn't nick it, if that's what you're accusing me of."

He laughed, a short braying noise. Shaking his head, he lowered it gently onto the table: pendant first, then the chain, coiling around.

"I'm just curious," he said. "It's a pretty thing." He took a seat and pushed it across.

Distrustfully, I took it and put it back on, stashing it beneath my shirt.

"What's the pattern?"

"I dunno. Some tribal thing, I guess."

"Certainly looks it."

I was quiet.

Heyman's eyes drifted over me. I imagined how ratty I looked: hair a mess; clothes creased like they'd made their way to me down the side of Everest; face blotted with dust—and, on my left sleeve, a slowly darkening line. I hadn't noticed it until it was pointed out, but apparently the space-grey sleeve had failed to hide the soft ooze of blood from my encounter with Burbondrer.

If I saw Carson again, I dreaded to think how he'd react to it. Probably faint dead away and crack his skull open like an egg.

I suppressed a grimace. *If* I saw him again. Which was not likely. He was somewhere in this building with me now, I figured, being asked about his side of events. We'd probably be let go around the same time—nothing they could pin on us, except for trespassing, I guessed, but even that was dubious after all the eyewitness accounts of men wielding daggers chasing after us.

I'd make a point of getting away quickly this time.

Although potentially not *immediately*. It was his fault I was in here, after all, and he deserved reminding of it.

Although … it was hardly his fault we'd been pursued,

was it?

I told myself to shut up. This was no time for sympathy or understanding.

"Run me through this again," Heyman said. He'd been taking notes, and he fished out the clipboard from under his arm, filled with scrawl. Completely impenetrable, by the look of it. He should've been a doctor. "You and your friend exited the Underground, Piccadilly line. What next?"

"He's not my friend," I corrected. "He's just some guy who started chatting to me when I was on the stairs, asking about places to visit while he's in the city."

"All right. Now, you're outside the tube station ..."

I recounted the story. Heyman listened, nodding along, asking follow-up questions in all the right places—did I see their faces, how tall did I think they were, did they say anything at all. All the same as before. Looking to catch me out, I guess, because he looked over and over his notes, adding to them only very occasionally.

When finally I was done, Heyman reviewed in silence.

No little holes—obviously.

He popped the clipboard back down, and eased back in his seat. An eagle eye met mine, gaze penetrating.

I did my best not to shift beneath it.

Not easy. It was like he was trying to peer into my soul. Probably what got him the job in the first place; the sort of look that could bring a person to break.

I didn't have anything to *break* over, and it still unnerved me. Under the table, I fidgeted, fingers tugging opposite sleeves.

"What?" I finally challenged.

"My boys pulled a few details on you."

I waited. "So?" But I felt the hairs on the back of my neck rise.

"Mira Traci Brand," he rattled off. "Seventeen. Second child of Jacob and ... Ileara?" I must've nodded subtly, because Heyman went on like I'd confirmed it.

"Computer says you ran away from home about three months ago; seventeenth of January." He leaned closer. "That would be you, wouldn't it, Miss Brand?"

I was frozen. Couldn't move an inch.

I should've run. Just left Carson and gone.

"You're from Colchester, Essex, is that right?"

I was aware of my nod this time, a jerky sort of motion I couldn't control. "Yes." The word sounded like a croak coming from my throat.

"Your parents from there?"

"My dad," I said. "My mum's from Lagos. Nigeria."

"They've been worried about you."

*Have they,* I almost said. There wouldn't have been even the remotest hint of belief in it.

"How've you been getting by? Seventeen-year-old girl, all alone in the city. This is where you've been, I presume? London?"

I didn't answer. Couldn't, even if I'd wanted to. My vocal cords were stuck. And if they weren't, what could I say? "I open gateways to other worlds and sell the things I bring back"? I'd be carted out of this room in an instant, chucked into the back of the nearest car, and taken to a padded cell in a loony bin somewhere.

"I see you travel with a flashlight," Heyman said. "Are you nicking things?"

I shook my head, once.

"I understand if you have," he went on. And there was no unkindness in his voice. He sounded ... sympathetic. "I see homeless people all the time, and it breaks my heart, it really does. To not know when your next meal is coming ... I get it, Mira. I do."

Good cop. That's all this was. He just wanted to bait a confession, nothing more.

But *what* confession? There was no confession to give! I hadn't *stolen* anything—at least from here. All right, I nabbed artifacts and trinkets—but no *person* was missing them, probably no creature at all, given the stupidly

43

ancient places they were squirreled away in. At *worst* I was robbing the graves of long-dead things from other worlds. It wasn't even like I'd taken custody of a doorstep to lay my head down at night!

I didn't say anything. Heyman didn't push—which was probably just another facet to his *good cop* routine. Instead he rose from the desk, stepped around me for the door.

"I'll be back shortly."

"You're leaving me in here?"

"Just for now. I won't be long." He lifted a parental sort of smile—and said, "Your parents are on the way. I'll bring them through when they're here."

Out he went.

Horror widened my eyes. They bored through the opposite wall, unseen.

*Your parents are on the way.*

Heyman had called them. Told them I was here.

They were coming to get me. To take me home.

It was over.

My adventure was over.

All my hopes, all my dreams …

Gone.

Just as soon as they stepped through that door.

# 7

No.

That was the first thought, when my brain kicked back into action. Outright refusal. I was not, repeat *not*, going back with them. No way.

Question was, how to avoid it?

The talisman.

Perfect answer. Ish. Mum and Dad knew well enough what it did, how it worked. If at first there had been any doubt, months of my absence would have only confirmed it: I'd pilfered a talisman and made my getaway. If I waited until they got here to collect me, the first thing they would do, the *very first*, would be to take it back. Clip my wings.

That would not do.

So I could cut through here …

But I didn't have the compass.

Worse still, there was a camera on me.

I glanced at it, hoping I didn't look too suspicious. Probably not, right? People in interrogation rooms by their lonesome probably glanced at the things all the time. Hard not to, when you knew you were being watched by eyes you couldn't see.

Would someone be watching it right now?

I doubted it. Paperwork to do, and all that. Plus how interesting was a scruffy-looking seventeen-year-old? Save for a cursory glance now and again at one of several monitors, I was pretty certain I was safe.

But where was I supposed to cut through? The camera was positioned in a corner, probably with a slightly fish-eyed lens. It would capture every wall. The only blinds spots were directly beneath—and under the table.

Which could work.

Brilliant. I'd just open a hole and drop in with the chair.

Resisting the urge to bite off a curse, I glanced at the camera again. Not ideal, not even close … but it was my only shot.

And if I popped out in the middle of the ocean?

I'd just … hold my breath, or whatever.

Edging the chair backward, I reached into my shirt and took hold of the talisman's pendant. Coiling fingers around it, I drank in its gentle warmth.

They were not taking this from me.

I eyed the camera one last time, raised a hand and drew a short line across the floor, hopefully where it was obscured by the table.

It was small; eighteen inches, if that. It widened into a circular maw, colors flashing within the shimmering white edge. Like a manhole cover, almost, if manhole covers were made by hippies in the sixties or seventies or whenever.

When it was wide enough, I thanked good genes (or irregular eating) for my size, stood, took a breath, and stepped through the hole.

For long seconds I was falling amidst a thousand exploding fireworks.

What if I dropped out of the sky? Or into the middle of a war? Or—

I fell out onto jagged rock. No time to roll, I thrust my hands out in front of me at the last moment.

Sharp white pain filled me. I yelped, lifted my palms. Blood trickled from both.

I stood. Glanced around.

The place I'd landed was like some alien world. I seemed

to have been thrown into a crater, onyx black, rock sharp and angular in every direction. Far off, beneath a night sky alive with three oversized stars, rock arched as though it had been thrown up in a molten wave and flash-frozen into place.

But the air was breathable, as it always seemed to be with these gateways, and save for another couple of wounds, one half of the trip had been successful.

*Just the second part now.*

I trudged awkwardly along the crags below, avoiding the sharpest jags. My shoes flexed uncomfortably; definitely not made for this terrain.

Fifty meters or so up, I found a flat-ish cliff-edge, towering toward the bloated orange discs lighting the night.

I gripped my talisman again, and cut another line.

As I stepped through, I prayed I was close enough to exit back into the station.

I *had* to be. I could not give up Decidian's Spear.

I fell out—

Right into the corridor of the police station I'd been brought to—and on my right, closed just as Constable Lawrence Heyman had left it, the door to a room I had just exited.

No time to enjoy it—or more likely dawdle, dazed, mouth hanging in a stupid O—because someone was coming my way.

I glanced frantically for an empty room.

Supply closet—that would do!

I ducked inside, pulling the door closed.

*Please, please, please do not be looking for pencils.*

I held my breath, waiting in the dark between racks, knowing my goose was cooked if the door should open …

The footsteps slowed …

My breath hitched. No …

Then he was past, disappearing up the corridor.

I closed my eyes. Breathed a long, heavy, totally unsatisfying sigh.

This *day*, man.

At least this way I could get my things back.

It was just a matter of finding them.

Waiting to be completely sure the coast was clear, and there were no sounds coming my way, I gently pushed down on the supply cupboard's interior door handle. Pushed it open … and leaned so I could peer out with just an eye.

Empty.

I let myself out, shooting a look behind.

Clear.

—at least, for now. From around a corner came—

"Just popping for a tea. Want one?"

"Yeah, go on. Two sugars, no milk."

"All right. Back in a few."

I jerked back into the supply cupboard, pulling it shut. For a tiny instant before it closed, I saw the break-room-bound officer come into view. By some small miracle, he was fiddling with his vest, eyes down.

I hoped the door's *click* was silent, and waited.

I wasn't going to get anywhere like this. The place was buzzing—and the second someone saw I'd gotten out of my room, I was going to have big questions to answer.

I pursed my lips.

I was not leaving without my compass or spear. No way.

Navigating the halls wasn't going to do it, or at least not this one. But maybe I could try my luck again …

In the dark of the supply cupboard, lit only by a soft bar of light coming in at the bottom, casting my toes in soft afternoon glow, I reached for my talisman, pointed at the door, and cut. A shimmering line extended across its surface, opening, full of lights—

"Someplace not totally dangerous, please," I whispered.

—and stepped through. Colors strobed around me, every direction, and then I was released, and fell into—

48

"*Aggh!*"

I was in the dark, and something, something *very, very close* stunk to high heaven.

I reached out, found wood, coarse and grainy. Damn near choking, I flailed up and down, until I found a handle. Shoving it down with all my might, I forced open a wide door twice the size of any human's and fell out into twilit grass that rose to my knee. Cool water clung to it.

I lay face-down, savoring air that didn't make me want to vom.

What was that?

Rotating onto my side, I cast a look behind me, and suppressed a retch.

Orc outhouse. Or at least as close to one as they got. They'd had the decency to erect walls around the place where they dropped the kids off at the pool, but there was no toilet bowl, crude though I might've expected. Just a dirty hole dug in the ground (and I mean *dirty*)—and zero paper ... or, like, leaves or whatever orcs use.

Before I rose, I checked to make sure I hadn't gotten any on me. Small miracle: I hadn't. Then I pushed to my feet, and surveyed the landscape.

Definitely not the same cratered world I'd landed in before. No surplus of suns to wreck the darkness, for one. The sky was purple here, and glittered with only a handful of sparkling pinpricks. A shroud of receding cloud streaked the horizon beyond a rise, dragging the rain with it.

In the opposite direction was a settlement, lit by torches. Far off, though; too far to trek to. And although perhaps these orcs might be more pleasant than the sort Alain Borrick had set on me—that was today, right? Yes, that was still today—I was low on time. Twenty minutes to run the two and a half miles or so out could make all the difference, with my parents on the way—and my things awaiting reclamation.

Something flat, though ...

Nothing. There were trees, beyond the outhouse, but though tall they were horrendously spindly. Even turning sideways, I wouldn't be able to pass through a gate—assuming, of course, one would even stick.

My gaze fell to the outhouse.

*"Urgh …"*

I wouldn't. Couldn't.

But I had no other options. So, putting on my best steely expression, and taking what might well be my last breath of fresh, untainted air, I stomped around the outhouse (giving it a wide berth, mind) to the rear.

Clutching my talisman, I cut open a new gateway on the back.

"Here goes nothing—*agg!*"

Choking on wretched, vile air so thick I could chew it, I passed through into the tumultuous lightshow … and dropped out again—into a plain room with one windowed wall—

A windowed wall looking into an interrogation room currently occupied by Carson and a familiar stern-looking police officer.

"… identifying some things for us," the officer was saying.

He pushed something across the table, to Carson, who looked desperately pale. If he were not seated, he'd probably be flat on his back, going by the look of him.

"I—I don't …"

But I tuned out if he said anything else, because then the officer shifted and I saw just what he was being asked to identify.

"Come on, lad," the officer barked. "I don't have all day."

"But I—I don't know what you want me to say! It's j-just an umbrella."

"Why did your accomplice have it open inside?"

My eyebrows knitted. What kind of stupid question was that?

"Sh-she wanted seven years' bad luck?" Carson stammered, and I exhaled a nose-laugh. I had to hand it to him; not totally terrible. Almost respectable, even, knowing he was on the other end of Sourpuss's toady grimace. "I don't know! I told you already—she pointed at the men following us, and—and then you turned up and they left!"

"Witnesses said they had knives."

"Cinquedeas," Carson corrected. "They're …" Then, clocking Sourpuss's death-stare, he silenced.

"Why would an umbrella stop someone brandishing a knife from attacking you?"

"It … it just did!"

I bit my lip. Sounded like Carson hadn't spilled the beans on the whole transforming umbrella thing. Again, had to give him credit; he'd done me a solid. On the other hand, maybe he was just trying to avoid being locked up in a loony bin for saying that an umbrella actually morphed into a spear in front of his eyes. That wouldn't be much of a vacation highlight for him.

But whereas I'd been given the ol' *good cop* routine, Carson had been shackled with the bad one. And though he might be holding his own just now, his voice quavered. I might not have long 'til he snapped, and the whole truth came pouring out.

My jaw tightened. Carson might be a bit of a limp rag, and I might still be ticked off over the whole screwing-up-our-escape thing, but I didn't want him to fall on my grenade. If that was anyone's job, it was … probably not mine either, but it was my task to punt the thing away, preferably into some orc pit.

Sourpuss had given up with the umbrella apparently, because he said, "And what about this?"

He threw something heavy onto the table, landing between the umbrella and Carson's manbag.

My eyebrows came down lower. Was that—?

Carson cleared his throat. "It's a compass."

Anger exploded in my chest. It was! Sourpuss had *chucked* my bloody compass! Narrowly catching myself from slamming a fist on the separating glass, I had half a mind to storm out of this room and into that one, open a gateway right beneath his big fat butt, and see him off into some far-off world where he'd end up in orc stew.

Of course, all that would draw attention, which I could really do without … so I clenched my fist instead, biting down a hiss of pain at the pressure on my sliced palms; the latest entry to my wounds catalogue. Good thing I'd chewed my nails down so far.

"A compass," Sourpuss repeated. He held it up, and it was just a simple thing; a bit antique-like, with some wood around the edges, but hardly bizarre.

"W-well … yeah. These lines are for degrees, see? The bigger lines are tens, and—"

Sourpuss hammered a fist on the table. It shuddered: strength and weight, slammed down in equal measure. Carson made a choking noise. Shoved back in his chair as far as he would go, his face was manic and panicked and pale.

*"I know what a bloody compass is, you Yank fool! What's she doing with one in the middle of bloody London?"*

"I—I don't know!" Carson's words came fast, more quivery than ever. He sounded like he was on the verge of passing out. "L-look, why are you asking me this? They're just n-normal things—"

*"These are not normal!"*

Carson continued, even faster, "And I don't know her! I haven't met her before today! I j-just asked her for travel recommendations, and th-then all this happened, and—"

*"ENOUGH!"*

At almost the same moment, noises from down the hall started in a muddle: voices, all vying for volume.

I tensed. Mum and Dad? It would be just like them to arrive and start squawking.

But then an officer called, "Officer Carmichael? We

need your assistance, please!"

Sourpuss marched around the desk, giving Carson a filthy look as he passed, which Carson flinched away from. Poking his head out of the door, he shouted, "I'm busy!"

*"Assistance please, Officer Carmichael!"*

Sourpuss growled. Whatever he saw on the face of his summoner must have been enough to convince him, though, because he turned to grunt at Carson, "Don't move. I'll be back." Then he stomped off down the hall.

I waited until he was gone, then poked my head out. Clear, in both directions. Better, the door to Carson's interrogation room was still open; I saw his back, suppressing quakes in his seat.

I darted in, pushing the door closed behind me.

At its creak, Carson jerked, turned around. Face blanching, he began, "I—" Then he saw it was me, not his interrogator already returning, and fear transformed into confusion. "Mira? What are you—?"

I pushed the door closed, stepped around him. "Getting my things back."

I took the umbrella first, looking it over. Didn't seem banged up or anything. And would it matter? Probably not. The glamour was illusion; if the illusion needed to take on wear and tear, I was pretty sure the spear itself remained intact. Although I did not intend to find out.

Strapping it to my belt, I picked up the compass. Scrutinizing it with hawk eyes, I scoured it for the slightest little ding. If I found even *one*, Sourpuss had something coming. And what might that be? The pointed end of my new toy, perhaps.

But it was pristine, and so I returned it to my belt.

Carson was gabbling. "… just on a nice trip to London, maybe meet some people—"

"Well, you met a whole bunch today," I muttered. Eyebrows twitching with annoyance, I said, "Why were they even asking you what my things were anyway? Come to the source, at least."

Carson's mouth hung.

"I … I didn't tell them. About the … you know …" He lowered his voice, and said, "The umbrella spear thing." Aiming for conspiratorial, he missed the mark, and just looked and sounded like a person on the verge of being sick.

And speaking of—

His nose turned up, eyes widening at me in disgust. "What is that *smell*?"

Damn it. Of course I'd managed to carry orc stink back through with me.

"I went through some things to get here." For good measure, I flashed my bloody palms. "See?" Pulling a disingenuous grin at his flinch, I stepped past.

The arm of a wall-mounted camera remained in the corner, but the camera itself was gone. I raised an eyebrow. My confidence in the Metropolitan Police had just taken a pretty disastrous nose-dive. Still, it did me a pretty big favor—and Carson too.

"Right, I'm off," I said, eyeing my compass as I stalked the walls. "It was nice meeting you."

"What? Where are you going?"

"Things to do, places to see." Casting a backward look, I added, "By the way, I forgot: the Apollo Theatre. Right near Piccadilly. I've been a couple of times. You'd like it."

Carson rose, seat scuffing on the floor. "I don't understand. You're—you're busting out? That's criminal!"

I shrugged. "Eh." Beyond caring, now.

"Well … well … well what about me?"

"What *about* you?"

"Aren't you going to—to tell me the plan?"

"Plan?" I scoffed, whirling on him. "Carson, there's no *plan*. I'm off out of here. The whole running from men with knives—"

"Cinquedeas."

"—thing was *super fun* and all, but this is where we part

ways." I consulted the compass again, suppressing a frown. Shadowed trees and the darkness, in every direction. Guess I had no choice.

"Look," I said, taking in the sad, sad look on his face, "they'll let you go once they know you're not a danger. And trust me, that won't take very long. For now, I recommend you stay here."

"And … and what about your things? The officer left me in here with them. When they come back and see they're gone …"

"You'll get a pat-down, they'll see you're not packing, and they get a little mystery to solve. Pretty soon they'll figure out that you had nothing to do with any of this." Compass deposited, I took my talisman in hand. The wall beside the door; as good a place as any to cut through. "Just tell them I came in and snatched them. That's probably the whole kerfuffle out there now; them realizing I've up and vanished."

"But—but …"

Conversation done. Time to go.

I smiled at him—"See you 'round, Carson."—and drew a white line onto the wall.

Carson gawped, eyes manic.

"*What is that?*"

"My exit strategy."

It widened, colors spilling forth, circling and zipping and arcing.

"*Geez. Oh geez.* First the umbrella, and now …"

"Pretty eye-opening day for you, eh?"

Carson's mouth did that goldfish thing again: open, closed, open, closed.

Then, just as I was about to step through, he said, suddenly desperate, with a craving note—

"Take me with you."

I hesitated. My head whipped round.

Incredulity must have lit my face, just the same as it had Carson's moments ago.

But unlike then, a hint of something else had come into his. Not fear, although there was more than enough of that (and I suspected it comprised a good sixty percent of his expression at rest anyway). No, Carson was lit with the tiniest little sliver of determination.

He snatched up his manbag, slung it over his shoulder, and stepped around the table for me.

"No," I said, holding up a hand. "You go out that door. See London. Have the adventure you came here for."

"But with you ..."

"My adventures are dangerous. There are orcs—yes, orcs, like I said earlier—and they're honestly one of the milder dangers out there," I added quickly as Carson's eyes somehow grew wider, "compared to furious dwarves, and svartelves and—and danger, and—blood, see?" I flashed my palms again. "I'm always coming back bloody. You'd hate it."

"But ... adventure ..."

"Seeing London is an adventure too! You can get a Boris Bike, or whatever they're calling them now ... or you never know; you might get spat at by an illegal minicab driver. All exciting stuff, yeah? Just stay here, and you can be on your way before you know it!"

I shouldn't have stayed to argue, I realized later. But for some reason, some little part of me thought I could convince him, that within the short period I'd been in Carson's company I'd got the full picture of him—mild and quiet and scared witless. And that with just that bit of force, he would back down and give up.

Instead, his face flickered with defiance.

"No."

I opened my mouth to argue—

Then Sourpuss's voice echoed up the corridor—"Not my job to find her!"—and it was coming closer.

No time left. Eyes on Carson for one last moment, I pleaded, "*Stay.*" Then I leapt through—

His hand caught me.

And as the door handle jiggled behind us, I fell into that ever-present, unending spiral of light … with Carson hanging on tight.

# 8

We fell into the forest my compass had promised, a landing made slightly harder by him thumping against me as we came down in a stumble, bright sparkles clouding my vision as my eyes reset after passing through the lightshow of the gate.

I whirled the moment my feet touched ground.

"You idiot!" I cried, shoving Carson in the chest. "Why did you follow me? I said to stay where you were! They would have let you go in—"

But Carson was not present for my reprimands. His gaze was past, sweeping over my shoulders and head. A look of pure astonishment covered his face, like a child setting sight on snow for the very first time.

I turned back a half-step, and took it in with him.

It was dark out. No moon here, but the sky was clear, and filled with stars.

Beneath the canopy, we ought not to have been able to see them. But here, every trunk, every leaf, was like glass. Starlight came through, bounced and refracted in every direction, filling every last point, gleaming down each and every tree, diamonds scattered on black. Refracted so many times that the forest had converted some ten thousand stars into millions.

"It's incredible," Carson breathed.

I let him have his moment, caught in the majesty of it

alongside him. If he hadn't been here, I wouldn't have taken any notice of this, because I would have been too busy trying to find a cutover back into London. I stared at the nearest tree, alive with the light, a crystalline sculpture alive with a rainbow of light here in this place of darkness. They really did remind me of diamonds, how they caught the light and sparkled.

Then it was time to move. Because if I was going to ever be in a position to buy some real diamonds, I needed to get moving.

"Come on," I said, pulling him into motion. "Enjoy sightseeing while you can, because we're not here long."

He came, feet dragging, eyes overhead. Good thing I had the sense to keep my eyes on where we were going, because he'd have careened into the dirt within less than four steps.

No path had been carved here, so I weaved in between trunks, one eye on the compass to ensure we continued in a straight line. I'd heard that without proper visual markers to orient themselves, a person ended up walking in wide circles. And although this place was pretty, it wasn't where I wanted to test that theory.

There were shrubs closer to the ground, creepers that had woven around the trees. They were glassy too, and each thin cable shone where the light from above seemed to condense in a speckled bar on its surface. It seemed a pity to traipse over them. But they sprung up behind us as though we'd never passed through, so I felt less guilty.

"Forest of Glass," Carson murmured some fifty meters from our starting point.

"Huh? Oh, uh, yes, very pretty." I squinted at the compass, then almost slammed face-first into a tree. "Look, can you watch where you're going? I'm not your minder; I can't deal with pulling you along and navigating at the same—"

A long howl went up in the night, too high, with an almost wheezing quality.

Three more answered it ... close.

I froze.

Carson, beside, did the same. His eyes found mine. "What was that?"

I grabbed his sweater. Eyes frantic, I motioned a chopping action, neck-height: *Shut up!*

He understood—or maybe was too scared by my reaction—because the only noise he made was a strangled-sounding swallow.

I surveyed, quickly.

Another wheezy howl, from maybe a hundred meters back the way we'd come ...

I pointed at a tree with a split trunk, low boughs protruding at forked angles. "Up here," I mouthed to Carson, then jogged to it. He followed. I cringed at the sound of creepers shifting underfoot as we moved through them.

"You first," I mouthed.

He eyed it. Then, in a soft whisper, almost too silent to hear: "I can't climb!"

"You have to, damn it!"

The wheezing howl filled the night air again. A friend joined it. Even closer, now; any second, those things would stumble upon the place where Carson and I had just entered this forest.

The noises galvanized him into motion. Planting a foot between the V where the trunk had split in two, he gripped for the nearest bough, and hefted himself up. Then, awkwardly, suppressing a grunt through a pained grimace, he shimmied higher.

"Next one," I breathed, climbing behind him.

He pushed onto his feet jerkily, bracing against the trunk. An image of him falling, trunk between the legs, conjured itself in my mind. Not funny; not right now. Nothing in the world could make me laugh at this moment in time.

Carson clutched the bough above. Legs wrapped around

the trunk, he somehow ascended, looking like some kind of strangely gangly monkey kitted out in a Halloween costume: *Class Dork*.

When he was up and settled, I climbed into the space Carson had just been ... and waited, breath held.

Above me, Carson's breathing was only too loud.

"Quieter," I whispered up at him.

Something scuffed in the dirt.

I tensed.

Ten meters away, maybe less, a dark streak passed by illuminated trunks. Blotting out stars like an eclipse blocks the sun, it seemed to carve out a spot of perfect darkness.

Then, a little farther up, another.

Scuffling.

One of the creatures howled. But this close, it was not at all like a howl—this was more like a baby's cry, high-pitched and warbling and breathy, coming through lungs caked with tar.

Its partner joined, and the whine drove into my ears, deep and penetrating and awful. I thought I would scream—perhaps this was how they found their victims, by driving them to such madness that they gave themselves away—and then it was over.

I closed my eyes.

I never, *ever*, wanted to hear that noise again.

More scuffing noises. Closer ... closer ...

They were right on us.

I dared to creep an eye open, and look down.

One of the things had stopped at the base of the tree Carson and I so frantically clutched.

It was almost a wolf ... almost. There was some boar in it too, making it both sleek and yet bulky. Two short tusks protruded from its mouth, perfect for stabbing, pinning. Its snout was squat, flat at the end, and working overtime as it sniffed.

Despite the millions of points of light dancing over it, the creature was near-black.

It dug around in creepers like a pig hunting for truffles—

And then, slowly, its head rose, up, up, up … toward me.

The breath caught in my chest.

The wolf in it didn't appear to touch its face, and except for the snout and tusks, neither did the boar. No, this was something out of a horror movie. A decapitated head starting to rot, there were sunken holes where its eyes should be. Its mouth, too, was a wide open maw, tusks exiting from darkness. There was no fur, and in the Forest of Glass's refracted light, it caught like moonlight over sand. Two bulbous growths, like tumors, stuck out below wilted ears—proto-eyes, I figured, sensitive to light and gradient changes.

Which meant, if we kept perfectly still …

The Sniffer ran its nose up and down the trunk.

Orc poo. It smelled me. Damn it.

I held my breath. How did I pick up that stink after just standing around the bloody outhouse for ten seconds?

The Sniffer reared. Three-toed feet pressed the trunk. It extended … I edged back, knowing in my head I was too high for it, animal instincts terrified I was hopelessly wrong.

It stood there, waiting.

Then, from low in its throat, came a low scratching sound. Vocal cords flexing, working …

Don't howl. Do not howl.

It didn't—

The noise it made was strangled … too human. *"Ahh … lo?"*

—and I instantly wished it had howled.

*"Ahh-lo?"*

Hello? Was it … was it saying …?

*"Ahh-loooo?"*

I closed my eyes. It couldn't see me, of that I was sure … but I could not look into its haggard face as its throat flexed in a way that it shouldn't be able to, and call a greeting to someone or something it thought was hiding scant feet away.

I tried to convince myself that this noise was just its cry. Like 'meow' from a cat, or 'quack' from a duck. It was not saying 'hello'.

*"Ahh-lo?"*

IT WAS NOT SAYING 'HELLO'.

The Sniffer paused, silenced. After long seconds of quiet, it shuffled its hold on the trunk, possibly looking for purchase—then, at last, it dropped onto all fours again. One last snuffle in the creepers underfoot, and it skulked away.

From somewhere far off, another in the pack loosed a howl. Much farther this time.

This one joined it—I pressed one hand over my ear, gritting my teeth—and then it disappeared.

I tracked its black shape vanishing among the lights shining throughout the trees.

When I was certain no shapes moved among their glow, I started to count Mississippis. Two hundred should do.

At sixty-eight, Carson whispered, "What was that thing?"

"Don't know. I think it was a predator, though."

"It sounded like it was saying …"

"I know," I said, cutting him off. I didn't want to think about it. Undoubtedly I would have plenty of time to do so over sleepless nights in the days and weeks to come—if I ever ended up back home. The way today was going, I was becoming less and less sure of it.

"Can we get down now?" Carson asked.

Part of me wanted to finish the count to two hundred. But I was sure enough that the Sniffer and its pack had gone, and as long as we were silent—and I directed us in the opposite direction to that last howl—I figured it was safe enough. Worst case scenario, we climbed another tree.

Actual worst case scenario: Carson and I got devoured by something out of *The Hills Have Eyes*.

I climbed down, and waited for Carson to follow. He was careful, and I almost wanted to shout at him to hurry it up. I'd only invite our friends back doing that though, and if Carson did hurry it up and ended up snapping an ankle on an accelerated climb down, we were both in trouble.

As he reached the bottom, I eyed the compass.

I wasn't quite sure where a gateway here might open out. It wasn't London, though; too run-down for that, unless it dropped us into a particularly grubby part of the city. If push came to shove, I'd take it … but I wasn't quite there yet.

"Come on," I whispered once Carson joined me.

Pushing through the trees, we trekked.

Once, another howl made its way to us, and we both froze. But it was so far off that the awful baby's cry really did sound like a real-world wolf, so we set into motion again, paces only very slightly quickened.

I kept my eyes glued to the compass, willing it to change, while trusting my ears to warn me of impending danger. It showed savannah, endless grasslands stretching off to mountains in the distance … America maybe, or Sub-Saharan Africa. Hell, outer Mongolia for all I knew. And then, just as the trees around us began to thin, the image on its face flickered, transitioning to—

"The O2 arena," I breathed.

At the same moment, Carson said, "Beach."

I looked up dumbly. "Huh?"

Sure enough, past a last small scattering of thinner, shorter glassy trees, the creepers underfoot petered out, and dirt was replaced with sand.

Carson jogged past me, out into the open.

"Wait!" I whispered. "You don't know if it's safe!"

Not, of course, that I'd have done anything different. So I followed, keeping half an eye on the compass to ensure it still showed the O2 as our exit.

The sand was almost perfectly white, and incredibly fine. It shifted gently under my feet as I stepped out, forming small divots that softened but remained as I passed. There were no other impressions in it, which meant either that the Sniffers didn't come out here, or that they *did*, and the tide had come in, smoothed it out, and it dried before this stretch was walked again. Either way, no complaints.

And the *sea* … so deep, and so perfectly still; not a wave in sight. Starlight reflected perfectly, as though someone had laid a mirror beneath the heavens.

For a second, I was overtaken by wonder. Part of it was childlike: the desire to plonk down on this beach, run my hands through the sand, dig holes that would forever fill themselves back in before I could go down more than a foot, or try to construct sandcastles, first with this dry stuff, then with water scavenged in a plastic bucket from the place where sand and sea kissed.

The other half was more adult. This part of me wanted *escape*. As though a fishing hook had impaled itself behind my belly button, compulsion pulled me to the water's edge. I would throw my shirt and jeans off, and just careen into this beautiful velvet ocean, sending ripples of my own over its perfect surface, making the reflected stars glitter and sparkle. It would be cold, perhaps, make my breath catch at first … but then I would lay back, held afloat, eyes closed, breathing in the cool scent of this glorious night, and just let the water wash my aches, my bruises, my blood, away.

I closed my eyes, imagining, holding onto it for just a second … and then let go. It was a nice fantasy—but it could be only that. There were things to do yet. Glory had to be sought.

Literally, almost.

I scoured, turning a slow circle.

"What are you doing?" Carson asked.

"I need a flat surface."

"Why … oh, for the—the portal thing?"

"Gateway," I said. "And yes."

"Is that how you found me?"

"Nah," I lied. "My constable friend was just as careless as yours."

Carson cleared his throat. "There's, err, a rocky section over there." He pointed. "See?"

Huh. "Good eyesight." I started moving.

"I should hope so. My prescription changed a lot when I was younger, but it seems to have settled now …"

"Right."

"I thought about laser eye surgery? But I read online that you have to have your eyes open for ten minutes. I mean, they give you drops and everything, but still … and they also, um, they have to cut a flap in your retina."

"Uh huh."

"Anyway, I'm fine with glasses. I like these."

I was pretty certain he was alone there, but didn't say anything.

The outcropping rose from the sand, and extended far beyond where I could see. Guess we lucked out with the pristine bit. I stepped onto a curving boulder, shaped almost like a buried fist, and looked for the flattest—and closest—area. Still the O2, thankfully, but I didn't trust it to remain that way much farther.

I settled for a plateau nearby. It wasn't perfect; the ends rose in sharp points. But it would suffice—although it meant a jump down, rather than stepping through.

Checking one last time that we'd still exit close to the O2, I said to Carson, "Come here." He joined, and with the talisman clutched in hand, I opened a gateway between our feet.

"We're going down?"

"No choice."

"Where will we end up?"

"London." I flashed him the compass. "Not exactly where I want to be in the city, but far enough away from the station that we'll manage for a while."

"The station," Carson echoed. "Do you think they'll be looking for us?"

"Course not. Why would they? We only vanished in front of their eyes—me on camera."

"You were on—?"

"The table blocked the gateway. As far as they know, I just … fell into the floor and vanished. Now do the same here, will you?"

Carson hesitated. He looked ready to ask another question—then I nudged him with my elbow. He teetered, and then stepped through the gap, disappearing.

I gave the beach a melancholy last look, and followed.

We didn't come out exactly at the O2, but close-by. It was just visible from the street we exited into, white edge curving like an upside-down bowl between two buildings.

Night was coming. Twilight had not arrived, but it was encroaching, and the streetlights were just coming to life with their dull sodium glow. In another hour, it would be full dark, and going by the grey blanket beginning to sweep across the sky, we wouldn't be treated to any stars. Even if we were, the night sky here on Earth would never compare to the one I'd just left behind.

Still, I glanced back at the mottled network of brick we'd come from, taking pains to memorize it. Maybe I could go back sometime.

Or not, given what waited in those woods.

I oriented myself, tracing my mental map for the nearest tube station. Thankfully, Constable Heyman hadn't seen fit to revoke me of my Railcard. It wouldn't have been the worst thing in the world if he had, but they were expensive, almost extortionately so it seemed to me at nigh on a tenner a pop, and I couldn't just throw those sorts of funds around willy-nilly.

It occurred to me that I'd need to scavenge up something to sell again, refill the coffers and all that. I'd have to make a point of finding some new gateways to temples; those were always good for a trinket or two.

"Right, that's me," I said. "Have a safe—what are you doing?"

I'd started on my way, and Carson had followed, half a step behind.

"What *is* that thing?" he asked, utterly oblivious of what I'd said, as well as the flat look on my face. "That … that pendant thing. And how does it work?"

"Talisman," I corrected. "And it … just works. I dunno." I lifted it to brandish at as I lied to him. It wasn't malicious; I just didn't want to get into a long discussion of how my world worked. "Never thought about it, I guess."

"Does it always go through to *that* world?"

"It, uh … no, it doesn't. I mean, if we went back through in the same places, then we'd come out there again, but …" I blinked, confused. I was trying to get rid of him, yet the rug seemed to have been pulled out from under me. Suddenly—whether through fatigue or just the ghost of loneliness—I couldn't help but answer.

"There are other places?" Carson breathed. "Other worlds?"

"Lots of them, yeah. One's where I got this." I indicated the umbrella. It swayed against my leg as we walked … together, which wasn't what I intended, but—

"And they're all here, attached to London?"

"Not *just* London. They connect everywhere." I frowned, a moment away from shooing him off—then I detached the compass, and lifted it to show him. "See this?"

Carson squinted. "Looks like water."

"It is. If I were to cut through a gateway here—" I pointed at a bulletin board at a bus stop "—we'd pass through and probably end up drowning somewhere. Whereas if we come a little farther …" Sure enough, just over the road, the compass image transitioned. A small pyramid on a squarish base loomed, coated in vines and nestled between trees with vast, dark trunks. "A gateway here would lead to this temple."

"We should go," Carson breathed.

*We?* I frowned at him. "No." Stowing the compass, the urge to tell him to leave resurfaced.

Before I could open my mouth to admonish him, he went on. "So how does it work, then? How are so many bunched up so close?"

"It's …" I stopped, needing to think. How was it Dad had first explained it? "Right," I said, turning to face Carson. "Imagine you've got two pieces of paper. One's a map of London, and the other one … it's filled with squares, okay? Really, really small ones. And each of those squares is its own world."

"So those sheets are laid over each other," Carson put in.

"Kind of, yeah, but not quite. It's more like … like that bottom sheet is crumpled up. So now, instead of orderly, it's all a big jumble. And actually, I guess there are like a hundred little crumpled-up balls of worlds, all together. London sits on top of those. And any place where part of the crumpled-up sheet connects, that's where we can travel through. Like here." I tapped the compass.

"What about the empty spaces?"

"Boundaries," I said. "The compass mists up when there's one of those. It doesn't connect—to anything. Go into a gateway there, you're gone. Poof. Finito."

Carson suppressed a grimace. Laughing nervously, he said, "Good thing you've got that compass then, right?"

"Right."

I set off again.

Carson followed.

I didn't complain.

For now.

"So where did you get the pendan—the talisman?" Carson asked.

Remembering Constable Heyman's faked concern—

*Have you been nicking things?*—my lips tightened.

"My parents. I stole it."

"Yeah, but where did it come from originally? Who made it?"

I opened my mouth to answer, when—

Up ahead, passing through a small throng that was arranged on a crossing, waiting for the light to change, I saw black.

Cloaks.

Carson saw them just a moment later. He squeaked, "They're back!"

"Quiet," I muttered. "I don't think they've seen us."

But they had, of course they had—because the first jabbed a fist at us, raising his cinquedea with his free hand—

"GO!"

And yet again, trailed by Carson and three men in cloaks, some two dozen meters behind, I broke into a run.

# 9

"Down here!" I ordered Carson, hooking a right down an alley.

Just a step behind, he followed, one hand furiously clamped on his satchel.

"What do we do?" he cried.

"This." I stopped. I was not in the mood to hold those guys off again. Also not particularly convinced of my chances if we needed to. Gripping the talisman, I shot a brief look at the compass—enough to know it was safe, not enough to fully take in what I saw in its face—I pointed at the nearest wall, and cut, a fast swiping motion.

The gateway widened …

At the mouth of the alley, three figures in cloaks and cowls burst into view.

"GO!"

I grabbed Carson—he squealed, eyes almost entirely whites—and pulled him sideways through the gateway.

For a dreadful moment I thought our pursuers would barrel through too. But the gateway shuddered closed, so it was only the two of us, floating in a sea of swirling dye—

Then we were upended, falling out sideways, through empty air—

And then, *CRASH!* We hit stone.

"Ow," I moaned, pushing up. *"Ow."* I felt like I'd run

headfirst into a door, or maybe leapt from a car speeding down the motorway, spanging into a road sign with enough force to leave a real Wile E. Coyote hole behind me.

Going by the noises Carson was making, he hadn't fared much better.

We'd landed on cobblestones, spaced well apart. They were lit by soft copper light. Dark spaces curved around them, the frail light unable to reach the bottom of the trenches. The butt of what looked like a cigarette lay in one of the troughs, only it was not quite the same as the ones you picked up from any of the million off-licenses spread across London's busy streets. No filter, for a start, and the tobacco hadn't been rolled in paper, but a pale, fibrous leaf.

I levered up, squinting.

We'd dropped into some kind of square. There was a tavern next to us, but the lights were out inside. Except for a door twice my size and three times my width, it might've been wrenched straight out of a fairytale: lots of wooden beams crisscrossing, thatched roof, and a sign hanging from the roof's peak. A name I couldn't pronounce was boasted across it: *KZ'GA'NTHZ*. Still, my lips tried.

"I think I broke something," Carson moaned. He pressed himself up awkwardly, looking for a moment like a nerd trying (and hopelessly failing) at a press-up. Then, on his knees, he gasped, "My glasses!" and patted them.

"They're fine," I told him, "just lopsided." Which was a shame, really. If Gok Wan rolled up to give him a makeover, those stupidly delicate frames would be the *first* to go—followed by pretty much everything else.

Carson took them off to check anyway. He barely scrutinized the lenses, which struck me as odd, instead focusing all his attention on the rims, the arms, checking the hinges were still intact. I didn't ask, and in any case they seemed to pass his test, because he put them back on his nose, though he didn't look the least bit happy.

"Why'd we fall like that?" he asked.

I pointed at the tavern's sign. "Gateway opened there, I reckon."

He squinted. "Kaz—kuz-gah … N-n …"

I left him to it, rising to my feet. Quick checks over my compass, talisman, and Decidian's Spear, then it was time to get the measure of where we'd ended up and figure out where the next connection to London might be.

I surveyed the square. Draped in crescent moonlight, it was lit by a single torch atop a post, some fifteen feet high. Folk were tall here, it looked like. Probably not an orc city—the unpronounceable string of letters on the tavern's sign didn't quite gel with them, even if the height thing hadn't been a mismatch—but I still didn't much fancy our luck if we should run into whoever might inhabit this realm of semi-giants.

Other buildings were arranged opposite a fountain that was wide and deep enough to fill an Olympic swimming pool. Most were dwellings, not unlike the tavern, with beams and stone and thatch, but there was also an open structure with an anvil and a fire pit, and beside that what I assumed was a shop, a crude helmet painted on its sign.

This place had *definitely* come out of a fairytale.

No one was around. The thin toenail moon was low. Going by the tavern's emptiness, I figured these were probably the early hours of the morning rather than the waxing night. So we were probably safe, for a while. A single chimney softly breathing smoke was a minor concern, but no lights were on inside, so it was probably the remains of a fire rather than anyone (or anything) up and about.

The compass showed a glimpse of the O2 seen from the alley where we'd made our escape.

Not for the first time, I lamented that it didn't double as a live camera feed. If the other side were visible in real-time, we could just wait, and pop back through once danger had passed.

Or not. I thought back to Alain Borrick and his orcs. They'd come for Decidian's Spear too. Was he on the same quest as me? If so, every second spent dodging in and out of other worlds was burning precious time.

"Up," I commanded Carson. "We're moving."

He obeyed, mouth open in dumb wonder.

I started a stride, eyes on my compass.

London vanished just six steps down the street, replaced with a view of orange outback. A boulder crested the very edge of the compass face, its curve begun and almost immediately cut off. Ayers Rock? Maybe. Or just a boulder.

It wavered to blue sky and nothing but after another thirteen steps—and then, just two after that, two images battled: rainforest on the left, and another, darker rainforest on the right. If I turned one way or the other I could pinpoint where the safe transition points were, but what was the point in that? Last I checked, London hadn't grown a little Amazon of its own, and that was still where I needed to be.

At a crossroads, I decided to take us left. Totally arbitrary choice, might come back to bite me in the backside, but never mind. Had to go *somewhere*.

After the compass had shown a beach, then total darkness, which might have been the bottom of the ocean or just the inside of a box, Carson started up.

"So … that umbrella …"

I pursed my lips. "What about it?"

"What *is* it, exactly?"

"A spear." Then, before I could help myself: "Decidian's Spear. Ancient relic. It got lost in the eleventh century, or thereabouts." I squinted as the compass flashed with yellow, images shifting too fast to take in, and backtracked just to confirm it was sand. "Now it's mine," I muttered when I resumed walking.

"Why's it an umbrella, though?"

"Glamour."

"Huh?"

"A disguise. It's masking itself."

"Right." He didn't quite take that in stride, which was good, because people in the real world didn't typically see spears turn into umbrellas and vice versa. If he had taken it in stride, he'd probably be well on his way to being a nutter.

Desert again. I huffed, and decided to cross the street. It was almost wide enough for three cars side by side, although I wasn't convinced the people here had figured out the internal combustion engine just yet. Probably still on horse-drawn carriages—and could you imagine the *size* of the things? Maybe elephant-drawn carriages.

"So what now?" Carson asked.

"'What now' what? I'm finding us a route back to London."

"I mean what now you've got Di—Decid—"

"Decidian's Spear."

"Right. What are you searching for next?"

An eyebrow rose on my face. "I didn't say I was searching for anything."

"You must be though, right?"

*Buzz off,* I was tempted to tell him. But I tamped it down in spite of myself and conceded after a moment, "Yes, I'm looking for something else."

"So—what is it?"

I caught myself before I spat something biting at him— *What, like you can help?*—and paused. Carson stopped almost too late, a split second from walking into my back.

I eyed him, lips tight, looking for—what? Confirmation that he was harmless, I guessed. And he gave it, shuffling his satchel and nervously clearing his throat. Always with the throat.

Starting up again, a little slower, I said, "I'm seeking the Chalice Gloria."

"The what?"

"Chalice Gloria. It's Latin." I tacked on, "Ish," before Carson could correct me; *"But there's no 'chalice' in Latin. There's 'cup,' but that's 'calicem', so shouldn't it be …?"* Yada, yada, yada. He was a pedant even in my imagination.

I continued, "It means 'Cup of Glory.' And it's been lost for thousands of years, so anyone who finds it is going to get a certain measure of respect in my world."

"Your world's not this one," Carson said, not a question, and then quickly amended, "I mean—London. Uh, Earth. Right?"

"I don't mean a real world. A metaphorical one; you know, my 'people'. Seekers of treasure. People who do what I do. That's what I mean."

Carson was quiet for a moment.

The compass flickered. I'd found an edge, and two images vied for the face. On the left was a bayou—and on the right, London, announced by the familiar angle of the Shard. I paused, twisting to find which direction I needed to go—left, which made no sense whatsoever, but fine—and then pointed.

"This way."

"We can get back to London here?"

"Somewhere around here, yeah."

We slowed. I watched, eyes mostly on the compass, as the Shard bloomed, pushing out the bayou with every step …

"So … these people," Carson began.

"Uh huh."

"Why does it matter that you get respect from them? They're strangers, right?"

I swallowed, throat suddenly dry. "Most, yeah."

"So why do you need the respect of people you don't even know?"

His eyes were on the back of my head, and I could feel them, boring a hole. I was glad not to be facing him; I'd never be able to meet his eyes.

"You wouldn't understand," I muttered.

"So … explain it. Is it a kind of fame thing?"

The Shard dominated, the bordering world pushed entirely from the compass's face.

Grateful for the conversational escape route, I said, "We can pass through here." I stowed my compass again. Carson looked like he wanted to say something, but I ignored him, gripping the talisman in one hand, and cutting a gateway beside the window of the adjacent house.

I nodded once it was open. "Through."

Carson obeyed after a moment's hesitation.

I followed.

When we were out, it was daytime.

Carson blinked in confusion. "What the—?" He looked at me, flabbergasted. "But—it was evening—"

"Time doesn't always pass the same in the other worlds." Which sucked, because yesterday had pretty much wrecked me. I'd been looking forward to getting back to my bed and enjoying some shut-eye. Now, going by the color of the sky and the absence of the sun's disc, we were more or less right at the beginning of the day again.

Unless I wanted to totally screw up my sleep, there was no choice but to power through.

Fortunately shops and off-licenses were about as plentiful as litter, so I could stop in and grab a few cans of 5-Hour Energy, and I'd be all set.

Now just the matter of cutting Carson loose—

He gripped his satchel by the strap, holding it close, eyes on me. "Where to now?"

"Where to—? *I* am going to Charing Cross. And you—"

"Can I come?" he asked. After a second's pause: "Please?"

I couldn't get words out for a moment, my brain apparently too tangled to keep up. But my feelings must've been clear on my face, because Carson continued, words coming fast like when he'd been under Sourpuss's penetrating glare, "Just until the city gets busier? Those guys might still be around, and—and I guess I don't want to be by myself. Please?"

"Why not call the police?"

"I … I mean, I could …"

He fumbled for words, looking … pathetic, no other word for it, even without the stupid glasses.

But though I longed to kick him to the curb now, get him out of my hair, guilt niggled at the back of my head. He was wrapped up in this now, whether I liked it or not—and whereas I had Decidian's Spear and my talisman, he had nothing. If *Skyrim* guy and his mates set upon Carson, he was done. I at least owed him what he asked: company until the streets were fuller, affording him better opportunities to blend in and make an escape.

"Fine," I conceded wearily. "But later today, after my next stops, you're going back to—where is it you're staying?"

"Russell Square," he said quickly. "It's a, err, hostel." And then, I guess because he had seen something in my face that didn't exist, he said, "It's only one-star, but it's not really that bad …"

Nice.

"Right. You can stick with me for now. But like I said: before today is out, I'm taking you back there, got it?"

Carson nodded, cleared his throat. "Got it."

I turned tail and marched off.

We stopped for an energy drink. I didn't quite have the change to make up one 5-Hour Energy, so I cheaped out, scavenging just enough for two generic blueberry-flavored cans. Nowhere near the amount of caffeine I was looking for, but beggars can't be choosers.

We rode the tube in silence, exiting at Charing Cross.

London was just beginning to pick up. The sun had risen enough to crest the buildings previously obscuring it. Before long, nothing would be able to blot it—and I'd be rid of Carson for good.

"Where are we going now?" Carson asked.

I pointed up the street. "The Strand."

"Oh! Trafalgar Square, right?"

"It's that way, but that's not where we're going."

I marched ahead. Carson jogged to keep up. I could've slowed down, really, but I liked this pace. Sugar and additives had infused me with an itch to get a shift on. Plus, Carson wasn't used to the exertion, and it kept him from talking.

"Do you think those guys will come for us again?"

Or not.

"I don't know."

"I hope not."

*Me too* ... I didn't say. Instead, casually: "At least they're not the orcs I dealt with earlier."

"Oh! You said—the purple stuff on your spear earlier, that—that was orc blood, did you say?" he asked with a conversational tone that was not entirely believable.

"Yes."

Carson hurried so that he was marching alongside me. He clutched the strap of his satchel tight to his chest, as though it might burst free and escape at any moment.

"Real orcs? Like from Mordor?"

*Lord of the Rings.* Figured. And probably not the films; Carson had read the books, from cover to cover, of that I was sure. A whole bunch of times, probably.

"You realize the concept of orcs comes from way before Tolkien, right? *Way* before. Anyhow, real orcs are like ... a scourge, I guess. They're invading worlds all the time." I nudged the umbrella bouncing against my thigh. "I ran into a few while I grabbed this thing."

"That's crazy," Carson breathed. Then, coughing nervously, he added, "They've never invaded *here*, have they?"

"What, London?"

"Earth, I mean. But I guess London, too."

"Not in modern times. I've heard a rumor they've been

79

brought through gateways a couple of times, but now we've got cars and trains, they get spooked. Dunno if that's true though." I shrugged. "Who knows?"

I brought us to a stop outside Tortilla, a burrito and taco place. It wasn't yet open, and I was thankful; the first of my energy drinks had been a nice pick-me-up, but it had also apparently reminded my stomach of just how hungry I was. Contending with the smells pouring out of the restaurant as the door opened and closed … no thanks.

Carson apparently had the same thought, as he eyed the sign. "But it's not open."

"We're not going in."

"Oh …"

I glanced up and down the street. People were milling about, but their eyes weren't on us.

More to the point, none of our black-cloaked friends had shown up.

Confident that we wouldn't be seen, I gripped my talisman and cut a new gateway in the brick alongside Tortilla's façade.

"In," I ordered. "Quick."

Carson passed through. I shot one last look up and down the street, left then right, and followed.

We dropped into …

*"Wow."*

For the first time since his unintended wisecrack at Sourpuss in the station yesterday, I found myself lifting an inadvertent smile at Carson.

The room was grand. A marble-floored library extended, shone to a perfect gleam. The room was almost circular, but angled—some geometric thing with about thirty sides, I guessed. Shelves packed with tomes, so high they required a stepladder to reach their top, were arranged at slight angles all the way around the perimeter, save for the arches broken by doors and a few blank walls. A fireplace burned in the far wall. Even from this distance, I could feel its magical heat licking my face, comforting and homey.

"Figured *you* would like it," I told him, stepping past. "This—" I swept open arms around the room "—is my hideout."

"Just … wow," Carson breathed. His mouth hung, jaw forgotten.

I snapped my fingers. "Follow."

He obeyed automatically. His loafers scuffed as he stumbled behind, eyes not remotely on where he was going. They were tracing the shelves, and then up, to the high vaulted ceiling. Long rods reached down from it, terminating in wide bulbs like rugby balls, shining with brilliant white light. So high above us that one of the inhabitants of the fairytale square we'd just passed through wouldn't have been able to reach one even if they stood atop a bookshelf.

"They don't burn out," I said. "Same as the fire. It's been burning since I found it. Never once had to drop a bit of kindling in."

Up and down went Carson's jaw.

I smirked, and turned.

Where the ribs of bookcases again terminated, doorways on the far curving wall led off to either side of the hearth. A kitchen, on one, contents all too meager, alongside a bathroom; and bedrooms, which had conveniently been made up when I first arrived. As was fair and right, I had commandeered the largest as mine.

Carson's eyes lingered on a blank stretch of wall beside the kitchen. A scrap of paper was tacked into it. "NEW YORK," it said in some stranger's neat, flowing script, for it led to an easy path through a forest of purple trees into a crossover at Central Park.

"You can get to New York from here?" he breathed.

"A few places, actually." I pointed back the way we'd come, and Carson turned to follow. "London's that way. Then there's Paris, over there … Hong Kong, just across from it … back behind one of those shelves, you can go to Rome. There are twelve connection paths in this room alone."

"The possibilities," Carson muttered.

"A world tour, right from my doorstep." I shrugged. "Can't deny it's useful."

I wandered into the kitchen, Carson following. The lights came on unbidden, illuminating stark marble surfaces, just as polished as the floor. In the corner was a fridge, like something out of a steampunk novel. An oddly misshapen mass of gears, it hummed away far more loudly than seemed necessary.

I stopped at it, pulled it open. Not a whole lot inside at all. A few vegetables—carrots, mainly, the tops sprouting in yellow-green—plus a single apple. A single-pint carton of milk stood in the door, but it had gone bad a few days ago, and I hadn't thrown it out yet. My one treat was a Snickers. I prodded it, turned my nose up. Going hard. Wasn't going to give up on it though. I retrieved it, took a bite … ugh … and then mumbled through chocolate-cake-filled teeth, "Uhm, I don't really have a lot, so … sorry."

Carson nodded. Still, his stomach gave a sorry grumble.

"So … how'd you find this place?"

"Flashed up on the compass as I was passing." I lied, chewing the remaining chunk of Snickers. Not very satisfying, but better than nothing—even if it was a whole lot tougher than I really liked. "Figured I'd cut through, take a look … ended up making it my home base, so to speak."

"I, err, like what you've done with it."

I filled two glasses with water, handing one to Carson. Mine I downed, not coming up for air until I'd chugged the whole thing. Cool, reinvigorating, and about a million times better than the remaining can of energy drink presently burning a hole in my jeans pocket.

I could do with a shower, or better yet, a long, hot bath, filled with bubbles; the sort that you came out of with a low-grade scald. Even with the burst of caffeine, though, I was likely to fall asleep in it—not good. For now I'd have to skip it, even if I was pretty sure I was starting to stink. Places to go, people to see.

"Right, time to go," I said once Carson had emptied his glass, and led us back out into the library.

"Where are we going now?"

"*I* am going after Feruiduin's Cutlass. But I need to stop off somewhere else first."

Carson tugged on his satchel nervously. "What about me?"

"You're coming too." But only because it would still be too early to shrug out of his clingy embrace. "But only on this one stop. As soon as I've got what we need, I'm taking you to Russell Square and seeing you off. Got it?"

He nodded. "Sure."

Somehow, looking at him, I got the feeling it might not be quite that easy … but I stifled it. Time was evaporating too fast, and every second was another in which Alain Borrick and his gang of green buddies pushed ahead.

Talisman in hand, I cut an opening back onto the Strand under the scrap of paper with "LONDON" written across the top.

"Go," I instructed.

Carson went.

I followed.

# 10

London: two blocks north of Kensington High Street Station.

The foot traffic was picking up now. On the one hand, that was good; once we were in and out, Carson would be out of my hair. On the other, the increased presence on the street made me wary. The cloaked men could … okay, not blend in as such, but as least use passers-by as a kind of blockade until they were ready to jump out on us.

I wondered who they were, where they'd come from. Sent by Alain Borrick, perhaps? Maybe, although how on earth he'd have been able to find me, and so quickly, was a mystery.

I silenced the thought. No sense worrying at things I could not produce answers to.

Carson, of course, was talking.

"… so do you *just* go through other worlds with that thing? Or can you kind of, I don't know, open a hole from your bedroom to your bathroom?"

My eyebrows twitched. "Why would you do that?"

"You could … I dunno … like, pee through it, or something."

"You can't see what's on the other side."

A pause. "Oh yeah."

"Gross, man."

"Okay, so not that, then. How about from your room to

the fridge?"

"No. Our world doesn't intersect other physical locations on itself, only other worlds. Why are you asking this? Do you just want to give up with the whole leg thing entirely and ride a mobility scooter everywhere?"

Carson flinched like the barbs in my words caused physical pain. "I was just wondering."

I made a "mrm" sort of noise.

Now he'd gone quiet again, I was safe to retract into my thoughts once more, no interruptions babbling away in my left ear like a radio host whose library had gone down and who had no choice but to fill air.

Feruiduin's Cutlass. Silently, my tongue traced the syllables.

I was certain that acquiring it would be just as much trouble as obtaining Decidian's Spear had been. But I knew how to get there, which made life infinitely easier.

Carson finally piped up again, "So what are we here for?"

"*We* are not here for anything. *I* am here because I need a spell."

"Like magic?" he asked, voice rising in surprise. "Magic is real?"

"Yes."

"So, does that mean … was *Harry Potter* true?"

I closed my eyes. "No."

"There's no Voldemort?"

"No Hogwarts either." That, or my invitation to attend had gotten lost somewhere en route.

"But orcs …"

"Dude." I snapped my fingers in front of his face. "*Potter* is fiction. Okay? End of story."

Carson quieted.

I sighed. "Magic is real, yes. But it's not easy to produce. For instance." I looked at him sidelong. "*You* couldn't produce magic if you tried."

"Could you?" he asked.

"No. Almost no one can anymore."

"So … where we're going … is it to see a person who can …?"

My lips pressed into a thin line. "Apparently."

I hated the very thought of it. Alone all these months, and suddenly needing to ask for help? I'd gotten by just fine, thank you very much.

But needs must, and all that, so I could only grin and bear it.

I read off numbers as we passed gargantuan apartment buildings; they were huge, red-brick affairs, six floors apiece. London property prices what they were, I doubted any single apartment went for a penny less than a million pounds apiece. To inherit one of these buildings would set a person up for life. More, even; probably could coast about sixteen lifetimes on that kind of dough.

At number 36, I said, "This is it."

Carson looked up. The building towered, so tall the morning sun couldn't find its way to us here.

"Nice," he said stupidly.

I climbed the steps, and rapped with a heavy iron knocker.

Barely before my arm had returned to my side, the door opened—

"Salutations, visitor! Pop in, yes?"

—and we were greeted by a clockwork butler.

"Uh …"

Carson reacted with a slightly more strangled sort of noise.

Happily, it said, "In you come, what-what?" And it stepped back, clanking away, to wave us through.

I obliged it, eyes raking it as I passed. It was a cheery thing, at least according to the smile that had been carved in its bronze-colored face. The mask did not cover it entirely, and gears were visible to either side, spinning frantically as it moved. A top hat, also made of metal, adorned its head. A slightly darker jacket formed the shell of its torso, the end of a long, spindly arm protruding from each inflexible sleeve. It tapered below that, a mass of gears and beams, to a pair of heavy-duty wheels.

Carson dawdled on the doorstep. Wide, wary eyes took in the mechanical butler.

"Please enter, visitor," the butler called to him, very Victorian-sounding and tinny. "I promise I shan't bite!"

Carson came, awkward and slow. "He can't bite, can he?" he asked me, skirting a wide berth around the contraption.

I shrugged. "Dunno. Probably wouldn't tell us if he could."

"Right you are," the butler said, perfectly cheerfully. Wheeling around, he extended his arms, whirring away as his joints flexed. When he stilled, a lower whirring continued as mechanisms inside turned and turned endlessly. "I presume you're here to see the Lady of the house?"

"This is a house?" I blurted before I could stop myself.

"Of course! Lady Hauk owns this entire building. It is *most* extravagant."

Damn. Six floors, all to herself. All right for some.

"Yes," I told the butler, "we're here to see Ang—Lady Hauk," I corrected. Best to be on most respectable behavior, even if we were only dealing with the rough (and somewhat outdated) approximation of human intelligence. "Please take us to her."

"Right this way!" And off the butler wheeled down the corridor.

Crimson walls, floors a deep mahogany … I could not help but take in its opulence. My library was one thing, but this … this was something else. "Majesty" would not do it, nor the scores of beautiful artwork on the walls, justice.

And supposing it did—well, it would immediately fall short at the *things* occupying the pedestals erected in this long, forking hall, or glimpsed through an open door.

Magical objects upon magical objects, one after another. Upon a fine silken cushion stood a golden cup, jewels encrusted in its surface. Hovering twelve inches above it was another, tilted on its side—and from it poured an endless stream of water. The cup below never overflowed.

Then there was a globe. Carved from wood, at first glance its oak surface was perfectly ordinary—until, that was, the Earth's continents flashed, replaced by the alien shorelines of another far-off world. A couple of seconds later it flashed again, and another set replaced it. Another flash, and the shorelines almost entirely vanished, save for a small ocean occupying less than a quarter-hemisphere. A mountain grew from the smooth surface, surely unimaginably massive given the size of the new blemish on this sphere. I longed to reach out and touch it, but I didn't dare lest the clockwork butler chastise me. In any case, it had vanished from the surface in another flash by the time I was close enough to do so.

Just where the corridor forked was a gear, turning slowly in the air, affixed to nothing. I wondered if this had come from the same realm as our escort.

Carson's mouth hung as his eyes hungrily devoured each object. It was hard not to do the same. Still, I did what I could to restrain my sensibilities. Hearts didn't belong on sleeves. Especially not mine: they were a mess of creases, and one was stained with blood to boot.

At the stairs, the butler ceased. Wheeling to face us, he extended one arm. "I must leave you—but my companion will join you at the top, and guide you to Lady Hauk. Pleasant visit, friends!"

I climbed, Carson followed, and as promised, a near-identical butler awaited us at the summit, the only difference being the slightly redder color of its faceplate.

"Salutations! To Lady Hauk, I understand. Let us be off!"

We climbed three sets of stairs like this. By the fourth, I was ready to ask if it would be considered impolite to crack open a can of liquid caffeine to see me through.

Fortunately, our last butler, faceplate almost black, finally directed us away from forking corridors and into a side room. "I shall pass you into the company of Lady Hauk, and will see you on the other side. Until then!"

I hesitated. The door the butler indicated was closed.

"Do we just go in?"

"Yes!" he chirped.

I exchanged a look with Carson and twisted the knob.

The room we stepped into was just as grand as I'd expected, going by the rest of the place. Bedecked in crimson and mahogany, a fireplace crackled on one wall below a mantel, a painting hanging above it depicting a quay filled with boats. An enormous grand piano filled one entire side of the room, and it played itself, melody slow and sweet.

Stood ahead of the fire, looking every bit as imposing as I'd expected her to be, in her wide-skirted black dress, a fat-petaled rose pinned in dark, swept-up hair above a thin and stern face—

"Well, well, well."

—was Lady Angelica Hauk.

"Who do we have here?"

# 11

She was an imperious sort of woman, and fit her title perfectly. Had I been born a Victorian girl, and brought before her for some indiscretion, I would certainly have cowed away from her unflinching gaze.

It was difficult not to do so even now, in twenty-first century London, when being a "lady" meant little more to me than having some land and a bit too much cash.

Filling my chest, I said, "I'm Mira. Mira Brand."

Carson, forgotten for a moment, nudged me. He whispered, "You did that reverse James Bond thing again."

I frowned at him, hard enough that he lifted an awkward smile and edged back a step.

Lady Angelica had not shifted. She studied with eyes like a hawk, penetrating, but unable to be penetrated in return.

"But of course you are," she said. "And what brings you here, young Mira? Come to live up to your famous name?"

Carson breathed, "Famous? Are you royalty?"

I flashed him another irritated look. "No more than you."

"But I'm American; I can't be—oh."

I ignored him. "I'm here," I told Lady Angelica, "because Benson recommended you."

An eyebrow, perfectly groomed and dangerously thin,

drifted half an inch up her forehead. "The broker?"

I nodded. "He said I could come to you—for a spell."

The eyebrow didn't dislodge. "I see." Taking well-practiced steps toward us, she clasped her hands, gaze on mine all the while. "And what precisely is it you require this spell for, hm?"

"I'm … looking for something," I said. "It'll help me get to it."

Vague. But Lady Angelica didn't push. Instead, she said, "And would you happen to have the *name* of this spell?"

"Yeah. I wrote it down."

I dug in my pocket, past my Railcard and a folded receipt from the morning's energy drink purchase. Among the few coins jangling in the bottom, all copper, was a thin scrap. I plucked it out. Folded so many times, it looked like a accordion by the time I unfurled it.

"Here," I said, and stepped forward to pass it over.

Lady Angelica did not reach for it, just peered at me from under that raised eyebrow.

"I, err, found it in a book. I can't say its name."

I fought back a flush of heated embarrassment.

She took it, holding it delicately between thumb and forefinger. Although written in small, untidy scrawl, I could see her eyes pass from left to right as she read it.

"Not too complicated," she finally said. "I can craft it, young Mira."

I waited. "The price?"

The soft curve of a smile crossed her lips. "Consider it a favor, hm?"

# 12

Lady Angelica guided us to a brewing chamber across the corridor. Filled with flasks and liquids of every color, it looked as though she had distilled the lightshow inside each of the gateways I opened.

"Pleasant brewing!" bleated the butler who had followed us, remaining at the threshold as we passed.

"Those things are weird," Carson breathed.

"I expect they must be somewhat peculiar if you're not used to them, yes," said Lady Angelica. She had already set to work, procuring stoppered flasks with purple contents from a rack. A label was stuck to the front, faded, text illegible. "They are, however, friendly, and of great use. For that, I find them invaluable."

"Where'd they come from?" Carson asked, transferring his puppy dog nosing curiosity to Lady Angelica. Thankfully.

"A world out of Delhi. It was utterly full of them, and just as friendly."

"Are they *alive*?"

"Oh, heavens no," Lady Angelica said, placing an armful of flasks down one by one on a surface beside a brewing stand. "They were constructed by a very prolific, brilliant inventor. I sought him out and requested he put together several that I might bring back with me. He was only too happy to oblige."

"We haven't seen anything like that, have we?" Carson asked me.

I wrinkled my nose, frowning. For the umpteenth time, I wanted to remind him that there was no *we*. It was just me, and a temporary tag-along, swept up in the ride.

"No," I said shortly.

"We saw this kind of forest," Carson continued in his usual babbling manner, oblivious to my irritation. "It looked like everything was made of glass. All the starlight came through, just reflected over and over again."

"It sounds beautiful," said Lady Angelica.

"But then there were these kind of dog things," Carson went on. "They were horrible, weren't they, Mira?" No answer from me, but he didn't pause for one anyway. "They howled, and it sounded like … like babies crying. Babies with asthma." He shuddered.

Lady Angelica had poured contents from half of her flasks into a larger beaker. Now she was adding the most gradual trickle from yet another, this liquid luminous green. She stirred with a glass rod all the while. The motion was so perfectly precise that *she* might be mechanical, like the butlers who'd escorted us to her.

"Some of the creatures in the worlds beneath are not to be trifled with," she said. "Escape should be conducted swiftly, and failing that, a solid evasion mounted."

Carson bit his lip. He cast me an aside glance, looking for a second as though he were weighing something in his mind.

At last, he said, "Some men chased us—in black cloaks. They had cinquedeas."

Lady Angelica paused her stirring. "The Order of Apdau."

"Who?" That was Carson, but I leaned forward an inch, interest suddenly piqued.

"An ancient order," said Lady Angelica. She laid the glass stirring rod gently on the surface beside her beaker, which had now gone white and cloudy, and lifted the cap of a five-inch glass test tube, like the ones from secondary school science. No liquid in this one; flakes of platinum material were nestled to halfway up. She tipped, tapping with a solitary finger, until one fell out. She dropped it into the beaker, whereupon it let off a belch of metallic gas and turned pitch black.

"What are they looking for?" I breathed.

"Decidian's Spear." She turned, peering at me with a stony expression. "Hence why they seek you."

I looked down at the umbrella at my belt, instinctively and guiltily. "How do you—?"

"Glamour is not impenetrable if you know how to look." Lips pursed, she rotated to the brewing stand. Setting the beaker upon it, she lit a flame. "I advise you to steer clear at all costs."

"We have been," I began.

She spun around again, a step closer to me before I could even blink.

"I mean this seriously, young Mira. The Order of Apdau are dangerous."

Yeah, well, both Carson and I could've told her that. At least now they had a name, though.

When at last Lady Angelica relinquished me from her gaze, she returned to the brewing stand. She twisted a knob to adjust the flame. It flashed white for a second, then reduced to a soft yellow glow.

"Your spell will take some time to prepare," she said.

I balked. "I can't have it now?"

"You can," she said, looking over her shoulder at me, "but it won't work. If you'd like it to function as intended, I recommend you return tonight, when the spell is complete."

My lips pressed into a thin line. Not only had I needed to rely on someone else's help, but now I was stuck in the lurch? Alain Borrick would be pressing for the cutlass even now.

But with no choice in the matter, I conceded. Another

trip to Kensington it would be, then.

We left the room, returning to the corridor and the butler with the black faceplate. He raised an arm.

"Greetings! Pleasant brewing, I trust?"

"As pleasant as brewing can be," Lady Angelica said. She started down the corridor. Carson and I followed, the butler whizzing around us to wheel along at Lady Angelica's side. For an older woman, she certainly pushed us to keep pace.

"Should I escort our guests to the front door, Lady Hauk?"

"No, thank you. I'll handle that myself."

"Of course! Have a pleasant day. Bon voyage, visitors." And he stopped dead in his tracks, like the brakes had been thrown and the power immediately cut. I glanced at him (it) as we passed; Carson did the same, mouth open wide, only turning again when he took a misstep and stumbled.

"Careful," I warned, voice low. The last thing I needed was for Carson to crash into the back of my apothecary. I'd probably end up coming back to a completed spell, but totally different to the one on my scrap of paper. Likely something that turned my head into a moose's, or something ridiculous like that.

By the time we reached the bottom, my legs were aching and tired again. Definitely needed to swig my second energy drink once we hit the street. Maybe, just maybe, it would give me enough buzz to drop Carson off, and get back to my hideout without wanting to curl up in a corner and fall asleep for twenty hours.

As we approached the front door, Lady Angelica slowed.

Carson, distracted yet again by the endless cup of water, nearly stumbled into her. I threw out my arm just in time to stop him. I shot him a dirty look; he returned it with an apologetic wince.

"Remember what I told you," Lady Angelica said.

Carson frowned. "About the butlers …?"

"The Order of Apdau are dangerous." She turned to peer at me, gaze unreadable, her lips tight. "Mysterious in equal measure, but very, very dangerous. Keep your eyes open. Your greatest chance of escape lies in seeing them before they see you."

"Right," I muttered.

Lady Angelica stared at me for a long moment. I did my best not to break her gaze.

"One last free and classic piece of advice for you, Miss Brand," she finally said.

'Free"—yeah, I'd bet. I didn't believe what she'd said about calling the spell a favor earlier, and nor did I believe what would come out of her mouth was without cost either. If she were anything like Benson, this advice would cost me a pretty penny indeed.

Lady Angelica's eyes brushed over my left arm. My sleeve, dark with a streak of blood, had rolled partway up my forearm. The long scratch left by my scuffle with mop-haired Burbondrer peeked out, two or three inches visible in raw red, crusted and scabbed.

Lady Angelica said, "Never let them see you bleed."

I followed her gaze, then met her eyes again. "Why's that?"

"Because they might continue under the misapprehension that they're near to beating you."

I stared, uncomprehending—was she referring to Brand lineage again?—but she said no more, turning away for the front door—though not before fixing me with the faint curve of a smile.

# 13

Lady Angelica guided us to the front door.

"Safe travels, Mira." To Carson: "And you, sir."

"Um." He cleared his throat, pulling at the strap of his manbag. "Thank you."

Lady Angelica stepped between us and opened the door. Somehow, she managed to look stately doing even this.

The sun was almost overhead now, so the long shadows of the road's extravagant houses had shrunk almost to nothing. The doorstep and the stairs leading down to the street were still cast in it, but halfway over the road, almost exactly at the center lines, sunlight was painted in a gorgeous bright bar. The buildings were all the more magnificent for the orange glow. If I didn't know better, I could swear we were approaching the height of summer, rather than having not long passed into spring.

The streets were not so busy here, but then why would they be? Sightseers and occupants of the neighboring apartments probably made up eighty percent of the street's foot traffic, with people passing through or lost comprising the rest.

Fortunately, with lunchtime looming, Russell Square would be positively heaving. A perfect time to rid myself of Carson.

I stepped out onto the expansive top step.

Just as I was about to say a final goodbye to Lady

Angelica, I paused. Someone stood at the bottom of the steps, on the street. A post was erected there, wrought iron bars bracketing either side of the stairs. A woman perched there, her back against it, arms folded.

As if she'd been waiting, she glanced around as Carson and I exited.

Our eyes met, then almost simultaneously raked down each other.

She was slightly older than me, I figured; nineteen, twenty, but not much past that. She was Asian, or at least had Asian heritage on one side of her immediate family. A scattering of freckles covered her face—out of place, in early April, which meant she must've returned from hotter climes in the not-too-distant past. Her hair was black, and cut short, just kissing her shoulders. Styled into waves that made her look like an anime character brought to life, her hair, her height—five-two? five-three?—alongside an almost delicately skinny frame made me think of a pixie.

She pushed out of her lean with her backside, thrusting it against the post to bounce to her feet. Rounding, she clambered the stairs with much more energy than I possessed. The unbuttoned shirt over her tank top fluttered. Holes were cut in skinny jeans, all the way from thigh to shin. Red Converse shoes slapped the pavement, somehow looking even smaller than I'd expected, and strangely flat.

"Ah, Ms. Luo," Lady Angelica greeted her.

Luo passed, gaze on me until the very last second. There was no warmth in her brown eyes. Her lips did not quiver in even the ghost of a polite smile.

In fairness, the same could probably be said for me.

I tuned out Lady Angelica's greeting to the ice queen and marched down onto the street.

At a streetlamp down near the next set of steps leading up to the neighboring building's door, I looked around.

Luo was just being ushered inside. She looked back at the same time I did, catching eyes—then the door closed, and she was gone.

Carson dawdled. Head craned right around, he stared after her.

"Dude."

Nothing.

"Dude!"

He jerked, like he'd fallen asleep and I'd set off one of those stupid air horns in his ear to wake him up. Spinning around, he cast me a guilty, wide-eyed look as he gripped his manbag between white knuckles.

"Sorry! I was …"

Checking out the Chinese girl?

Instead, I said, "Hurry up. I want to get to Russell Square."

"Why are we going to … oh." His face clouded. "I mean, yeah, I guess I should be getting back to my hostel."

"Yes, you should."

I hoped he'd just shut up. Yesterday—or today? It all seemed the same, seeing as about twelve hours had been chopped out of our lives, condensed to just twenty minutes—I had been bitten by some strangely forthcoming little bug that was perfectly happy and willing to entertain this fish out of water (nerd out of math club? I shook my head). But that willingness had deserted me. I was ticked off thanks to a combination of exhaustion and the need to just twiddle my thumbs and wait for my spell—and on top of it all, something about Luo on Lady Angelica's doorstep had rubbed me up the wrong way.

All I wanted was to offload Carson, get back to my hideaway, and finally enjoy some well-earned rest.

Unfortunately, my snippiness was either lost on Carson, or ignored, because just ten steps up the step, he blew out a breath and said, "So … those Apdau people. Creepy, huh?"

"Mm-hmm."

"And they're looking for your spear? Why do you think

they want it?"

"Haven't the foggiest," I said. I did, of course; a powerful object like this would outshine those cinquedeas any day.

"Maybe they're looking for things too? Do you think they have talismans of their—?"

Something elastic must've snapped, because I whirled on him, eyes boring into his. Four inches taller though he was, Carson was a pushover, and he flinched back like a lion in a zoo had suddenly gone for him behind the glass of its enclosure.

"Look," I said, fighting to keep my voice as level as possible. "Could you just … not *talk* anymore? Please? I have had it up to *here* today." I indicated my eyebrow.

"Um …"

"I am tired. I am stressed out. I have had to babysit you since yesterday afternoon. And although I am very sorry that you ended up being swept up in this, my patience has pretty much run out. The only thing keeping me going right now is this." I prodded the pocket holding can #2. Body heat had long since stripped it of the chill it possessed when I bought it. "So would you please, *please*, be a dear, and let me have some peace?"

Carson's mouth opened and closed. I pictured it getting stuck in a loop like that forever, him never finding the words to answer me, just gulping for air like a fish plucked out of the sea.

"Okay," he said. "Yeah, I—I can—can do that." He nodded, cleared his throat again. "S-sorry."

If I had more energy, I might have felt some semblance of pity for him. But right now, I neither had the capacity to ask if I could've handled the task of asking him to shut up a little better, nor the ability to feel bad for failing to do so.

So I grumbled, "Thank you," and swiveled, heading off again.

Carson's footsteps did not follow me.

I glanced back at him.

He'd frozen in place, like a rabbit caught in high-beam headlights, stuck as their little brains froze up—right before being smeared across the road.

Or maybe he was wondering whether he should just get out of my hair now; escort himself back to Russell Square. It would be the more honorable thing to do.

"Move it," I ordered.

But if that was what he had been wondering, he chose not to. At my instruction, his legs shifted back into motion. Nodding jerkily, he gripped the manbag close and trotted along behind me.

I held in a sigh as I trudged back to the tube station. Perfect opportunity for him to show some spine, and he'd still ended up crawling on the floor after my ankles. I dreaded to think what Carson's future held.

Thank goodness I'd never have to think of him again in just an hour's time.

# 14

I remembered, back before I ran away, when I was doing my research. Most of it was about other worlds, but I spent some time trying to get the measure of London, too, from everyone's best friend: Google.

Of course, that wasn't really possible; the only way to really come to understand a place was by living in its streets. But I distinctly remembered, even now, sitting in the library in Colchester, at a slow, chugging computer, as I looked up every place in London I could think of, and being incredibly taken by one particular piece of information. You see, at some point the boffins at Google must have tracked GPS data from people's mobile phones—or just sat out in places with clipboards and calculators, tallying passers-by—because many of the locations also showed a little bar graph of how "busy" a place was, broken down by hour and day.

Of course, for most of London, those bars were pretty high all the time. But the absolute peak was most often in the hours between midday and three p.m.: lunchtime.

I didn't have a phone to check anymore—too hard to keep the thing topped up, and why did I even need it anyway? It wasn't like anyone called me. And I got bored of texting and Snapchat lenses within the first five minutes—but if I *did*, I would bet any sum of money that Russell Square, at 12:26 p.m., matched its rounded peak almost perfectly.

It was heaving. The paths winding their way through the park were a constant stream of traffic, like the routes of endlessly busy worker ants. Under trees just now re-growing pale leaves were hordes of people arrayed on the grass: businessmen and women in suits and jackets, chowing down on sandwiches or pastas or sushi; a half-dozen groups of teenagers were spread on blankets, enjoying picnics, probably visiting for the day from some other corner of the country; an old married couple, who must've been at least seventy-five, sat side by side, reading. The old boy kept sneaking his wife glances. When she caught him, she nudged him and laughed, and granted him a peck on the lips.

Utterly sickening, in the best, cutest way.

"Right," I said, at a fork in the path. "This is me."

I turned to Carson. He'd not spoken a word since I reprimanded him down the street from Lady Angelica's. And although I was absolutely, positively, one hundred percent grateful for that, the bone or chunk of brain or whatever was responsible for feeling guilt was just starting to wake up again. Not feeling particularly *nasty* as such, but I was distantly aware that Carson's first experiences in London had been kind of a hot mess. Rounding that out with a good telling-off was probably enough to send him back home, writing England off forevermore.

He gave me a nervous look, unable to hold my eyes. He coughed. "Um. Well, err. Thank you for walking me back."

I didn't say *fine*, because it wasn't. Instead, I told him, "Have safe travels, all right? And check out all those places I told you about."

He nodded. Glanced at his shoes. My face. Then off over my shoulder.

"Right. Will do."

Okay then.

"Well, see you."

I turned to walk away—

"Wait!"

Pausing, I looked over my shoulder at him. If I lifted an eyebrow, I expected I'd be some kind of chav picture of Lady Angelica. The look I gave was a flat one, though.

"I was just, err, just wondering if you, um … if you had thought of anywhere else to visit."

I frowned. Now, really?

"No, I haven't. But I'm sure if you ask any one of the kind people out here, they'll be able to recommend you someplace."

And I turned on my heel, stepping away once more—

"Mira!"

Ugh. *What.*

Carson laughed nervously. "Those, um, those things that Lady Hauk had—th-those butlers. They were pretty … pretty cool, right?" Another nervous rattle of laughter.

Now I did lift an eyebrow. "Mate. Come on."

If looks could be spineless, the one he gave me definitely fit the bill.

"I'm leaving now," I said. Turned—

"Wait, Mira!"

He jogged up to me, caught me by the wrist.

I yanked it free, whirling on him.

"What do you think you're playing at? I've got things to do! I told you earlier, I've had enough of babysitting you!"

A young woman, very early twenties, walked by. She wore sunglasses, which made me want to say, *It's bright, but it's not that much like summer yet, love.* Although their dark lenses masked her eyes, the turn of her head in our direction was plain to see, as was the lowering of her eyebrows. She frowned, lip pushing down a beauty spot.

Great. We were beginning to cause a scene. Probably looked like some couple whose relationship had finally sputtered out on the streets of Camden.

Carson opened his mouth. Whether it was to argue, fire off some retort, or simply to let it hang before closing it again, doing that infuriating goldfish thing—how was it possible to be sick of a person's tics within less than twenty-four hours of meeting them?—I would never know. Instead his eyes drifted behind …

His face paled.

Behind us, people were suddenly screaming.

I turned on my heel, pumped with adrenaline.

Russell Square had thrown itself into action. Picnic blankets were abandoned as people climbed to their feet, bolting across the wide expanse of grass. The path emptied as others fled.

Striding toward us, cinquedeas drawn and glinting in the sunlight, they came:

The Order of Apdau.

# 15

My first thought was to do as Lady Angelica had said: to run.

But though the Order of Apdau made for us—for *me*—a large component of Russell Square was emptying in our direction. It was like that Indiana Jones thing; *why run from the boulder whilst remaining in the path of the boulder?* Hook a left out of there, damn it!

Net effect was that the crowd became too thick to make an escape.

Something else, too. I didn't *need* help or advice from anyone. I could do things my way, just like I had been.

And right now, feeling like I was sleepwalking, I had had enough of running.

I slipped the umbrella from my belt, extending it. It burst to full-length in an instant, glamour dissipating as it grew to its full size.

I brandished Decidian's Spear, teeth gritted.

"We've been through this!" I yelled. "I'd urge you to listen!"

The Order stopped just out of reach. Cinquedeas drawn and in hand, they looked poised to spring at any moment. I would have to trust that the adrenaline suddenly pulsing through my veins would be enough to keep me on my toes and fight them off.

And then what?

Didn't know, and right now, didn't care.

I jabbed air. In the midday sun, the dried orc blood had taken on a subtle blue sheen.

"I'll use it," I warned again. "Just watch me."

The Order seemed to converse in perfect silence, assessing …

Then the lead swung his cinquedea and barreled forward.

"Damn it!" I grunted, swinging the spear for him.

He dodged, throwing up the sword.

Spear and cinquedea clanged.

Barely before I had retreated a step, readying myself to swing again, another launched in from the right—and the third came at me on the left.

I bit back a string of curses, spinning.

Decidian's Spear slammed metal. A high-pitched whine shrieked, starting and ending in just a fraction of a second. Then I was darting sideways and back, feet working like one of the guests on those dancing shows, bringing the spear around—

This member of the Order was too close. He'd already passed the spear's bloody tip. Best I could do was whack him upside the head—

He ducked as it sailed over—

One hand thrust out, catching it. Still carried by momentum, I tripped—

"Hey!" I yelped.

Apdau #3 bared clenched teeth beneath his cowl. He swung up with the cinquedea in his free hand—

Leather sailed out of nowhere, smashing him in the face.

*"TAKE THAT!"*

He staggered back, releasing Decidian's Spear.

Left of me, Carson swung his manbag around. His mouth was wide open, caught between a snarl and a cry of fear.

Apdau #1 lunged—

"Carson, look out!"

He twisted.

A cinquedea sailed.

Carson ducked, almost too late, battle cry becoming a squeak of fright—I swore I caught sight of a tuft of brown hair flutter from where the blade just whizzed past his head—

Then I was swinging again, loosing my own roar.

The spear clashed, metal on metal, blocking one blade—

I dragged it around—

Metal flashed, and I jerked back as it sailed overhead—was that a tuft of *my* hair deserting me now?!—and then pushed forward, stabbing for the nearest cloaked man's midsection. He dodged back, though he didn't need to; I jerked back so the pointed tip stopped short of where he'd been standing.

For all my words to the contrary, I wouldn't kill these men. *Couldn't* kill these men.

But if it was my life or theirs …

One of the cloaked men was halfway through recovering. He planted his feet, pivoting, cinquedea just beginning to swing—

*"LEAVE HER ALONE!"*

Carson swung again. The manbag slammed the order member in the face, sending him staggering back—just what was he *packing* in that thing?—and then—

"Carson!" I cried.

He twisted around as another man leapt—

I swung the spear around—too slow, damn it!—

Carson hissed as the blade sailed across his midsection.

"NO!"

He stared in utter shock, totally uncomprehending.

Frozen to the spot, I did the same.

Time seemed to stand still.

He reached down, face paper white and eyes bulging as his fingers wrapped his sweater just where his ribcage ended, and lifted—

A hole had been sliced in it.

There would be blood, I was certain—

But then the hole widened as he pulled it open.

The shirt underneath was intact.

I didn't even have time to gasp, "They missed," because suddenly metal flashed again. I yelped, staggering sideways to dodge, bringing the spear up—the blade collided with the spear's handle, in the space between where each of my hands was planted. I grunted, biting my tongue as the force pushed me earthward and I fought to keep hold—

Another blade swung, low. I kicked up a leg. Air rushed past in a frigid breath—

Then I was rising—

Before I'd managed to, another swing crashed hard into the end of Decidian's Spear. The impact was almost enough to knock me off-balance again. I lurched backward, planting my foot to steady myself—

"BRAND!"

The cry split the air. I twisted for it, Carson doing the same.

There, across the way, was—

Luo?

She bounced on her heels just up the path. Body like a spring, coiled to the point of maximum tension and ready to erupt, she jerked her head at me, eyes icy.

"This way!"

Easier said than done!

I needed to buy us an out first though, otherwise we weren't going anywhere.

Spinning, I pushed all my energy into swinging Decidian's Spear in a wide arc.

"GET—LOST!"

The Order of Apdau dodged back as it sailed through the air—

"NOW! MOVE IT, CARSON!"

Then we were sprinting.

Luo didn't wait for us. Tearing into motion the moment she saw we could make a get-away, she sprinted with the speed of an Olympian down the path. I pumped my legs to keep up, grunting, torn between wanting the spear in hand to defend myself and wishing it would return to its umbrella form and make this escape slightly easier.

Carson barely kept up. On instinct, I gripped the spear one-handed and clasped his wrist.

"FASTER!"

Luo leapt off the path onto the grass. She shot a look behind us—the Order of Apdau were gaining, if my ears did not deceive me—and then, gripping something in hand, she chopped an arm through the air, neatly running it over the ground beneath.

The telltale blinding white edge of a gateway spilled across the grass.

"In here, quick!"

"What about you—?"

"I'll close it behind us! Go!"

I crossed the last of the distance in three great strides, leapt—

The compass!

—and then vanished from Russell Square, drowning in spiraling lights.

# 16

Wet.

Definitely not in Russell Square anymore.

Carson popped out next to me. He landed in just as ungainly a fashion as I had: the instant his body realized he had gone from land to an unending expanse of water, he flailed, gasping, arms thrust out and sending salty waves across my face.

"Quit splashing me!" I complained. "Just kick your legs."

Carson obeyed, although it looked as if it took great effort to do so.

Beside him, his manbag floated. Bobbing up and down on the water's surface, it looked like debris drifting from a wrecked ship, waiting to wash up on a shore a thousand miles off.

"Where are we?" Carson asked shakily.

I frowned. "No idea." I'd thought too late to give the compass a look.

But then, would it have mattered if I had? The Order of Apdau were much faster than we were. The only reason we'd got out in the first place was thanks to the help of our pixie-like accomplice. We didn't have time to sprint across Russell Square until the compass showed someplace more hospitable, let alone for me to cut us a gateway.

Speaking of our Asian friend, she popped in, much more gracefully than Carson or I had.

A stab of dislike went through me.

"Where are we?" Carson asked again.

I cut over him. "Who are you?"

She appraised me with a cold look. Even treading water, she looked so put together.

Kitted out in my shabby shirt and dark jeans whose stains were hidden only thanks to their color, I tried to push out a flush of self-consciousness.

"That doesn't sound much like a thank you, Brand," she retorted. "I just saved both of your arses."

"Thank you," Carson bleated.

I resisted the urge to prod him with the end of spear. (Just a little prod, mind.)

"Are you following me?"

Luo laughed, a short incredulous sound that was clipped, started and ended in half a second. "Why would I be following you?"

"You were outside Lady Angelica's—"

"I was paying a visit to Lady *Hauk*, not that it's any of your business—"

"—and then you just crop up in the middle of Russell Square like some—some—some *deus ex machina* elf girl—"

"*Elf girl?*" she repeated, face gone from cold to offended in a heartbeat.

"—and send us through to who knows where!"

"*Yeah.* I got you out of there." Luo sneered at me. "And again: I'm *pretty sure* that deserves a thank-you, Brand."

I pressed my lips into a line.

Kicking water beside me, Carson looked like he wasn't sure whether to try to convince me, or simply disappear into the sea like a human jellyfish.

"Fine," I muttered at last. "Thank you."

"You're welcome." Luo flicked her hair out of the water. "And for the record, I'm Heidi Luo."

"Carson Yates," he said softly.

"Mira Brand," I begrudgingly added. "Although by the sound of it, you already know that."

Heidi neither confirmed nor denied it.

Carson asked her, "Do you know where we are?"

"A water world," she said sniffily, "although that much should be fairly obvious. Lucky for us, this one's warm."

"There are cold ones?"

Heidi gave him a mildly perplexed look. "Yes."

"Is there *any* shore here?"

Heidi shrugged. "I haven't mapped it, but I know it, generally. From research."

From here, at least, there didn't appear to be any shore in sight. Kicking myself around in a slow circle, I could see only miles of endless, uninterrupted blue. A fat disc almost twice as large as the sun I knew best lay fairly low in a clear sky. No birds—which meant if there *was* a shore somewhere on this globe, it certainly was not nearby, assuming birds here had evolved in a remotely similar fashion to those streaking the Earth's skies.

Of course, I knew by now that this was by no means a given.

"So how do we get back to London?" Carson asked.

"This world connects to the Embankment tube station below us."

Carson stammered, "B-below?" He seemed to suddenly remember he was in wide ocean, where anything might lurk, because panicked eyes darted around the eddying waves he sloshed into motion around his awkward doggy-paddle.

"It's not far," Heidi said. "Ten feet, give or take. We came out somewhere shallow."

"Ten feet isn't *that* shallow."

"It's like three meters, dude," I grumbled.

Heidi started, "All we have to do is swim down—"

"Great," I muttered.

She paused, icy look on me again. "What?"

I didn't want to say. To put it into words—*I've had to*

*trust a stranger twice today already, and I don't want to do it a third time*—would sound stupid. But with Heidi frosty and waiting, and Carson's eyes bouncing between us like they were following a ping pong ball, I had to say *something*. So I begrudgingly forced the first excuse that popped into my head.

"Just that—there could be anything down there."

"Yeah; a gateway back to London, and a whole lot of water."

"Says *you*."

Heidi rolled her eyes. "Look, while we're all treading water, the surface isn't steady enough to open a gateway back to Russell Square. Plus it's been, what, three minutes? Your Apdau friends won't be far gone. Even if we could get through, you're only going to end up with a fight on your hands again—and *I* get the joy of saving the day."

Fire lit in my chest. "And why's that? We were holding our own just fine before you rocked up."

Not true, and Heidi knew it; she'd interrupted only moments before my legs went out from under me.

But unlike me, she was apparently unwilling to argue, because she rolled her eyes and said, "Whatever. I'm going down and opening a gateway out of here. Follow, or don't." And after a great inhalation, she disappeared under the surface. I caught a glimpse of red as her Converse trainers kicked, and then they too had descended past where I could see them.

I simmered.

"We could at least *try*," Carson said gently.

"We don't know what's down there," I muttered. Stupid, stupid excuse. Nothing had dragged us under yet; seemed doubtful by now that anything would.

Carson bit his lip.

"What?"

"*London* is down there."

"Well, you best get going then, hadn't you?"

He hesitated, torn. Then, with a last fleeting look, he took off his glasses, folding them into one hand, then sucked in a deep breath of his own, and disappeared beneath the surface. The last glimpse of him I had was his manbag trailing those terrible loafers.

I figured he'd pop back up after a moment. Limp rags tended to float, didn't they? But he didn't, and so I was alone, grimacing by myself atop a world-spanning ocean.

Just ten feet away. That's how far London was.

I harrumphed, like a horse.

"Damn it!"

And, sucking it up, I willed the spear to return to its umbrella form. Clipping it onto my belt, I checked it was affixed, then inhaled, and dived.

Heidi was right: ten feet, that was all that was in it. Not enough height to stack me twice, nor even enough for two Heidis, one balancing on the other's head.

A shimmering gateway was already open on the sea floor, which was dark and just as perfectly flat as I expected the sea had been before the three of us landed in it. The gateway's edges were tinged blue, and wobbled as my arms worked to take me down, down.

Heidi waited, breath held. Carson had already gone through.

She jerked her head at me. *Get a move on.*

I wouldn't just trust her instinct though, even if Carson had. Fingers fumbling as they continued to prune, I detached the compass from my belt.

I squinted at its face.

Sure enough, through a veil of blue, I saw the sign for the Embankment Underground station.

I swam through, not looking at Heidi as I passed. Probably had another thank you to prepare for on the other side. And oh, how I looked forward to it already.

Lights swirled around me. I held my breath in them; water would have passed through with me, and if I breathed now I'd inhale a lungful. A dim part of me hoped Carson did not make that mistake—

Then I was expelled in a fountain in a toilet stall.

Carson was up already. Sopping wet, he'd already replaced his glasses on his nose. He coughed, wringing his sweater out. Fat lot of good it did.

"Ugh." I shoved up, bracing myself on the toilet roll holder. My bulging eyes glared at the toilet. "Did we just—?"

Then Heidi erupted from it in a final shower of wet, confirming to me that yes, we had indeed passed back into London via a public toilet.

I prayed with all my might that it had been *clean* when we came through, neither yellow nor bobbing with something floating and brown—

"Get out," I ordered Carson. The words came warbled. Pretty sure I wasn't far off chucking my guts up. "Go!"

He opened the door, and stepped out. I strode after him, Heidi following—

A line of sinks stood opposite. A middle-aged woman with curly, greying hair had perched at one. Bag on the counter, open and forgotten, she clasped a tube of lipstick. Her eyes *had* been down at her feet, mouth drawing down in disgust at the sudden deluge of water around her heels.

Now she caught sight of us in the mirror. Her mouth hung, words dead on her tongue beneath huge eyes.

"It's out of order," I said, as helpfully as I could before beating a hasty exit.

# 17

We huddled onto the station's platform.

Carson mumbled, "People are, um, looking at us."

Yeah, no surprises there. We were sopping wet from head to foot, a fat puddle extending from our feet—and not slowly, either. Onlookers shooting us confused eyes steadily moved farther away as our personal pool widened on the platform. In true British fashion, of course, not one person said a word.

On the plus side, the wet and the ebbing remains of adrenaline from the clash in Russell Square had livened me up good and proper.

When the train pulled up, the three of us were the only people to board at the doors we selected. The passengers clambering off gave us utterly baffled looks. One asked his partner, "Should we have brought an umbrella?" Another skidded as he stepped out, legs jack-knifing before he got them under control. The few remaining in the queue decided to try their luck elsewhere, and made their way to the door at the opposite end of the carriage.

Despite the midday rush, by sheer luck there were three empty seats next to each other.

We dropped into them, each with a *squish*.

Ugh. Should've spent ten minutes crouched under the hand-dryers. Wouldn't have come even close to ridding us of the wet, but anything was better than sitting in slosh.

I'd taken the leftmost seat. Ten seconds after I sat, the man beside me let out a yelp. He looked down at the space between us, eyes bulging.

I followed his gaze.

I'd overflowed. Tan jeans now sported a much darker spot along the full length of his right thigh.

"Sorry," I offered lamely.

He shot me a hard look, but didn't say a word, rising and edging away from our latest pool, now growing in the aisle.

Beside Heidi, her neighbor seemed to be enduring it. Same as the passengers directly opposite. One woman lifted her bag before the advancing wave met it; the others remained stoic as the pool crept around their shoes.

When the doors closed and the train started into motion, Carson mumbled, "We should've found towels."

"From where?" I breathed. "I know you haven't been here long, but in the time that you *have*, have you *ever* seen a towel stand in a tube station?"

"I meant on the street or something."

"Sure. We should've headed up and found the local seaside shop, maybe picked up a couple of buckets and spades while we're at it."

"But there's no beach near Lon—oh."

I did my best not to roll my eyes. If I started, I might never stop.

We were quiet until the next station, just three minutes up the line.

Half of our carriage were up on their feet the moment the platform came into view. Almost all, I noticed, were passengers in our direct vicinity. The woman opposite clutched her bag in her arms like a rugby player barreling across a pitch. Two seats down, a middle-aged businessman with sallow skin and tired, weary eyes rose, then slipped and fell heavily into his seat again. I winced, ready to apologize, but he righted himself and made his way to the doors without even a glance.

A handful of new passengers climbed aboard. Most, however, stepped in and saw two women and a man looking like drowned rats in the seats opposite, not to mention the watery bay that seemed to have devoured half of the carriage's floor, and they climbed straight off to find a seat elsewhere.

With most of our neighbors gone, Heidi extricated herself, dropping into a seat opposite.

Her anime-character hair was flat to her cheeks. I took a moment's pleasure in enjoying it before remembering that I probably looked about the same.

When the train started up again, Heidi asked, keeping her voice low and measured, "So where are we going now?"

My nostrils flared. *"We?"* What was it with hangers-on this past couple of days? "The only place *we* are going, me and Carson, is back to Russell Square so I can drop him off."

"But those guys ..." he started in a whine.

"Don't worry," I griped. "I doubt they're hanging around, hoping we pop up again. They're probably halfway across London by now."

"But what if—?"

"But nothing." I rounded on him, teeth gritted. "We had this talk earlier, Carson. I'm finished babysitting."

"Harsh," Heidi muttered.

"None of your business, is it?" I countered.

"I'm just saying. You don't need to be insulting."

"How am I insulting?"

"By calling it 'babysitting'. He's not a kid. He looks older than you."

"I really do, don't I?" Carson mumbled.

I ignored him, still on Heidi. "Not that I particularly care about what you think, but I've been dragging homeboy over London for close to twenty-four hours now." Not quite true, with that lost time in the fairytale square, but that wasn't for her to know. "In that time, we've been set upon by the Order of Apdau three times, had to escape into an abandoned building, been *arrested* and escaped the station, had to climb a tree made of glass to avoid being eaten by a creepy blind wolf thing that I'm pretty sure *could speak English*, and taken the world's biggest bath, courtesy of you. I haven't slept, haven't eaten, and haven't had a moment's peace without Yankee Doodle here yammering away at me."

The guilty little fragment of me would feel bad for this later. But now I'd started, fatigue mingled with anger had stripped away my social graces and I couldn't stop, whether Carson was perched immediately beside me or not.

"He is an albatross around my neck that I don't need, and which I never asked for."

Heidi's eyebrows had drawn right down her face. She frowned, and I was reminded of one of my primary school teachers, who had overheard me telling Suzie Bates that she couldn't play with me and my friends because she had a nose like a parrot's beak.

"What a wonderfully charming girl you are," Heidi bit off.

"Butt out."

"No, I won't." She leaned forward, across the aisle, hard eyes on mine. Again, I had a flash of a teacher doing the same, a different one this time over a separate infraction. "I'll grant that I don't know much of your story so far, Mira—"

"Then don't comment on it."

"—but the Order of Apdau are looking for *you*. Not Carson, here; you, Mira Brand."

I pursed my lips. "Whatever."

Heidi's eyes flashed. "Sure. Blame him. It's all his fault, of course. Not for one second could trouble possibly be attributed to *famous* Mira Brand." The word 'famous' rolled off her tongue with all the sarcasm in the world.

"And what's that supposed to mean?"

"*You're* the one going around causing problems. Starting things with orcish hordes?"

Alain Borrick's smarmy leer flashed in my head. It was replaced with a flash of falling, then the awkward clash with Burbondrer.

"How do you know—?"

"Word travels." Heidi reclined. One leg crossed over the other. "I get that you've got a lot to live up to, but could you maybe consider handling yourself a bit better? You don't get glory for infuriating people and starting fights."

I bristled. Whether she realized it or not, she'd cut far, far too close to the nerve. I wanted to kick back with some barbs of my own—but what did I really have? The best I could call her was a know-it-all. And anyway, if not for her, Carson and I might still be in Russell Square, possibly in pieces.

As much as it turned my stomach to admit it ... I *owed* her.

The train pulled into the next station. A few last passengers exited the carriage. They were replaced in equal number, though these new ones also took seats at the farthest end of the carriage.

I quieted, grateful for the interruption.

When our journey resumed, I got back to the most important matter at hand.

"We're going back to Russell Square," I told Carson, "and you are going to say goodbye, *properly* this time, short and sweet. And then we're going to go our separate ways, and God willing, never see each other again. Got it?"

He licked his lips, bottom then top.

"I could help ..."

"No, you couldn't."

"I'm sure he could," said Heidi.

I pretended like she hadn't spoken. Which was difficult.

"When those Apdau guys came for us, I got a couple of good hits in," Carson said.

I gritted my teeth. Fine. But I wouldn't concede. Most

people probably got a few good punches in when their lives were on the line. All Carson's manbag-swinging proved was that his flight response could, on occasion, be overridden by the fight response.

"I could help you on your quest—" he began again.

"Tell me what you'd do if you crossed paths with a black-eyed howler."

Carson paused. His eyebrows drew in, imprinting the shadow of a comma between them. "A what?"

"A black-eyed howler. What would you do?"

"I, err …" His gaze drifted to Heidi as though she was a lifeline.

I snapped my fingers in front of him, got him to refocus.

"Black-eyed howler! What would you do, Carson?"

"I would, um … I would …" He cleared his throat, swallowed; it clicked. "I don't know what one of those is."

"Exactly." Straightening in my seat, I grumbled, "You're about as much good to me as the morons in Geordie Shore."

In the corner of my eye, Carson's face flashed in confusion. "Do you mean Jersey Shore?"

"See?" I said to Heidi. "No good to me. I'm better off doing what I've always done, and going it alone—for my sake, *and* his."

"Going it alone *where?*" Heidi asked.

"None of your business."

"No, go on. Enlighten me."

Carson said, "You said you were looking for—"

"Quiet." I silenced him with a hand: *stop*. Like a warden guiding traffic around a busy car park.

Heidi said, "Come on. I'm *curious*, all right? Plus I saved your arse back there. The least you can do is entertain me."

No. Not going to happen.

But … she *was* right. She had saved us.

And maybe I wanted to brag. Prove a point, and all that;

show her that much as she had rescued me and Carson, I was more than capable. That *this* Brand was more than meeting the bar everyone else seemed to think I was jumping for.

Plus, with the hair plastered to her face, her drowned-rat look helped take out a bit of her sting, too.

Carson opened his mouth again.

I cut him off before he could begin. These was *my* quest, damn it. The geek wasn't going to tell it for me.

"I'm after the Chalice Gloria."

Heidi waited, as if there were more—and then her face broke with disbelieving laughter.

"What's funny?"

"*You*—" she pointed "—are looking for the Cup of Glory?"

"What's so funny about that?"

"That's crazy, even for a Brand."

"What does she mean—?" Carson started in my ear.

I was talking over him already. "How is that crazy? I'm a *Seeker*, just like I figure you must be, with your bracelet there. I *seek* things, and so I'm seeking this."

Heidi let out another short staccato laugh.

My blood started to boil.

"Yeah, well, good luck with that," she said. She shook her head. "Cup of Glory. Oh my days."

"I don't understand," Carson muttered. He was looking between us again like he was following a ball batted back and forth.

"The *Chalice Gloria*, Cup of Glory, is like the Holy Grail for treasure seekers," Heidi explained to him. "And it's been lost for … how many years now, Mira?" She didn't wait for me to answer before continuing to Carson, "It's a pointless exercise, is what I'm getting at. Others have tried and failed." Glancing at me, she added, "I guess now there's another one to add to the list."

"Hey, I found Decidian's Spear all right, didn't I? Step one of the process, done." I unclipped the umbrella and brandished it. "You want to tell Carson how long *that* was lost for, up until yesterday?"

Heidi's gaze slipped over it. Her mouth opened, ready to bite off some retort. But I had her; she'd seen it with her own eyes in Russell Square.

When she met my eyes again, there was a begrudging kind of respect in them.

"Well done," she said, slow. "But the Cup of Glory—that's a whole other ball game. You need two keys—"

"And I've got one," I pointed out, tapping the umbrella.

"That's not the point. Feruiduin's Cutlass is just as lost, and if the stories are true, you'll need *both* to get to the Chalice."

"What, and you think I just got lucky in finding this thing? Seekers spent whole *lifetimes* looking for Decidian's Spear. It took a seventeen-year-old girl in London's West End to find it again on an April afternoon. I know what I'm doing. I found the spear, and I will find the cutlass too, *and* claim the Chalice Gloria as my own."

Heidi quieted.

Finally, after a long pause, she said, "You know where to find Feruiduin's Cutlass then, do you?"

"Yes," I said with more than a touch of Heidi's own sniffiness, "I do."

She seemed to assess for a moment—and then a bemused, lopsided grin split her face. "Well, now this I have to see."

"No—" I started.

But: "Me too," said Carson over us both. "Just one question, though. What exactly does this Chalice Gloria look like?"

# 18

London, the Strand; currently dawdling like creeps just outside the Tortilla restaurant.

Strangely *wet* creeps.

I ignored the latest glance fired our way, this from a lone young man exiting Tortilla. His steps slowed for just a moment as his eyes swept down.

Move along. Just move along.

"You wanna remember to use that next time," he called, and pointed at the umbrella at my belt. Then he was off, smirking over his shoulder.

"Thanks for that," I muttered.

"We look stupid," said Carson. "Can't we just go through?"

"It's lunchtime," I retorted. "You see all these people out here? I cut through now, we'll be seen."

"I thought everyone in London was wrapped up in their own thing," Carson said.

"Yeah, and most of them are. But when you get three people stood awkwardly in the middle of the street like us, soaked from head to toe like they've just been splashing around in the fountains over there in Trafalgar Square," I waved a hand to my right, "that tends not to hold true anymore."

True enough, another passer-by, this one a middle-aged bespectacled man a long way into the process of balding, pointed at the spear-become-umbrella and said, "You know that thing's more than for just looking pretty; it protects from showers too." His overweight wife, hanging onto his arm, tittered.

"You're a real gem," I tossed after him. He ignored me, though.

"We can't stand here forever," Carson said.

"Look, let's just wait for a big enough crowd to pass, and duck in then," said Heidi. "There's one coming now, see?"

Foot traffic was like vehicular traffic: it came in stops and starts. A handful of people would pass, all separated; then a crowd of some dozen or more, like a clot. True to Heidi's word, one of these clots was coming our way. All of them in worlds of their own, they stumbled along, totally oblivious of the congealed mass of people they had been swallowed into.

We waited. I clutched my talisman tight, free hand at my side but ready to jerk up at a moment's notice and open the gateway.

The blob overtook Heidi—

"Now!" she whispered.

Carson and Heidi huddled close. I sliced a line, praying that it was hidden between ourselves from the thirteen or fourteen people passing by, and that they obscured any white glow from making its way to the rest of the street.

The gateway opened—

"In," I said, already stepping through.

"I'll close," Heidi started. I assumed she would have finished, 'it when we're through.' But the words were lost as London swept away, and I passed through the familiar swirling lightshow.

I landed back on my feet in the library under the "LONDON" sign.

Carson followed. And lastly, bringing up the rear, was Heidi.

"Closed," she said. "I assume unseen, too—*whoa*."

"Don't touch anything," I said, all of a sudden a librarian. "Not until we've dried off."

"You've got a bathroom here?" she asked.

"In the back. And towels. This way."

I headed down the library's central spine. Heidi and Carson fell in behind me. Although he'd seen it before, he took the place in much the same as she was: by craning his neck, eyes drifting over the lights, enormous shelves, across tomes which had been lightly dusted in the long years since they were last retrieved.

I wondered, as I went: why had I even entertained bringing them here? I was supposed to be freeing myself of the anchor that was Carson Yates. As for the debt to Heidi, I considered that repaid. She knew what the 'famous Mira Brand' was up to; more than that, she knew that the Chalice Gloria was still out there, and that I knew where. Anything beyond that didn't concern her in the slightest.

So why was I here, not alone like I intended, but joined by Yates and Luo?

It was, I supposed, to prove a point.

Where the last shelves ended, and the floor opened out into the space before the fireplace, desks were arranged. I suspected there had once been chairs, when this place actually was used as a library, so patrons could sit for a spell. Today, only one remained: a battered thing, stained very dark, with a deeply uncomfortable seat.

As I made for the kitchen, Heidi dawdled at one of the tables.

A small collection of books remained on it, abandoned in a stack. There was also a newspaper, so old the text on it had almost faded to the color of the paper.

She bent over, sideways so the drips from her hair would not land on its crumpled surface.

"November 11, 1912," she read off. "Has this place been disused since then?"

"It was empty when I got here in January," I said. "As

for the other hundred and five years, I couldn't tell you."

I led us into the kitchen. Trying that trick of opening the steampunk fridge door and hoping the contents had miraculously changed since the last time, I was disappointed.

"You, um, want a carrot?"

"I'm fine, thanks," said Heidi. "Ate before I got here."

On cue, Carson's stomach gave a sorry grumble.

"Carrot?" I offered, holding one out.

"Um … maybe we can just stop off somewhere so I can get something when we're back in London."

"Suit yourself." I stowed the orange vegetable. Didn't blame him really. I made steps to eat healthy (energy drinks today ignored, of course), but even hungry I wasn't likely to snack on a carrot to keep me going. Especially not this one. The telltale leafy sprouts at the top showed just how long it had been in here. And it had grown a whole bunch of stringy white things down the sides, too. Totally harmless (I didn't usually bother peeling them off if I was cooking), but not very appetizing.

I attempted to fill out the hole in my stomach with my last apple, made a mental note to rustle up the funds to buy some more, and filled myself a glass of water.

"So, this Cup—" Heidi started.

"Not yet." I held up a finger. "I'm not talking about anything until I've changed out of these clothes and dried off."

"I can get behind that," she said, nodding. "Have you got anything in my size?"

Hmph. It wasn't enough that I was saddled with her, but now she wanted to borrow my clothes, too?

"Doubt it," I said, looking her over. "My stuff will come up a bit big on you."

"That's fine, I can deal with that."

Carson cleared his throat. "What, um, about me?"

"Definitely not," I said. "Unless you want to walk around the streets of London in a tank top?"

He didn't. Which was unfortunate, because after the day I'd had, I could really use the laugh.

Once I'd stripped, dried, and changed, I dug out some things for Heidi to wear. I made a point of finding my least liked t-shirt, a red and black thing with a band's logo printed on the front. It was mostly faded by now, not unlike my interest in their music. I wouldn't have even had it if I hadn't packed on such short notice, snatching it from the top of a pile awaiting hanging. Then, I'd figured I'd replace it at the earliest opportunity. Months later, foisting it on Heidi was probably as good as I was going to get.

Carson, I gifted a towel. He took off his glasses and manbag, and rubbed it over himself with little vigor. His hair stuck up in spikes that were about as close as Carson would ever come to looking 'cool.' Then, of course, the eyes shifted down to his sweater plastered to him, with a great gaping hole through to his shirt, and the paper-thin illusion was quashed.

Heidi returned to the kitchen, breaking the awkward quiet with a, "Much better."

Her hair was arranged in those same loose waves she'd had outside Lady Angelica's. Still damp, they'd regained about half of their previous volume. Without a hairdryer on hand to help things along, it was about as close as she'd come here; sun and air would have to do the rest.

In the shirt and tank top and jeans she'd shrugged out of, she didn't look particularly incredible. Not super fashionable, but not out of place either. She *had* looked put-together.

Now, in my clothes, she looked anything but. Even if they hadn't been a couple of sizes too big for her, my jeans looked ratty, the bottoms fraying at the back where I'd spent months treading on them. The band t-shirt was the same, crumpled and dull.

I felt a self-conscious stab opposite her. Was this what I walked around looking like?

If Heidi thought the same, she had the good grace not to mention it.

She took in Carson's spiky brown hair. "Looking good."

A laugh almost burst from my lips. I held it in; I figured he probably needed this one.

"Y-you think?"

"The hair, sure. Suits you. The clothes stuck to you … not so much."

He laughed nervously. "Yeah, I thought as much. No danger of this becoming the latest fashion trend, right?"

Bang on there, buddy.

"So, this Cup—" Heidi began, picking up from before our pause.

"First things first," I cut over. "The Chalice is mine, and mine alone. We've got to be clear on that."

"All right," she said.

"I'm serious. I'm letting you on this trip with me only because you're so insistent. I don't want *you* here, and I don't want you here." This was to Carson. He shuffled awkwardly and avoided my eyes. "But if you're intent on coming, even *helping me*—" another look to Carson "—then we need to be in agreement before we go even a step further."

"Okay," Heidi said, "got it. Chalice is yours. You don't need to tell me twice."

I eyeballed her, debating whether or not she was trustable.

Potentially. She was connected to Lady Angelica at the very least, which was a good sign.

Besides, going by the look on Heidi's face, she still didn't believe I had any idea what I was talking about anyway.

"Okay, then," I conceded. "Now that's out of the way: the Chalice is held in a temple. As you've already made clear you're aware, Decidian's Spear acts as a key. The *second* key is Feruiduin's Cutlass."

"Thanks for repeating our conversation on the train,"

Heidi said sarcastically.

Carson's lips silently worked at the name Feruiduin. "How do you spell that?"

"F," Heidi started.

"This isn't a spelling bee, so it's irrelevant," I cut across. "What's important is how we get it—how *I* get it."

"I'm listening," said Heidi.

"It's … a little dangerous," I began.

"Keep talking," said Carson.

I looked at him like he'd gone mad.

At his side, Heidi did the same.

Carson hesitated. Tugging his manbag's strap tight to his chest, he said, "What?"

# 19

From over my shoulder, Heidi said, "That's not good."

We were on King William Street, outside Regis House. An eleven-story high-rise, it made the apartment buildings in Kensington, and Lady Angelica's house, look positively dinky by comparison. Ornamental trees were planted off the curb, spindly trunks rising from wooden planters. More than a few cigarettes had been stubbed out in the closest one. Stay classy, London.

The time was approaching three o'clock now. We'd been slowed so Carson could nip into a little corner shop and pick up a sandwich. He blanched at the price of the first one he chose, settling instead for tuna and cucumber.

"Do you, err, want me to get you anything?" he offered.

Heidi had declined, and so had I. Now, midsection feeling like an enormous black hole once more, I wasn't sure if I regretted doing so. I hated the idea of taking anything from Carson—or anyone else for that matter.

Still, I lamented, lips pressed into a thin line, I'd saved him from the Order of Apdau outside Piccadilly Circus, and kept him clear of danger in the Forest of Glass. If anything, *he* owed *me*. Buying me lunch seemed only fair, in the scheme of things.

The sun was sinking now, shadows growing across the streets. A breeze had picked up, bringing with it a chill that reminded me that no matter how bright it was, we were still just a couple of weeks into spring. At least the short-lived warmth had done something to dry Carson out. He was still damp, of course, but his hair looked mostly normal again (although he kept running a self-conscious hand over it, I spied from the corner of my eye), and his clothes weren't clinging to him quite as much as they had been back in my hideout. He probably wouldn't be totally dry by nightfall, but I figured however the afternoon went, he'd be back at his hostel by then, high and dry and out of my hair at last.

"What's not good?" he asked, peering over my shoulder.

"Boundary," said Heidi.

I held my compass so he could see. The image was split almost directly down the middle. Both sides were dark, but coals flickered in the one on the left: a distant campfire, by the looks.

"We've been going up and down for ten minutes," I told Heidi. "It's not getting any better."

Carson said, "Can't you find where the edge disappears?"

"No," I said shortly.

"I'm telling you, it's going to be in one of those somewhere." Heidi pointed at the store fronts to left and right of the grand glass doors into Regis House itself: Waitrose and Pret a Manger respectively. "Maybe even the office itself."

"Brilliant," I muttered. "Let's just pop open a gateway on the side of a box of corn flakes, shall we?"

"Well, is that our only option, or isn't it?"

My lips thinned. My research showed a slightly back-and-forth trek ahead of us before we would come close to where we needed to be; a jump back into London would be necessary after passing through this next gateway. Accessing this midpoint from here was going to be impossible, though—which meant finding a connection point to the darkness on the right side of the compass was a necessity.

"Fine," I grumbled. "Which do we check first?"

"Waitrose," said Heidi immediately. "Easier to loiter in a supermarket."

We made our way inside.

This Waitrose was small, and even boasted as much: 'little' stood atop the Waitrose logo in white letters. One of the convenience branches, this particular shop had sprung up like so many others to take advantage of London workers too lazy to put together their own lunch, or caught short and needing to grab something for dinner on the way home. Everything was overpriced, even by the combined standards of London and Waitrose, itself a knock-off Marks and Spencer as far as I could tell.

We wove through aisles, me with an eye on the compass all the while. No suspicious looks here; Carson looked like he'd been caught in a short-lived if somewhat intense shower, so except for the occasional squinted glance as a shopper tried to recall whether or not it had rained today, we made our way around the shop without much notice paid to us at all.

By the time we reached the end, the thin line of my lips had become even thinner.

"Not in here," I muttered, heading out the door.

"Let's try Pret a Manger, then."

"How are we supposed to sneak around a bloody sandwich shop?" I hissed. "Let alone cutting a gateway through." I didn't want to even *think* of the possibility that a safe connection point might be in the men's toilets.

"Just act natural," Heidi said, holding the door into Pret open for us. "Walk like you know where you're going."

"I *do* know where I'm going," I griped. "I just don't understand how I'm supposed to get there with half of London watching me over baguettes and overpriced coffee."

A serving station greeted us almost immediately, curving alongside the door and then making its way farther back into the restaurant. A small queue was arranged already.

Two servers busied themselves making drinks. The fellow at the end of the line, who was somehow even shorter and skinnier than Heidi, and sported a thick coating of facial hair, was alternately evaluating a display of cakes and trying to catch the eye of one of the staff.

Cake. God. *Cake.*

Sugar cravings be damned. More important things going on, remember?

The rest of the restaurant was open plan, round and square tables arranged in some semblance of order on a polished hardwood floor, very light in color. Only a third were occupied, most of these by the windows. A couple of occupants glanced our way in typically nosy British fashion as we stepped inside, then resumed people-watching through the glass.

I stepped in—

*"Yes,"* I hissed almost immediately.

"Got it?" Heidi asked.

I showed her the compass face. The boundary had vanished instantly, not pushed away but simply gone in a single step. There was only darkness now, the faintest glow coming from somewhere to the left. Less than ideal, usually, but right now I swelled with excitement.

"But where do we cut through?" Carson asked.

I glanced up. No one inside was really looking our way. But we still could hardly open a gateway on the wall. Uninteresting as we might be, I figured a great long bar of shimmering white light would probably change that pretty quickly.

Fortunately, at the very end of the counter was a drinks cabinet. Filled to the brim with what looked like all thirty-eight current variants of Coca Cola, or however many there were, fruit juice and bottled water were relegated to the very bottom. No price list printed on it, like the cabinets I tended to cross paths with (in off-licenses, mostly), but I bet they were expensive.

If we just ducked around the side …

"I'll need you to block me from view," I told Heidi and
Carson. Mainly him, though I was grudging about it. Heidi
would block little more than my left arm. At least thanks
to his height, Carson had *one* use. "I'm opening it here, on
the side of the cabinet."

"In view of the street?" Carson asked, eyes wide.
Something flashed in them; not fear, but excitement.

"It's the street alone, or street and the restaurant. Now
let's—"

"Are you all right there?"

One of the servers had called to us. She looked at us
expectantly, eyebrows raised and mouth open. Opposite
the counter, the man eyeing the cakes followed her gaze,
looking none too pleased we were keeping him from the
slab of coffee cake the server was midway through placing
on a plate.

"We're fine," said Heidi, smiling politely. "Just
browsing."

"All right." And the server went back to the cake man.

"Let's be quick," I said. "Come on."

I maneuvered to the edge of the drinks cabinet.
Checking one last time that the compass still indicated the
dark place on the other side, and no hint of the
encroaching boundary toward the street, I clutched my
talisman, feeling its warmth. Carson arranged himself very
close to my back, blocking as much of the window as he
could—it wasn't anywhere near enough—and Heidi
pressed in from the other side.

I dreaded to think what we'd look like to anyone who
should glance our way now.

Which was all the more reason to do it quickly.

I cut a line.

The gateway shimmered, opening wide and bursting
with light—

"In!" I whispered, already going.

Through lights, I swirled. I wished I could twist behind
me to see if they had come fast enough—but forward

momentum was retained, and in this surfaceless space between worlds I had nothing to brace against to turn, so I had no choice but to hold my breath as lights whizzed by, reds and greens and vibrant purples like a rainbow poured into water—

Then I was out, and blind.

# 20

Not blind. It was just dark, that was all. And there was light *somewhere*; we'd seen it in the compass, so incredibly frail but absolutely leaking in weak shafts into this deep grey expanse.

Heidi dropped in behind me. Though I couldn't see, I could tell by the sound that she'd landed spryly, infinitely more graceful than my stumbling lurch into the darkness.

I hoped she was the only one, that she had followed behind me and closed the gateway on Carson, bringing my entourage down to one—but then he came, staggering awkwardly like he'd been shoved.

"Hey!" Heidi snapped.

"Sorry—geez, it's *dark*."

"You're stepping on my ankles!"

"S-sorry!" More scuffling. "Does anyone have a flashlight? I can't see—"

"No one can," I whispered. "Just stay quiet, all right?"

"But—"

"*Shut up,*" I hissed. "You want some cave monster to come and find us?"

"Are we in a cave?"

There was a thump of flesh, closely followed by a breathy "Oof!" from Carson. Sounded like Heidi had elbowed him. He quieted after that though, so I would make a rare point of thanking her when we knew the coast was clear.

I waited, trying to absorb every sound in the darkness, waiting for my eyes to adjust. Trickling came from somewhere. In the opposite direction there came an occasional click, very light, as though some small creature had crawled over loose stone and sent one or two pebbles rolling no more than six inches.

If there were any other noises, I could not detect them—although given how heavily Carson was breathing, practically right in my ear, I'd probably miss a rock band playing just feet away, amps turned all the way up to eleven.

"Okay," I whispered at last, digging in my pocket for my flashlight. "We're clear."

Thankfully I'd had some spare batteries in my hideout, since I hadn't managed to reclaim the confiscated pair from the police station. Even more thankfully, despite being submerged in the ocean of another world, it still worked.

I brought it out and clicked it on.

Cave. High-roofed, dark, empty. The ground tended downward on our left, climbing much more steeply on the right.

Carson exhaled in relief. "So we're in the right place?"

"Looks like it."

"What was the other side of the boundary? It looked like a campfire."

"Fire nymphs," said Heidi. "Hostile. You'd have needed asbestos knickers to get through that."

Carson gripped my shoulder with a panicked hand. "But there are none of those fire things in here, right?"

I shrugged out of it, shooting him a dirty look he probably didn't catch as I swung the flashlight around. "You see anything glowing and red?"

"No."

"Then we're probably in the clear."

"At least here," said Heidi tightly.

"Right. Which is why we should move. Come on."

"Which way?"

I gave a mental double-check to my research. "Left," I said, pointing. And thank goodness for that: it was much easier to traverse in this direction. "Watch your step, though." I threw this over my shoulder to Carson. I trusted Heidi could move. Him, on the other hand … knowing my luck, he'd step into the trickle, his feet would go out from under him like a cartoon character stepping on a banana peel, and then he'd sail out of sight, yelping every time his coccyx slammed stone until even that sound was a distant memory.

It would rid me of him, though.

Not that I was anywhere near cruel enough to entertain just abandoning him if he *did* vanish into the bowels of this world. It would make life a heck of a lot easier if I were, though.

I picked my way across rock. The tunnel's floor rose and fell in knobbles, sleek and rounded. Not a lava tube, by the looks; I'd not traversed one myself, but I'd seen enough photos in my research to know this uneven a floor was not typically a feature. No, this cave had been carved by water, eroding the softer material and softening the remaining edges over the millennia. It was kind of pretty, though I couldn't help but wishing I'd packed better footwear.

Now that my eyes did not need to fight the pitch, and my ears, though still pricked, were no longer listening as intently for danger as when we'd first stepped through the gateway, I could let my other senses loose.

The air was beautifully cool on my skin; not remotely like the chill of the April breeze outside Pret a Manger. A definite dampness hung in it. I'd gone camping in France a couple of times when I was younger, and most mornings awoke with a sheen as though dew had permeated my tent and condensed on me instead of the grass. If we were to camp out here for a night, I was certain we'd all wake with that same covering of moisture.

The smell was gloriously earthy. A soft watery tang hung in the air too, tainted with the coppery tang of unfiltered particulates. I could drink in the scent all day—especially having spent the past two and a half months in London, riding stuffy tube carriages filled with endlessly re-breathed air, or walking busy streets thick with traffic, exhausts coughing smoke into the sky every hour of the day. Here was *natural*. And unlike those stupid bottles of overpriced water "sourced from a mountain spring" (a dodgy tap off an allotment in Peckham, more like), *this* kind of natural was exactly what I craved.

"So," Carson said, "where are you from, Heidi?"

"Err—Croydon?"

"And you have a pendant thing as well?"

"A what?"

"Talisman," I muttered without glancing back.

"Oh. Yeah. Mine's a bracelet, see?"

"Um … kind of. Mira, could you—"

"I'm not lighting her up for you, if that's what you're asking. You'll just have to wait to see it when we get outside, or get back to London."

"We're going back to London?"

"Well *I'm* not planning on spending my life in a cave. *You* are free to do whatever you please, however." I moved my compass into the beam of my flashlight again, squinting at its face. "Now could you please shut up for a minute? I need to concentrate."

The rocky surface made our trek slow. My flashlight didn't help matters: it was a dinky little thing, the sort you'd clip onto a keychain. Even in the sheer, almost all-encompassing darkness, the shaft of light it cast was still dim. No more than fifteen feet ahead of us was illuminated before the dark crept in again.

We'd gone maybe three hundred feet from our starting point when the ground leveled out, although it felt like longer. Still knobbled in that awkward, uncomfortable way, the flashlight's reflection glinted: water had pooled, forming little islands. It was no more than maybe two or three inches deep at the most, but I still pointed it out to Heidi and Carson, and made deliberate effort to step on each of the miniature knolls.

"There's a light up there!" Carson suddenly bleated.

"Hey!" Heidi shouted. "Stop *grabbing* me!"

"Sorry—"

She huffed, stepping away from him and falling in alongside me.

"Told you," I muttered.

"The light—!" Carson said, joining me on the other side.

I looked away from my compass, which was currently showing what looked like a war-torn city if the crumpled buildings and cratered streets were anything to go by, and followed Carson's finger.

Sure enough, there was a single point of bright light up ahead. It came through a hole in the ceiling, which I realized now was even higher than I'd thought. Two by three inches wide, this tiny shaft explained the practically invisible glow in the face of the compass on King William Street.

Directly beneath it, we stopped to look up.

So high above us, and so small, it was impossible to tell what the sky might be like out there; clear blue, cloudy, decked in storm clouds. Against the darkness of the cave, the light was simply a white glow.

"Well, we're not getting out that way," Heidi said.

"Right." I started to move again, flashlight sweeping, its dullness was terribly obvious again now.

Soon the distant trickle restarted. I'd thought we left it behind, but there was another in front of us as the cave began its downward crawl again.

It split off into two directions. The leftmost was larger, and by the look of the sheen underfoot, this was where the tiny stream continued on its way. The right-hand path, meanwhile, was far smaller. Rather than the path forking, this was more like a tendril extending from a trunk; the hole loomed out of the wall, four feet wide but almost eight tall. The flow of water had made it just as smoothly misshapen as the floor.

"Which way?" Heidi asked.

"Left again," I said, and commenced leading.

"Can you see London yet?" Carson asked.

"Not yet. We've got a ways to go."

"Unless," Carson piped up. "Unless ... unless this is one of those places where time passes differently, and we're so far in the future that London has—"

"Turned into a crimson bog?" Heidi asked.

"It could happen."

"Time can condense *hours*," I said, "not however many thousands of years it takes nature to reclaim the biggest city in England. Pretty sure the only way it gets abandoned now is if humanity bombs itself into oblivion. Or if Liam and Cheryl break up." They both looked at me, Heidi rolling her eyes and Carson with blank ones. "What? They're adorable together."

"The temporal shrinkage is related to the gates, anyway," Heidi said. "That's where you get out of sync. As soon as you've set foot in a place, one second there is just the same as a second anywhere else on planet Earth."

"Oh." A second of quiet, broken by the soft babble of water. "But *what if*—"

"Sorry. Bored now."

After another leftward turn, Heidi picked up the conversation. "How do you know we're going the right way?"

"Because I conduct thorough research." I flashed a sarcastic smile she probably didn't see in the darkness.

"Books?" Carson asked.

"Uh huh. Not the sort you'd find in the London Library, though. That's another one for your sightseeing list, by the way. I expect you'll be right at home there."

Within another hundred feet, the path forked again,

both rising this time. Water spilled down from both routes, draining into the small "pond" at the bottom. Springs? Maybe. Could be the remnants of the water source that had carved this place out.

Still no sign of London, I confirmed with a look at my compass—but then I knew that. We had yet another left-hand turn, which I directed us on.

Quiet descended between us again. Our feet on rock broke it, steps careful—or not, in Carson's case; he scuffed every few feet, occasionally biting back grunts as he stubbed his toe where he'd miscalculated a step.

"How much farther?" Heidi griped after ten minutes.

"Not much."

"Aren't there any slightly quicker ways to where we're going? Or any brighter?"

"I should've bought a bigger flashlight," Carson muttered.

"Or one at all," Heidi grumbled. "Better still, a flashlight *and* a muzzle."

I shook my head, huffing a breath out of my nostrils. This was getting to be too much like corralling children.

Carson reached my side and asked, "If you made us a port—a gateway now, where would we end up?"

Going by the sand-colored stone buildings laid out on the compass's face, probably Uzbekistan. "Nowhere we want to be," I answered.

"And—and are there ever borders on this side to avoid too?"

"Plenty," I answered.

"But those gateways all lead out to our world," Heidi put in. "It might be London on one side and Antarctica on the other, but you're always coming out on planet Earth. It's when you're going from Earth to the worlds beneath that the gates could lead to anywhere—and I mean *anywhere*."

"Mira said it was like—like loads of crumpled up pieces of paper, laid under London. And where they connect is where you open gateways."

"Crumpled up balls of paper?" Heidi made a 'huh' sort of noise with her throat. "I never really thought of it like that. But yeah, that sounds pretty—"

"Found it," I cut across.

Heidi and Carson stopped and peered.

"It's just dark," Carson muttered.

"I think I can see *something*," said Heidi. She bowed closer, squinting. "Although whether or not it's London …"

"It's definitely London," I told her. "Hold this, can you?" I passed her the flashlight. She took it, and I gripped my talisman, pointing to the nearest wall. "We'll cut through here."

I sliced open a gateway with a downward swipe.

The glow from its edges was dazzling compared to the flashlight beam. I squinted. It felt like someone had switched on a floodlight and pointed it right at me.

"See you on the other side," I said, and I stepped through.

The other side was, as promised, dark.

I realized, too late, that I'd left the flashlight in Heidi's hands. Damn it.

Carson blundered through next. Then Heidi popped in, preceded for half a second by the weak beam of my flashlight. After the gateway and its interior lightshow, it was once again terribly dim. If only Decidian's Spear had transformed itself into a big ol' Maglite.

"Thanks," I said, taking it from her.

"Where are we?" Carson asked.

"King William Street tube station." I swept the flashlight around. "Abandoned, obviously."

The station was derelict, looking a bit like Carson's post-apocalyptic London had come to pass. Split into two sections, we'd come out on the top level. No getting on a train from here—the platform was down a set of stairs—but the curvature of the ceiling and walls was telltale. A squared steel pipe ran along the very center, tube lights mounted to the either side of it. We could find a switch, but there was no way in a million years that they'd turn on.

The tiles were dirty. Dark stains marred them in full clusters. These had a very sooty look to them, as though a fire had been ignited directly underneath. Corresponding stains were reflected on the floor. In some places, tiles were missing, leaving rectangular holes.

Stale air invaded our noses, worse for the time we'd spent in the cave system. It did not quite have the unpleasant taste of the traditional Underground; there were no passengers to bring coughs and sniffles and leave them lingering. But there was an unpleasant scent amidst the trapped oxygen: like mildew, almost, but it caught me much deeper in my lungs.

"Geez," Carson breathed. There was a note of horror in his voice. His eyes had gone wide, eyebrows drifting high above the delicate frames of his granddad glasses.

"You wanted a tour of London, didn't you? I'd say you're getting one."

"I wanted to see nice places."

"This isn't nice?"

"I'm with Carson on this," Heidi said. "This place gives me the creeps. Our destination is through here?"

"Somewhere," I confirmed.

I led the way, flashlight sweeping.

The upper level was long, and split into several rooms, each more or less the same as the last. A metal beam rose to the ceiling in one, blue paint chipped to high heaven. The entire bottom two feet had either been stripped of paint entirely, or been dyed black. The curious child in me wanted to run a finger along to check, but I knew better. If that was a coating of something, it would surely be smoke, and the black fingertip I gave myself would take a long, long time to wash off.

The tile stains changed color, becoming coppery orange.

These looked like they came from something leaking, streaking earthward and fading.

On either side of a doorway were several posters.

Carson dawdled.

"These are from the war," he said.

We backtracked, me only really because Heidi had.

"The station was used as a makeshift air raid shelter in World War II," she explained.

Carson bowed to peer at a smaller sign tacked on beneath a poster advertising national security certificates.

"'Special notice to late arrivals and early risers,'" he read. "'Please spare a thought for your fellow shelterers and refrain from making any unnecessary noise.'" He looked up at me and Heidi in turn, eyebrows knitted. "The German fighter planes couldn't hear people in here, could they?"

Heidi shook her head in disbelief. "Read the next sentence."

He squinted at it. "'Please remember others may be asleep'—oh."

She and I exchanged a look. Like I had found myself doing more and more this past day and a half, the hard fight against rolling her eyes was readily apparent on her face.

"Come on," I said. "This place stinks; I want to get out of here as soon as possible."

Stairs led between the station's upper and lower level. Another tatty WWII poster remained at the bottom: a cartoon of two women talking, above the captions "Don't forget that walls have ears!" and "CARELESS TALK COSTS LIVES." The wallpaper of the room the women sat in was a stylized version of Adolf Hitler's face repeated over and over. Here, like the cave, the floor was damp.

"Ugh," Carson groaned as he stepped into it.

"Could be worse," I said.

"Probably will be," Heidi added. "I remember reading that the station was partitioned when it was converted into an air raid shelter. Some areas are lower than others. They'll have collected more water than this."

"Do we *have* to go this way? Couldn't we just find some other gateway to wherever it is this cutlass thing is?"

"Maybe. But I don't have a lifetime to mess around and search for it. As it stands, this is our way through."

"There must be *other* connection points, though …"

"It's just a little water," Heidi grumbled. "You weren't complaining back in the cave."

"I was stepping around it. And it's … it's different here anyway. This stuff is, like … stagnant World War II water or something. I don't like it."

"If there are other options, I don't know what they are," I told Carson. "So we're using the station." Swinging around as a boundary flicked up on the compass's face, I tried to dissolve it for a moment before giving up; neither were what I wanted anyway.

"This is the problem with Seekers," I continued. "There aren't a whole lot of us. So there aren't a whole lot of *maps* to places like the one we're going, especially not when things like this—" I knocked a fist on the station wall "—make them even more difficult to access. Only option then is to go blind, just exploring and exploring forever—"

"Which is a nice quick way of getting yourself killed by a barbed shambler," Heidi finished.

"B-barbed—" Carson cleared his throat. "What's, err …"

"You don't want to know."

For a moment, that confident little spark he'd shown in my hideaway seemed to ignite behind his eyes. But it dimmed just a moment later; he'd decided that no, he really *didn't* want to know after all.

"Or you could disappear in a border you didn't know was there," I said, taking a little joy in his plain discomfort.

"The compass is a nice touch," Heidi said with clear admiration. "Family heirloom?"

"Yes," I said coolly.

"So how did you find this place?" Carson asked, reinserting himself into our conversation.

"Research. Read it in a book somewhere." One of my parents', although I kept that to myself.

"*Sites of Ancient Iniquity*?" Heidi asked. "I read that one ... although I don't think I remember it mentioning anything about Feruiduin's Cutlass ..."

"Something like that."

I paused, frowning at the compass. I leaned forward just an inch—

"Here."

Both Heidi and Carson joined my side, peering down.

"Right on the borderline," Heidi murmured.

Sure enough, if I tilted just a couple of inches to the left, the compass face flashed with white and blue: a wide expanse of snow, a mountain very faintly visible in the distance with a bright cap. But to the right—

A temple, all sharp-edged stone, under an angry red sky.

"That's it," I said.

"I don't like the look of that," Carson mumbled.

"It's right in the corner," I said, pointing.

"I'll cut us through," Heidi offered, stepping up. "You need precision, and I've got smaller hands."

"Right."

She selected a spot, right up at the very edge of the room. It was so close to the adjoining wall that we'd need to turn side-on to pass through; the gateway would never open wide enough, especially not for Carson's larger frame and that manbag clutched at his side like a leather growth.

Heidi slipped her bracelet down so she could grip it between her fingers. She exchanged a look with me—I nodded back—and then sliced her hand down.

Somehow, her gateway seemed more perfect than any of mine. My edges always had a slight sway, like my hand was not quite steady when I made the motion. Hers was smooth. The light did not shimmer so much either, just glowed, an ethereal halo widening around a churning spiral of color.

"Ladies first," Heidi offered, waving me forward.

If that was the rule, I was pretty certain it meant Carson should go through the maw before I did.

I stepped forward, taking in a breath.

So, so close now.

I stepped into the light, carried forward as the disused platform left me behind and I moved through spirals, combining and exploding and fragmenting in a kaleidoscope—

Then I was thrust out into empty air—and darkness.

# 21

I frittered with my flashlight. Somehow passing through the gateway had stopped it from working—that or its dousing in water earlier had just now caught up with it. I flicked the switch back to the *off* position, then on again. It did nothing.

Heidi was through second.

"Whoa," she muttered, voice low. "Mira, you there?"

"I'm here," I said. "Just trying to get my flashlight—aha!" After a thump, it flickered back into life, soft yellow beam shining right into my face. Nothing like a bit of percussive maintenance.

"Carson coming?" I asked, hoping that he'd had a change of heart and decided to figure out a way back onto London's streets.

But my hopes were dashed: on cue, he fell out of the gateway midway up the wall, and gasped, landing ungracefully.

"Where are we now?"

"Right where I want to be," I said quietly. "Now would you just keep your voice down when we drop in anywhere? My compass doesn't exactly show a live feed of what's on the other side. I'd rather not you alert anything with that foghorn voice of yours."

"Sorry."

I pivoted, shining the flashlight around us.

Although the compass had professed otherwise, we hadn't landed outside of the blocky structure, but within it; probably a side-effect of just how close to the boundary we were when we went through. Being inside did make our lives easier—but only by a touch. We might be right next door to Feruiduin's Cutlass … or miles and miles of labyrinthine corridors away.

This temple was nothing like the one from which I'd made off with Decidian's Spear. The hard-edged square aesthetic from the outside was carried over to the interior, too. The corridor we were in was constructed from huge stone bricks, each as tall as my knee. They were not exactly even, so some stuck out by a half-inch, while others were recessed. Looking close, I couldn't see anything remotely resembling cement sandwiched between them, which meant either that they were held in place by rods, magic or, more unnervingly, the structure supported itself.

I had an uncomfortable feeling that it supported itself.

Faint script was inscribed halfway up the walls, weaving from brick to brick. At first I thought the extravagantly calligraphic text had been carved in while these blocks set. But they did not appear to be concrete of any sort; no, I was fairly certain that every single one of these bricks had been hewn from solid rock.

I listened. Heavy breathing from Carson, as was par for the course. I couldn't detect anything else, though.

"I think we're clear," I said quietly. "But let's keep our voices down and our steps quiet as we go, shall we?"

My research hadn't told me exactly which direction to take once we arrived, and in any case how useful would a direction have been without any reference points? So I flipped an imaginary coin and set us off toward the left, flashlight penetrating the darkness.

"Weird," I muttered as we went.

"What?"

"The needle shows us traveling on a perfect easterly

vector." I showed Heidi the compass. "Not even a couple of degrees in it."

"Precisely engineered," she said.

"Hm." I eyeballed the uneven bricks in the walls, protruding or pushed inward just slightly with no real rhyme or reason, at least as far as I could make out. It didn't make me think of precision engineering.

Carson brought up the rear, manbag held close in front of the wide gaping hole in his avocado sweater. "This place seems alien."

"That's because it is."

"It is?"

"We're in another world," Heidi told him. "Counts as pretty alien to me."

"Elves built this place," I said. I pointed at the script flowing alongside us, tempted to run my fingertip across its soft grooves, and equally worried I might bring the place down on us. "Whether or not they're still here, of course, I couldn't tell you."

"Elves are real?"

"A whole lot of things from ancient myths are real," I retorted. "Like orcs, remember?"

"Right, right. So orcs are real—and *elves* are real. What about dwarfs?"

"There are dwarfs in *our* world."

"What? No, no, not little people—"

*"Dwarfs."*

"—I mean like little guys with battleaxes and Viking helmets and big bushy beards."

"Pickaxes too?" Heidi put in sarcastically.

"Yeah!"

"Keep your voice *down*," I hissed.

Carson's cheeks colored. "Sorry, Mira."

I bit my tongue to keep it from going off. I'd heard that about forty times from him so far, and he *still* hadn't learned. I wished I'd acquired a muzzle before leaving London, or at least a roll of duct tape to close his bloody mouth with.

Thirty seconds of blissful silence later, he spoke up again.

"So, if all this stuff is real, are you *sure* that *Harry Potter*—"

Heidi burst out with an incredulous laugh.

I glared at her.

She slapped her hand in front of her mouth. "Whoops."

To Carson: "*Harry Potter* is not real. Now can you stop asking?"

"I was just wondering—"

"Yeah, I heard, last time you asked me." I shook my head and massaged the corners of my eyes with thumb and forefinger. "I don't understand why I need to have the same conversation with you more than once for things to actually take root in whatever you have in there that passes for a brain." A peanut, possibly. Although some birds had brains the size of a peanut, so maybe even that was too generous.

Blissful silence, for almost a full minute this time, before …

"You know," said Carson, "when we spilled out of the Embankment station, from the toilets, it was kind of like a reverse version of that part in *The Deathly Hallows* where—"

"Read another effing book," I told him.

"Ain't nothing wrong with *Harry Potter*," Heidi said. Still, she folded her arms and turned away from him; a begrudging sort of defense.

When I was finally about to ask just how long we'd been walking in a straight line with no deviation and no forks, we were presented with a wider room. Cubic and just as square as the tunnel, with the same calligraphic script on those uneven blocks comprising the walls, it splintered with three doorways: one straight ahead, and two to either side. The left and right passages were open, ready to pass through.

The center passage, though, was closed off by a door. Solid stone, its surface was unbroken and perfect.

On the floor before each of the passages, new script flowed.

I squinted at it. "Can you read that?"

"Um ... no?" Carson wittered.

"Me, genius," Heidi grunted. She knelt beside me, tracing fingers over the text. "This one—" the left "—says something like *cantonment*, or *barracks*, I think. And on the right, we go to, um ... let me think. This one means ... ah, it's *cache*, I think. So storage of some kind." She glanced up at me. "You reckon that's where Feruiduin's Cutlass is?"

I shook my head. "Too easy. What's the middle one?"

Heidi ran her fingers across it.

"*Atrium*," she said immediately.

Hmm. "I wonder ..."

Heidi asked, "What?"

"Step back a second."

She reversed. I handed her the flashlight as she went.

Reaching for my belt, I unclipped the umbrella, springing it open—

It grew to full length, glamour dissipating before our eyes, so once again I held Decidian's Spear.

Although Heidi had seen me swing for the Order of Apdau with it in Russell Square, she hadn't exactly had much time to admire the thing. Now she did, loosing an amazed coo. She stepped forward, eyes fiery with reflected light as they swept its sleek body and traced the tip. A trace of orc blood remained, but it was faint. Self-cleaning, possibly—or maybe just the short stint in the water world had been enough to dislodge most of the acrid purple ooze.

"Decidian's Spear," she marveled. "Named for the monk Decidian, and lost in the Crusades." Her gaze joined mine. "You really found it."

"Why do you need it here?" Carson asked.

"These temples," I said. "They're … I don't know, exactly. They're in different worlds, but the objects inside them are … connected, I guess. I don't really understand it myself." My eyebrows knitted. "Anyway, it's like, each relic is part of a key—like just one of the teeth, or something. The first one is necessary to get the second, and *both* of them are required to get the Chalice Gloria."

"The Cup of Glory," Heidi whispered. Her disbelief on the Underground had been—not totally expunged. But it was getting there; a daring sort of fire burned in her eyes.

"Decidian's Spear is the first relic. Feruiduin's Cutlass is number two. And if I'm right about this … the only way we get to the cutlass is with the spear—through here."

And with all of my might, I thrust the spear at the partition blocking the passage ahead—

The air suddenly turned elastic. The spear pressed, fighting tension—

Then a rocky noise filled the air, like stones being dragged. And before our very eyes, a hole carved itself in the rock, maybe two inches tall, growing wider and wider, until it took the shape of a letterbox. Only it was not perfect, not like the edges of the bricks making up this strange place; it took on an irregular, starfish-like shape, but thinner on the legs, with a bulbous round center—

"The umbrella," Carson whispered. We both turned to look at him with wide eyes. "I—I think it wants the spear as—as the umbrella."

I nodded, letting Decidian's Spear regain its glamoured form. Then I stepped forward—electricity seemed to crackle in the air around me, ready to arc at a moment's notice—and slotted the umbrella into the hole.

Perfect fit.

A soft green glow ignited around it.

"I think you're meant to take it now," Carson whispered. His voice had taken on a strangled quality.

I retrieved the umbrella from the slot, stepped back—

The rock leading down the central passage split in two,

perfectly down the middle, along an invisible seam. It creaked as it pulled away, the rumble of stone on stone so loud that I honestly thought for a moment that the place was going to come down on us—

Then it silenced. The door's segments now flush with the wall, the passage to the atrium loomed beyond. And from far up its length came a low red light—like the angry sky I'd seen in the face of the compass.

# 22

We all stared in open-mouthed wonder.

It worked. It really worked.

"Let's go," I said, jerking into motion.

Heidi swept along behind me. Even Carson seemed to gain his footing and keep pace.

This new tunnel was tighter than the others. We could barely stand all three in a line, and were he another couple of inches taller, Carson would have needed to duck to avoid clonking his head on the ceiling. Heidi aimed the flashlight straight ahead, but it was not necessary: the glow of angry sky painted the entire thing in a deep, hellish red. Every stone brick that seemed to be out of place, jutting toward us, threw long dark shadows behind it. Even the script, so beautiful from the way we'd come, had taken on a deranged sort of look, like the scrawl ripped from a nightmare.

The corridor was short.

As we came closer to the end, I broke into a jog. Up ahead—

"Oh, *geeeeez*," Carson moaned.

The "atrium," as the elves had termed it, was a grotesquely huge cube. Not unlike the resting place of Decidian's Spear, we came out probably halfway up. But this was so much larger: two hundred meters were clear below us, leading to swirling, misty darkness. The sky frothed and heaved, lightning drawing great flashing arcs overhead, casting searing white forks amidst a sea of blood red on black.

A long, perilous walkway connected our ledge to the central platform. Joined by two others to either side, and I presumed another directly opposite, they were two feet wide, no more. Enough to walk across—but one wrong move and it was goodnight, Vienna.

The central platform was larger. I craned sideways to check it was indeed mounted on a spire of rock, and not simply connected to these pencil-thin bridges. Open at the edges, stone pillars were constructed just off from each of the corners, holding up an angular roof twisted forty-five degrees off-center.

"Is—the cutlass—" Carson sounded as though he could barely breathe, let alone force the words out. He tried again—"Is that—" and was cut off by a deafening boom of thunder, a flash of orange lightning streaking across the red sky. He squeaked, noise lost amidst the thunderclap.

Just this one time, neither I nor Heidi admonished him. Both of us let out yelps too.

"We're not seriously going across that," Heidi said shakily when the boom had subsided.

"Yes, we are."

She closed her eyes, wincing. "You know, maybe the other way, with the storage …?"

"Sorry," I said. "It's here. I can feel it."

I could—and it was nothing to do with the buzzing static in the air from the storm surging over our heads.

I eyed the bridge, biting my lip.

Two feet wide. Not like I was walking a tightrope or anything.

I took a step out—

"Mira!" Carson squeaked. He almost grabbed me to pull me back, but thought better of it. My heart still pulsed with fear, though. It would be just like him to set me off-balance and send me to my grave.

"What?"

"I—Mira, what about the storm? If the wind kicks up, you're—you're gone!"

He had a point.

But ...

"It's safe," I told him—and stepped out, far beyond arm's reach.

"MIRA!"

"We'll be fine!" I called back. One foot after the other, one foot after the other, and *do not look down.* "You think they'd put Feruiduin's Cutlass in a room open to the sky where anyone could get it? There's, like ... a force field or something, I don't know."

*"How can you know that?"*

"I just do!" Didn't. But I had to get to it some way, right? "Now get a move on!"

Heidi made a defeated sort of noise behind me. I assumed she stepped on, because Carson bleated, "Heidi—oh *geez.*"

"Come on!" she yelled back.

Lightning forked overhead, lighting my vision from the top with a momentary white bar. The boom followed instantly. I braced, holding steady for a moment lest I trip—then I was going again, counting step after step after step, eyes on the central platform every single moment—

*"I'll just, uh ... I'll just wait here, okay?"* Carson called.

"LIVE A LITTLE!" I belted back.

*"That's exactly why I'm not following you!"*

But we were creeping farther along—I must be closing in on halfway now, I was sure—because a distant whine came from Carson, and he cried, *"Oh, geeeeeeez!!"*

I paused, dared a glance behind me.

He was crawling, body as low as it would go. He'd positioned his manbag on his back, like a snail carrying its shell. Though it was hard to tell from so far, his lips seemed to be moving; I imagined him whispering, panicked, "Don't look down. Don't look down."

It seemed a sensible thing to say, so I could hardly fault him for it.

Another blinding fork carved the sky, throwing the central platform into stark relief.

The boom was deafening. And unexpected—with no warning, just one brief fraction of a second between lightning strike and the rolling clap that followed, I was caught off-guard. I screamed without thinking, body flinching—

I took a misstep—

"MIRA!"

—and caught myself before teetering over the edge.

Still, I caught a long, hard look into the swirling abyss below. Black, streaked with churning deep grey mist, it stared back at me hungrily.

My foot had landed half on, half off the edge of the bridge. I shimmied back, not daring to lift it to do so, until I was dead-center again.

Damn, it really *was* perilously thin. Maybe Carson had the right idea with his crawl. Low center mass, much more difficult to knock aside—plus he could grip either side of the bridge as he went with L-shaped hands, fingers always forcing him to stay as close to the middle as possible.

"Are you okay?" he called, a note of panic in his voice. It was him who'd shouted my name, I realized, as I wobbled on the precipice.

"I'm—fine!" But I didn't sell it. A quiver shook my voice. And still I stared into that misty void below us, waiting for me to be knocked over, to consume me as I fell end over end into whatever painful death awaited. "Let's ... let's keep going, okay?"

Body rigid, I forced it into motion, tearing my eyes away from the abyss. Refocus on the platform—on Feruiduin's Cutlass. I was close. Almost there. Definitely over halfway now. All I needed to do was put one foot down, then another, until I got there. Simple.

With maybe twenty feet to go, another blast of lightning

ripped a blinding arc across the sky. My vision flashed again, and the crack that followed was just as deafening as the last. And though I flinched, this time my body was primed to lock itself down, so I froze, teeth gritted, waiting for it to end.

"We—we good?" I shouted when it had silenced. I no longer dared a look back.

"Still here," Heidi called.

From farther behind her, Carson added, "Yes!"

Good. Entourage intact.

Although, none of us had made it to the central platform yet. I shouldn't be counting my chickens before they hatched. Twenty feet of bridge was still plenty of time for a lightning strike powerful enough to cleave the world in two, and send me tumbling over—and then I wouldn't be counting chickens at all.

But I got there; mercifully, I got there. I staggered onto the platform, loosing a shaky breath I hadn't realized I'd been holding.

Pure adrenaline had kept me moving. Now, it deserted me. My legs turned to jelly, and I fell to my knees. Perfectly smooth tan stone reached up to meet me, and I let myself clatter to it with complete willingness. After that ordeal, I'd probably welcome the embrace of broken glass. It would slice me up like a paper garland, but I'd be alive. And right now, I wasn't sure I had ever been so thankful. (I had, of course. When rational thought returned, I'd recall being this thankful just yesterday, after miscalculating that first jump in the stupid game of parkour needed to acquire Decidian's Spear.)

Heidi joined me maybe fifteen seconds later.

"Are you okay?" she asked, voice tight.

I still hadn't moved from the ground. My head was down, eyes closed, between firmly planted hands.

"Just give me a second here, all right?"

Heidi obliged.

I figured she must have looked back at Carson, because

she called, "Almost there!" It wasn't quite encouraging—she sounded a little flat to me—but it was at least something. And after forcing him through something that had shaken me so heavily, I had to admit: limp rag or not, Carson deserved all the encouragement he could get.

He made it to the platform, scrabbling up behind me.

"Geez," he whispered. Though strained, a note of disbelief crept into his voice. "I can't believe I just did that."

Yeah, me neither.

A hand touched my shoulder, very light and careful.

"Mira?" he asked.

"I'm okay," I said. Just came far too close to being snuffed out of existence, that was all. It barely even constituted a crisis.

"You made it," he said. "We all did."

I pressed lower, forehead against the stone. It was cool. Calming waves seemed to radiate from it through my skull, finding all the little places where my brain had knotted itself into a tight wad. As though touched by softly massaging hands, each tense coil began to loosen.

And something about Carson's hand on my shoulder seemed to help, too.

"You ever wonder if maybe you're not cut out for something?" I murmured.

Carson scuffled to a crouch at my side.

"Lots," he said. "All the time. I mean … just getting on the plane and coming over here. That was scary."

He went quiet for a while. Not like the silences after being berated by me—or, increasingly, Heidi. Nor was this the silence of a man whose words had run dry. There was something in his voice that suggested he had receded, falling into a black void of his own where it was him and only him. If I could summon the will to push up and just look at him, I was certain his face would be somber, as it so often was, but in a new way, a different, deeper sort.

Finally, he spoke again.

"You're cut out for this, Mira Brand."

Was I? I'd been told the answer was *no* for so long. All that pressure, piled on all the time—and still I faced it, from Lady Angelica, from Heidi. *Living up to your famous name?* I couldn't escape. And now, having brushed with death, running on fumes, it all seemed to come back.

And yet—

*You're cut out for this, Mira Brand.*

It came from Carson. *Carson*, who didn't know what I faced, had known me less than two days—and yet he was honest, almost to a fault, the way every little thought seemed to spill from him at times.

He had seen something.

"I *am* cut out for this," I murmured into stone.

From Heidi: "Huh?"

I pushed up. Opened my eyes. My back cracked, a little pop from midway down that was satisfying and good.

My first look was to Carson.

He met my gaze, face serious. He was paler than normal, and sweat had slicked his hair, sticking it to his forehead. A distinctly grey tinge painted him, although it was on the way out even as I looked at him. But there was concern in his eyes too, worry—for me, who'd sputtered out before both of them.

"Thank you," I said.

He nodded.

I rose. Carson dropped his hand, retraining it on his manbag's strap, and stood with me.

Heidi leaned against one of the pillars. Not something I'd have dared, but she was so feather-light, she could probably support herself quite happily against a tower of Jenga blocks without knocking it over. Arms folded across the faded punk band logo, she nodded at me. A slightly icy look had crept into her face again.

"Moment over?"

"Yeah," I said. "Ready to move."

"Good." She pushed herself up with her backside, same

as she had on the rails outside Lady Angelica's, and strode forward. Her gaze drifted over Carson momentarily, a veiled expression of distaste briefly crossing her face before it vanished.

Fugue broken, I took in the platform properly.

It was five meters by five, or thereabouts. Amidst the pillars, right in the center, stood a pedestal. It rose to just below my ribs, and on it, floating perfectly a couple of inches above the pedestal's smooth surface, suspended by (I assumed) the same sort of magic keeping the storm's atmospheric effects from bleeding down here, was Feruiduin's Cutlass. The blade, slightly curved, was inscribed with calligraphic elven script. Onyx in color, it tapered to a devastatingly sharp point. The guard and hilt were bronze, almost gold. We were reflected in its perfectly polished surface, misshapen and out of proportion.

I stepped for it, breath catching.

"Thought seeing it would put some life back in you," Heidi said. She strolled around the pedestal's edge, eyebrow raised, one finger tapping her chin.

"Can you just take it?" Carson asked.

"No," said Heidi.

"But it's just sitting there."

"Over here," said Heidi, waving me over.

"Here's the thing," I said, joining her side. Carson followed, coming around in the other direction. "For a race venerated for their wisdom and intelligence, elves have a certain blind spot."

Heidi smirked.

Carson asked, "What's the blind spot?"

"They think everyone is either as smart as they are, or a total idiot. No middle ground. Hence this." I pointed.

Opposite from where we'd come in, a stone slab was affixed to the pedestal's surface. Wedge-shaped, it flowed with more elven writing.

"What is it?" Carson asked.

"A riddle," said Heidi.

"Here's the other thing," I told him. "Remember I mentioned orcs before? As you might expect, orcs and elves are sworn enemies."

"Why?"

I shrugged. "Elves had things orcs wanted, I guess." I waved the question away. "Point is, with the orcs constantly besieging their strongholds and temples— pretty much any place where something valuable might be held—the elves designed all their security features with orcs in mind."

"So …?" Carson asked, looking a little lost.

"So they left a little riddle here, knowing—sorry, *thinking*—no orc would be able to answer it. Because *of course* orcs are utterly stupid creatures with barely a brain cell between them."

"They're not?"

"Some are, same as some people," I said. Heidi snorted where she bent over the slab. "But there are also a bunch of very smart orcs too."

"So what does the riddle say?"

Carson and I both glanced back at Heidi. She was reading, fingers tracing the script for subtle elements the human eye was not as adept at detecting but which an elf would pick out with ease. Her eyebrows were drawn as low as they would go, and the short-lived snort was long gone, her face set in a determined sort of bafflement.

"It's something condescending, whatever it is," she answered. "But the way it's written is really obscure." She turned up her nose. "I can't recall if Muirhannon was a third age philosopher for them or a second age dramatist."

Carson glanced to me. "Could an orc answer that?"

"Probably not. But elves, all high and mighty, wouldn't have believed they even had a chance.

"More to the point," I continued, stepping closer to the pedestal, "they would *also* have believed orcs to be too stupid to simply ignore their riddle, and do this."

I reached forward. The same energy that had surrounded the door leading to the atrium, as well as Decidian's Spear atop the spine, crackled around my fingers. But just as I thought, there was no force field, no security measure worth a damn—and my fingers closed on the hilt.

I pulled it free of the slightly elastic-feeling place in the air where the pedestal hung, and lifted it.

Lightning split the air with perfect timing. Despite the blinding white glow, it was barely reflected from the onyx blade, metal seeming to devour the light.

Carson jumped at the boom. Behind me, Heidi seemed to do the same.

"No way," she said when the noise had quieted. She stepped to my side, eyes awed. "Feruiduin's Cutlass. It's ... it's here." She reached out to touch it. I let her, holding it steady so she could trace fingers across the script pressed into the blade. "You have it."

"Told you." I took the cutlass in, in all its glory. "My research paid off."

Carson cleared his throat. "But doesn't this seem too easy to you?"

"Hm?"

"I mean, we end up in a corridor that's in a perfect straight line from this atrium. We get in here—and the bridge, that wasn't pleasant, and the storm ... but then there's this riddle, and yet you can just walk up and take the thing?" He glanced between me and Heidi with wild, concerned eyes. "Isn't that too straightforward?"

"Like I said: blind spots. Now let's—"

I'd stepped away from the pedestal—and my skin seemed to ripple as though passing an invisible barrier. The static feeling in the air dissipated at once.

The moment it did, the bridges shattered. Every one, on all four sides, broke into pieces, like some oversized hammer had crashed down on them. Carson shrieked in panic—

The shattered bridges tumbled into the abyss, leaving no more than a couple of feet of what had once been our way across attached to the platform, jagged like shark's teeth.

Carson spun back to me. "What were you saying about blind spots?"

"Huh. I guess I, err … I was wrong."

# 23

"Wrong? *Wrong?*" Carson's voice was high-pitched and panicked. His knuckles were white around the strap for his manbag like it was an anchor, the only thing holding him from following the broken remains of the bridges into the swirling abyss below. "We're *stuck* here! With no way across! How are we supposed to get back?"

"Cool it, Poindexter," Heidi said.

His eyes flashed with confusion. "Poin—oh, sure, *this* is the time for insults! In case you failed to notice, *Lucy Liu*, we just lost our only way back across!"

"And what a shame you must find that, considering how quivery you were climbing across it in the first place."

Carson opened his mouth to spit back some fire of his own. I cut him off by stepping in between them, free hand raised.

"We *all* hated the bridge," I said. "Let's not turn on each other now, okay? We've come this far."

"So how do you propose we get out of here?" Carson asked.

"I've got this, don't I?" I patted my talisman. "We cut open a gateway. Simple."

I passed the cutlass to Heidi to free up both of my hands.

Before I relinquished my hold, however, I said, "It's *mine*. I found it; it comes back to me when we're done.

Got it?"

*"Comprender."*

I let her take it.

"And be careful," I added. She didn't strike me as the sort to take her simmering annoyance with Carson much further than insults, but he already had one nice big hole opened in his sweater; I didn't want him to leave here with another one.

I detached the compass from my belt. "I don't remember seeing anything in my research about exit points around the pedestal. But we're on a flat surface, which is perfect for a gateway, and so ... oh."

Carson waited a second, then prompted, "Oh?"

"It's a, uh ... we're at a border."

He and Heidi crowded in at either side, peering at the compass face.

Split in two, one side was thick with pelting hail, a dark expanse of lifeless trees just barely visible beyond the sheeting ice. And on the other ...

"Well, I mean, it's definitely London," said Heidi. She touched it: a slice of the London Eye. An idle finger traced the curve between cabins before the border terminated its arc. "Only question is, how do we get to it?"

"Can't we just open a gateway and hope for the best?" Carson asked.

I debated. Possible, but unlikely. "I don't fancy our chances. We could end up on either side, or worse—and more likely—in the ether between."

"But we won't be here."

"No, but do you really want to tackle that?" I flashed the compass so he could see the deluge of hailstones.

"But we won't be *here*."

"It's just a little ice," Heidi muttered.

"And no canopy."

"Those woods *do* look pretty dead," Carson conceded after an awkward second look.

"We don't know how long we'll be out there before finding a safe place to open a new gateway. And even if we stumble on one immediately, it might take days of bouncing around to get back to London, *weeks* even."

Heidi huffed, folding her arms. "Well, we'd better pin down where the connection point is, then, hadn't we?"

I strolled around her, holding my compass out, and walked the platform. Although confined to a fairly small circle, at no point did the boundary in the compass face budge. I even held it right out to the edge, and still nothing.

Back at my starting point, my eyebrows knitted.

"Nothing?" Carson asked.

"The boundary didn't move, no."

"I guess we'd better make do with hail then," said Heidi.

I hesitated, eyebrows lowering. "I wonder ..."

I crouched.

Carson asked, "Mira, what are you—?"

"There's a pillar holding this thing up. Maybe London is ..."

Sure enough, as I brought the compass right to the platform's floor, the boundary shifted. The London Eye grew on its face—but it still took up no more than two-thirds, with that remaining third still comprised of dead forest and inclement weather.

"Excuse me," I said to Carson, creeping to the edge. "Can you, um, like hold onto my other arm? So I don't fall?"

"I ... I'm not very strong."

"Well, I don't weigh a whole lot. Please?"

He would decline, I thought, and it would be Heidi's job to step up instead. But though his expression sagged, and a touch of that queasy grey crept back into his cheeks, he nodded, and followed me to the precipice.

Orienting myself sideways, body as low as I could possibly make it, I extended my left hand to Carson. He wiped the sweat from his palms on his trousers, and took

171

it.

My other hand, the one holding the compass, I lowered.

I forced myself not to let my eyes drift to the darkness below. Somehow, despite the gelatinous wreck I'd turned into, they still wanted to go—to stare death into the face.

Instead I gazed at the compass as it lowered … and the boundary shifted sideways farther still, bringing the London Eye to a full three quarters of the view.

"It's down there," I said, clambering to my feet and returning to the platform's center, and the safety it provided. "If we can get a gateway on the pillar, we can get back out on the Thames."

"How do we do that, though?" Carson asked.

"Easy," Heidi said. "We'll just rappel down with your manbag."

"It's a *satchel.*"

"It's an embarrassment, that's what it is."

"Shut up," I begged, "please? I need to think of something. Just give me a few minutes without arguing like a pair of children."

Heidi didn't look particularly happy about it, and to his credit, neither did Carson. But they both quieted, Heidi ambling to a corner to resume her cold lean against one of the pillars.

I sank down by the pedestal. Knees bent, I rested my elbows on them, head in my hands.

*Think, Mira, think.*

At least when I'd acquired Decidian's Spear, the cleft in the roof had allowed vines to spill in and seal my get-away. This place had nothing but rock.

Maybe attempting to abseil with Carson's manbag *was* our only option. Question was, what did we affix it to?

Even better question: how much weight could it manage? It put up with Carson gripping it like a lifeline well enough, but I doubted it would support Heidi, let alone me or Carson.

Carson sank down next to me. His face was tense—but

still that worried gleam flickered in the back of his eyes.

"Maybe we just take our chances," he said.

I shook my head. "No."

"But it's just a coin flip. Fifty-fifty. If we lose, we just … find another way back."

"It's not that easy, Carson. That one of the problems with going blind—you know, besides ending up in a fire nymph camp or any other deadly predicament fate might throw at us. We could end up stumbling right into something lethal, or ending up hitting the boundary by mistake." I peered at the compass face. "This is close."

"Surely it's not *that* difficult though. We just—we find civilization, and make our way to London from there."

"Most of our world *isn't* civilization, though. It's desert, or rainforest—and something like sixty percent of it is just water."

"Seventy-one," Carson murmured. "Oceans are about ninety-six point five percent of that."

I fixed him with a sidelong look. He lifted a nervous sort of smile.

"We've got to get back to London." I paused, closing my eyes. "Anywhere else is just ammunition."

"Ammunition for what?"

"My parents." And there it was, the thing I'd been trying so hard to avoid thinking of, and yet at the same time could not get away from, no matter how I tried.

Carson said, low, "They put a lot of pressure on you." It was not a question.

"You could say that." I sighed. "They're … difficult. It's the whole reason I ran away."

"You ran away?"

"You didn't think I grew up on the streets of London by myself, did you? I'm seventeen, Carson." Sarcastically, I tacked on, "A *kid.*"

"I didn't know. I just assumed … I don't know what I assumed."

"I ran away."

"Why?"

"Because I was sick and tired of them riding me all the time!" I'd raised my voice, the shout lost to the atrium's cavernous void. "Sorry."

"I'm sure they were just worried about you," Carson said quietly.

I snorted a laugh from my nose. "Funny way of showing it."

We were quiet for a while.

Carson broke the silence.

"I wouldn't mind having parents who worried about me like that. Especially with …" He waved a hand around us. "You know. This stuff."

"You wouldn't say that if you had them."

"Well … mine are dead, so I guess we'll never know."

I paused, caught for a moment. Carson had delivered it so matter-of-factly. Plain and simple, without any of the heartache I was certain I would glimpse in his eyes if only he would look my way.

"I'm sorry," I said. "I didn't know."

"Of course you didn't. Why would you?" He shrugged, a rise and fall of the shoulders that might have been the answer to a question like, *Where should we go eat?* or *Do you know which movie you want to watch?* Not this.

"It's why I'm here, you know?" he continued, and now he did look at me, and there was something in the back of his eyes, something that had *always* been there, and now, here, he had shone a dim flashlight beam on it and let me see. "In England. I needed to … get out, for a while—of … America. Home."

Lightning exploded.

Before the rumble had ceased, Heidi was stamping across to us—

*"ALAIN BORRICK!"* she roared as she passed.

I fumbled, stumbling to my feet and whirling.

And there he was. So very distant, on the ledge around the atrium's edge, but three things confirmed it. Two of them—dark hair, and that dark jacket enshrouding his V-shaped chest—would have been enough to raise my suspicions.

What made Alain Borrick's presence utterly unmistakable, though, was the orc army flooding out of the tunnel behind him.

# 24

Carson scrabbled up alongside us, panic washing his face. "Who's that?"

I rounded on Heidi, talking over him. "How do you know Borrick?"

"I've crossed paths with him before," she said grimly.

"Who is he?" Carson repeated.

"Another Seeker," I said, "but this one's got his own personal army."

That army was presently spreading across the atrium's ledge—the *entire* ledge. Turning a short circle, I could see them flooding from the other three tunnels, where the bridges had connected to this central platform. We were surrounded on all sides.

"You know him?" Carson asked me.

"I met him briefly yesterday. He wasn't very happy with me for managing to get my hands on Decidian's Spear before him."

"Which means he's going to be *so* chuffed that you grabbed Feruiduin's Cutlass first too," Heidi said.

"Well, what do we *do*?" Carson asked.

"We're safe for now." And taking great joy in her taunt, Heidi shouted across the chasm, *"SORRY, ALAIN! LOOKS LIKE THE BRIDGE IS OUT!"*

He did not call back to us, instead walking back and forth along the ledge's terminus, hands clasped behind his back. From so far, he was a stick figure, but each action was perfectly visible: clad in so much black and deep purple, he formed a kind of silhouette against snot-green orc skin and chipped red armor.

"Oh, geez," Carson whispered. He looked like he was on the urge of hyperventilating. "Those are—those are—"

"Orcs," Heidi finished for him. "Good observation, genius."

"Oh, geez."

"Don't worry," I said in my best reassuring voice. "They can't get across to us. We're safe as long as—that. Doesn't. *Change.*"

A pair of orcs had brought something forward. From so distant, it resembled a fat brown roll, furled over and over. I squinted, trying to make out—what were those *lines*? It looked like a pile of sticks, maybe the width of my forearm each, tied at either end with much more rope than was strictly necessary.

The orcs laid the roll on the last fractured remains of the broken bridge. They stepped back, replaced by Borrick, who lifted a hand—and waved.

The roll instantly began to unfurl. One end affixed to the ledge, it flew out, uncoiling at a terrific pace toward us—

"Ladders!" Heidi cried. "They have *ladders!*"

"Magical roll-up ladders," Carson added, rapt with awe and horror all at once.

I stumbled back, knocking into the pedestal. Turned.

Replacing all four shattered bridges, ladders unwound of their own volition. They came right for us in a horizontal line, never sagging, never dropping into the churning darkness below us. It was as if each was suspended on a set of invisible hooks.

The ladder from Borrick was almost upon us.

I yanked the umbrella from my belt. It had been attached by a small metal book; now that clinked off, bouncing at my feet and then careening over the edge.

The spear extended.

I leapt forward with it, ready to stab—

The rope ladder slammed the edge of the platform, the perfect length.

I swung down—

The air surrounding the ladder's edge was suddenly solid. Decidian's Spear rattled off, unable to make contact.

"No," I whispered.

"Mira …"

I stabbed again, pushing with all my might. But no matter how hard I shoved, I could—not—make—*contact*!

"Heidi?" I called.

"Cutlass won't do it either!" she shouted back. "I think it's just the end, though; if we could crawl out—"

"Mira!" Carson cried.

I looked at him. He was pointing over my shoulder.

I turned—

Orcs were thundering, sure-footed, over the ladder. It barely moved under their weight, nor did it sag. They might have been running over the top of a steel set of monkey bars, rather than a perilous length of rope and wood suspended over certain death.

And not just this one. A desperate glance behind showed me that they were coming down *every* ladder. In just seconds they would be upon us.

"Right, change of plan," I said. There was a panicky note in my voice. I fought to keep it at bay. "Heidi, you, err, you know how to use that cutlass?"

"Swing it at bad guys?"

"Good enough!"

Carson: "What are we doing?!"

"We're going to have to fight."

"But—but I don't have a weapon!"

"Just stay behind me!"

I didn't have time to say more. The nearest orcs were finally upon us.

I jabbed with the spear at the red and green train

178

hurtling toward me. The leading orc braced, pushing forward with a shoulder to meet the spear. I jerked it higher at the last second, stabbing for his face. He squawked, and twisted, foot missing a step—

Then he was falling over the brink. Another tried to grab hold—but he overbalanced and went down too.

More were already rushing forward to replace them.

I backpedaled, shooting a glance behind me.

Four bridges. Three of us.

We couldn't cover them all.

"Carson!" I shouted. He was staring with bulbous eyes from the pedestal, his manbag gripped tightly between his fingers as a makeshift shield: he'd positioned himself between me and Heidi, on our side, where we covered two adjacent bridges.

Orcs on the two opposite were short seconds from reaching us.

"I need you to cover one of the bridges!"

"B-but—but *how?*"

*"Swing your manbag at them!"*

"But they're *orcs!*"

*"Just do it, damn it!!"*

Credit to him: when hopelessly cornered, as we had been by the Order of Apdau in Russell Square, he could put up a fight. There was no resolute nod, no flare of determination—but he leapt around the pedestal, legs almost skidding out from under him before he righted, and flew for the bridge opposite Heidi.

*"GET OUT OF HERE!"* he shrieked, a sound rivaled the storm overhead—and then he was swinging.

I had time to admire one orc lurch over the edge, so caught off-guard by a five-foot-eleven American nerd swinging a satchel at him—then more were on me, and I had to swing Decidian's Spear in a long arc. It sailed—the orc nearest ducked, but his friend behind him didn't, executing a perfect Olympian dive before he realized his mistake—he wailed, grabbing out for anything he could manage to find. In this case, it was the first orc's pauldron. His brutal fist closed around a spike of bone, and pulled. Orc #1's face had just enough time to contort in terror— and then both were sailing away.

"THIEVES!" came a roar from behind us.

I pivoted.

The last bridge was crested.

Damn it! Why hadn't I managed to pick up at least *one more* hanger-on?

I threw myself into motion, swinging Decidian's Spear up and over my head. The tip sailed a smooth arc, silver and faintly purple—then it was jabbing for this new threat as I dodged Heidi's swing of Feruiduin's Cutlass to skirt the pedestal—

The orc threw up his shoulder. The spear slammed it— bounced off, totally harmless—

"RELINQUISH THESE STOLEN ARTIFACTS, SPINELESS THIEF!"

*"Spineless?"*

From Heidi: "When did this one meet Carson?"

"I'm—not—*spineless!*" Carson swung his satchel overhead like he was doing the hammer throw. The next orc on his bridge yelped and stumbled, one foot disappearing through the gap between horizontal rungs. The orc behind lurched into him, then bounced off.

"These—artifacts—are—*mine!*" I shouted, stabbing and stabbing. This new orc, face a network of scars, dodged each blow. "You're not having them!"

He growled, teeth bared.

I'd stab him right in that stupid fat head of his.

I thrust forward—

Scarface caught the spear in his grip.

"Wrong," he growled—and pulled.

I yelped, suddenly lifted—

*"Mira!"*

The orc swung. I went with it, like the end of an oversized fly-swatter—

Hold on!

—then he jerked it, loosing my fingers, and I was sailing clear. I screamed as I flew through empty space—

Then my back slammed one of the corner pillars, and I landed with a grunt.

No breath. No breath left in me.

"MIRA!" Carson cried.

Scarface lifted Decidian's Spear, temporarily overtaken by wonder. His eyes gleamed across its surface—

*"GIVE IT BACK!"*

The shriek came from Heidi. She leapt, looking for a protracted moment like an actual ninja, the cutlass over her head—

Then it sailed down.

Scarface squawked. The spear clattered—as did all of his fingers. Purple erupted in a gouting fountain.

I scrabbled forward. Heidi kicked the spear clear—it spun toward me, and I slammed a hand down on its hilt—

*"HELP!"*

I pivoted for Carson—

The platform was filled, orcs pushing in—

And there he was, clutched between two of them. He struggled, hands still clasped around the strap of his manbag, eyes desperately wide—

Then they were carrying him back over the bridge the way they'd come.

*"CARSON!"* I cried—

Then the stumpy remains of a hand clouted me in the stomach, and I was sailing backward again.

# 25

I slammed the pedestal. Its hard edges drove into my spine. My body flexed involuntarily to absorb it—but still I screamed, sure for an instant that my back would break, that my adventure ended here, with paralysis before death—

"Let's just *relax* a moment, shall we?" The voice that spoke was calm, collected. Alain Borrick was savoring his victory, I suspected, but he wasn't lording it over us.

Yet.

I slumped. My every breath was heavy. My eyes longed to close, to just give up and let it be over.

Somewhere beside me, Heidi landed awkwardly

"You can lower that thing, you know," Borrick told her.

She spat back, "I'm not lowering anything for you."

I pried my eyes open.

We were surrounded by orcs. Only a small space remained clear, an uneven triangle around me and Heidi—and strolling through it, arms behind his back, lips a thin, distasteful line, was Alain Borrick.

My fist tightened around Decidian's Spear.

He squatted before me. Not touching the spear—not yet—but close.

"Young Mira Brand. So very determined to live up to her family name."

I just barely held myself from spitting in his face.

Up close, he was just as handsome as I'd thought in the temple with the spear. Jaw square and defined and perfect, he could well be the model on a Men's Health magazine, or the frontman in a rock band adored by hordes of young women, or the leading man in a movie. In another life, I might have been attracted to him.

Here, surrounded by his army, and Carson's wails diminishing as he was carried away, I hated him.

When he spoke again, he seemed to have channeled Heidi's icy fire.

"I would very much like for you to hand over Decidian's Spear and Feruiduin's Cutlass."

"I have half a mind to slice your head off right where you stand," Heidi sneered.

"And then you'll be pounded into mincemeat by my army," he said, surprisingly calm.

"Worth it," Heidi muttered. But she made no move to carry out her threat.

"What do you even want them for?" I asked. Stupid question, obvious answer. But I needed time—time to think my way out of this mess.

"The same as you; the Chalice Gloria, of course." His nostrils flared with irritation. "You might be the youngest Brand, but you're not that idiotic to think you're the only person on this quest, are you?" He rose—and the question seemed to have set something off, because as he began a short back-and-forth stomp, the words continued to spill out of him.

"I spent so long on *research*, all this time, and finally find the entrance only for a *Brand* to get there first! Then you just make off with it, and the one orc who actually has a chance at stopping you—"

Burbondrer, I realized, but Borrick was past it, thought unfinished.

"So we move to head you off at Feruiduin's Cutlass, thinking we'd separate you and the spear before you opened the gate—and we're *still* too slow!" He curled his hand into a fist, and slammed it against a pillar.

Then his eyes were on me, seething.

The fist shook at his side.

He was going to hit me.

But he didn't. Instead he stepped close again, looking down on me with just as much anger and hate as I tried to channel into staring back up at him.

"I'm not a bad person, you know," he said. A calmer note crept into his words now. "We're just two sides of the same coin, searching for the same prize. That's all. And ... tell me, Mira." He crouched, looking deep into my eyes. "If it was wrenched from you when you were so close, you would fight for it. Wouldn't you? You'd do everything in your power to take it back?"

I didn't answer.

He rose.

"I'm not a bad person," he repeated.

Not buying it.

"I'll make it easy," he continued. "Your friend—Carson, is it?—in exchange for the spear and the cutlass."

My breath caught. "If I don't—what will you—?"

"He'll be harmed," Borrick said shortly.

Damn it. I *should* have cut him loose.

"What do you say to that?" Borrick asked. "Your lives—plus his, of course—in exchange for your artifacts. I'd say that's fair. Wouldn't you?" He asked this of an orc nearby, who responded with a nod. To another, he repeated, "Wouldn't you say so?" A second nod came back to him.

He squatted again. Came closer. Closer.

I tightened my hand on Decidian's Spear.

The toe of his boot covered its shaft.

"Carson for the artifacts," he whispered, face so near I could feel his breath on my cheek. "A simple trade. What do you s—?"

"MIRA, MOVE!"

Heidi snatched something from her pocket, and threw it at her feet. It exploded in a shower of light, flying like sparks—

I shoved up in an instant, lifting the spear, shoving Borrick in the chest—he shouted, and an arm swam out to get me. It sailed past my leg, flailing blindly in the light—

Then Heidi had her hand on me, and was pulling me—

*"Where?"*

*"The ladder!"*

We staggered—an orc roared, close by, and I dodged its grabbing fist—

Then the short-lived explosion of light was gone.

We were right on the precipice. Heidi ran out first.

Just walking on top of monkey bars! That's all!

I followed.

"AFTER THEM!" Borrick shrieked.

Orcs blundered after us.

I picked up my feet. "Do not look down!"

From ahead, Heidi called back, "Still don't want to risk the ice?"

"No!"

"Then hang on!"

Heidi sliced Feruiduin's Cutlass in a low arc.

Out here, there was no magical resistance. The blade cut smoothly through the ladder—

I started to scream. *"What are you—?"*

*"Getting us out of here!"*

The ladder split clean in a horizontal line—

Without anything to hold it, our end sagged, dragged down by our weight, platform side still held firmly in place.

I dropped toward it, grabbing with my free hand for a rung, gripping, screaming as we descended like a pendulum—

"GATEWAY!" Heidi roared.

But to do that I'd have to let go!

The ladder swung to its lowest point—

Upended, we shrieked, falling—I squeezed tight to the

185

last rung, catching a terrifying momentary glimpse of the black abyss swirling hungrily—

Then we were rising on the second half of its swing, and the tall pillar upon which the platform was erected was swinging to meet us—

With it came our only guaranteed path to London.

I closed my eyes—I couldn't believe I was doing this—and released, flying through empty air. One hand clutched my talisman; the other, still gripping Decidian's Spear, swiped desperately ahead of me as I sailed, and Heidi flew alongside me, roaring as thunder split the air with a deafening peal, and orcs loosed angry battle cries as their quarry slipped away, and the hungry darkness below came ever closer as we dropped—

The gateway burst open on the pillar. I had a fraction of a second to hope, pray, that we wouldn't miss—

And then I was weightless, shrouded in a cocoon of vibrant light.

# 26

Twilight had descended over London by the time we returned to Tortilla, and stepped through to my hideout.

Neither of us had said a word on the way here, just walked in stunned silence.

Though it had only been … four hours? Five? since I'd last stepped foot in here, it felt like so much more. So much had changed.

I bustled into the kitchen without saying anything. My cheap energy drink still pressed into my hip. I pulled it out and stowed it in the strange fridge, which made me think of exploded, oversized and rearranged mechanisms of a watch. It hummed along, the interior light flickering. So empty.

I shuffled to the counter. Glass in hand, I was about to fill it—and stopped.

Carson.

I closed my eyes, leaning on the countertop, head in my hands. His face came back time and time again. That first nervous look he'd given me outside Piccadilly Circus, trying to force friendliness in the face of his fear at being in a new place—at going it alone, without the people he loved. The fear when the Order of Apdau had chased us into the under-construction building down the block, and I hustled him behind me on the stairs to keep him safe. Hurt, at my barbs, and Heidi's, delivered without diplomacy. Determination, when he swung his satchel in Russell Square, and again as Alain Borrick's army descended on us. And concern, for me, on the platform housing Feruiduin's Cutlass. Because in spite of all the terror I'd led him into, and all my snapping, all my effort to shove every flaw he had in front of his nose, for all of my outright nastiness to this man—in spite of all that, he was a good person.

Now Borrick's army had him.

And it was my fault.

Heidi sauntered in behind me, but stopped in the doorway.

For the first time, she spoke.

"What's up? I thought you'd be happy. You got the cutlass."

"I don't deserve it," I mumbled.

The room was quiet, the only sound between us the hum of my steampunk fridge.

"Come on, Mira," Heidi said, voice bright. "Of course you deserve it. You found an object that has been lost for centuries. *Two of them*. And now the Chalice Gloria—it's yours!" She stepped for me, touched a hand to my shoulder.

I shrugged out of it, turning on her. My eyes flashed, equals parts anger and anguish.

"What?" she asked. "Why're you looking at me like that?"

"Carson got taken because of me."

Disbelief sent Heidi's eyebrows twitching together. "What's the problem? You wanted him gone. You said it yourself. Now he's out of your hair."

"I wanted him to go back to his tour of London," I snapped back. "Not be held hostage by orcs in a world he has no way out of!"

"Borrick is a Seeker too; he and his army can travel just the same as we can. And once they see that Carson is just as useless as a bargaining chip as he is as a sidekick, they'll let him go."

"You don't seriously *believe that*, do you?"

Heidi floundered. Just for a moment—she was far too collected in general to become stuck for more than a second—but the truth was blatant on her face. She knew Alain Borrick. And if she didn't, she had heard his response when asked what would happen to Carson: *He'll be harmed.*

"Mira," she began heavily. "I was on that very same platform as you this afternoon. I heard you talk about your family life. And even if I hadn't ... do you think I wouldn't know? You're a *Brand*. This is in your blood. Decidian's Spear, Feruiduin's Cutlass, the Chalice Gloria ... those things are your calling, just like a thousand Seekers before you. You can't be suggesting that you'll give it up for some guy you met on a train."

"I didn't meet him on a train," I murmured.

"You've only known him a day!"

"That doesn't matter!" I cried, voice shrill. It echoed out the door, bouncing around the library between untold numbers of books.

Heidi quieted. Watching. Waiting.

"If I'd known him an hour, a day, a month, or a year, the fact remains: I got Carson caught up in this mess. I've got to get him out of it. Even if that means ..."

I didn't finish.

In the quiet, Heidi finished for me.

"Alain wants the spear and the cutlass," she said softly. "If you want to save Carson, if you play by his rules ... everything you said to Carson, about your family pressuring you—you kiss goodbye to all of that." Words hard, she said, "You *fail*, Mira."

"And I prove them right," I murmured. "I show them that I'm not a true Seeker. Just like they said."

All this research, all this time—if I went back for Carson, the whole thing was over. I passed victory into Borrick's hands—and Mira Brand, the child, would leave empty-handed. The ultimate chance to prove myself, to the world, to *them*—evaporated, gone in a puff of smoke.

I'd come so far. It had taken it out of me in a way I hadn't realized—and faced with a fridge that was perpetually almost empty, I was forced to admit that I had only just been scraping by. But I had found Decidian's Spear before anyone—and Feruiduin's Cutlass too, damn it! I had both the keys needed to retrieve the Chalice Gloria, and walk out triumphant—

And now I was considering giving it all up?

I couldn't. Surely I couldn't.

But then Carson's face swam in my mind's eye again. His hand on my shoulder as he stooped beside me when I came apart after the bridge. Queasy, yes, but riddled with worry nevertheless. And then his admission beside the pedestal: that his parents were gone.

He was alone in the world.

That was why he'd reached out for me. Not for travel recommendations—or maybe not entirely. He was a lost soul, cast out and wandering—and wasn't I, too? Maybe he felt it in me as we clambered the stairs out of the Underground, some ethereal thing that could not be touched or seen. He had *reached out*, nervous and awkward and uncomfortable though he might be; he had overcome all that to prove something. To *be* something.

Just like me.

"I'm sorry, Heidi," I said. "I've come a long way on this journey ... but some things are more important."

Her brow creased. "What are you saying?"

I took a steeling breath.

Had to say it out loud.

Cement it.

"I'm rescuing Carson Yates," I said firmly. "And if that means giving up the Chalice Gloria ... then so be it."

# 27

"You're not serious. You can't be. There's no way—for *Carson*? Look, Borrick sucks, but, I mean … I don't think he'll do anything fatal …"

Apparently, under duress, Heidi Luo resorted to the same kind of babbling that Carson did.

"I am deadly serious. One hundred percent." And it was true. I didn't *like* it, necessarily—chucking away everything you'd worked for at the drop of a hat was probably not something *anyone* got to immediate grips with. But after saying it aloud, my resolution grew. "I have to do this. It's the only thing that's right."

*"Carson?"* Heidi repeated. "Carson Yates?"

Despite myself, my exhaustion, Carson's life dangling by a thread, I couldn't help but laugh. "Yes, Carson Yates. He of avocado sweater fame."

"I'm sorry," said Heidi. "You've got to walk me through this. Just today, this morning in fact, you laid into him within just ten minutes of us crossing paths. Remember that? On the tube?"

"I was tired. Stressed. And I am aware that's no excuse, by the way. But even if I hadn't been, why would it matter? Carson's in danger, it's my fault, and I also have the means to save him."

"You likened spending time with him to *babysitting*."

"Yeah, well, I guess if I'd been thrown into worlds full

191

of monsters and was pursued by creeps in cloaks on my first day in London, I'd react poorly too." Eyebrows knitting, I went on, "And what's up with you, anyway? When we first met, you at least fought in Carson's corner. Within a couple of hours you went all ice queen, and now you're suggesting we let the orcs eat him?"

Heidi straightened. She turned her nose up, expression cold. "His glaring failures became apparent to me, just like they did to you. And I don't have time to play around with failure." If she weren't wearing my ancient band t-shirt and a pair of dark, creased jeans that were too baggy on her tiny frame, she'd have looked very much the stereotypical popular high-school girl, looking down on some well-meaning misfit. Except, you know, Asian instead of blonde, or whatever.

"He's a write-off, Mira," she continued, "plain and simple."

"*A write-off?*" I asked, incredulous—and not just at Heidi, but at me, too, because hadn't this been my opinion of him just six hours ago? "He may stutter, and be scared, and hold onto that stupid manbag of his like it's the only thing keeping me from floating away from this world. But he's brave, too!"

*"How is he brave?!"*

"The Order of Apdau set upon us in Russell Square. We were outnumbered, and whereas I had a spear, he had nothing to protect himself from those cinquedeas they carry. And *still* he came to my rescue."

"By swinging a *satchel*."

"What does that matter? If anything, it makes him braver! I don't know about the world you live in, but in mine, canvas doesn't hold up so hot against *knives*, Heidi! And again, in the temple. He held off the orcs alongside the two of us, and gave it just as good as we did."

"Not good enough," she pointed out through tight lips. "He got carried off, didn't he? This is his own fault, really."

"We got overrun. Only by sheer luck did we escape. It could easily have been us in his shoes."

Heidi's lips grew thinner still. She folded her arms. For her minute build, she looked like a sullen teenager with poor fashion sense.

"How do we even *find* him?" she muttered at last, glancing at me. "We don't know where Borrick took him."

Or if he was even still alive, after our get-away.

I stymied that thought. He had to be. He was a bargaining chip. Bargaining chips didn't just get tossed away the moment the enemy made a clutch escape.

"He knows I'm looking for the Chalice Gloria," I said. "And he knows I have the keys to get it." I patted the umbrella I'd shoved into my pocket, bright yellow and red canvas sticking out.

Feruiduin's Cutlass had been a little less subtle in its transformation. On our exit alongside the Thames, it had turned into a Bluetooth speaker. Awkward and bulky, and undoubtedly even more ridiculous if I tried to fix the thing to my belt, it had ridden in my lap on the tube ride to the Strand. Luckily, only one teenaged boy, probably my age or a bit younger, had been kind enough to say, "Nice boombox, love," as he sidled past me to his seat, to the great amusement of his three friends.

The speaker sat on the countertop now, sleek and black and unassuming. Both our eyes traveled across it.

"Stupid glamour," Heidi said, appraising it flatly. "It could at least turn itself into an iPhone or something useful. Or something that looks less stupid to carry around London." Then she conceded, after what looked like a very torn moment: "At least if Carson were here he could shove this stupid thing in that bloody bag of his."

My heart skipped. Yes. She wasn't a totally lost cause. Because I would do it alone, absolutely I would—but that didn't mean I wanted to. Not this time.

"Please do this with me," I asked. "You know it's the

right thing to do."

"And just let Borrick make off with the Chalice Gloria?"

"Last time we were here, we agreed. Right in this very room, in fact. The Chalice Gloria, as well as the artifacts needed to gain entry to it, is mine. That means if I choose to give it up—to let Alain Borrick have it in exchange for Carson—then you have to go along with it." Technically not, perhaps, but I'd like to see a lawyer argue that one.

Heidi considered for a long time. Too long, almost.

Then, at last, she sighed. Slumping against the doorframe, she raked fingers through her black hair.

All at once she looked very tired.

"You didn't finish your thought a moment ago. How do we find him?"

"Borrick's been researching the Chalice Gloria too, right?"

"So he says."

"Which means he's probably figured out where it's stored. And knowing that I have the keys in my possession to enter it ..."

"He'll have gone there to wait for us," Heidi finished. "One step ahead of you at last. Perfect."

"So we meet him there," I said. "And then we end this."

"We'll be outnumbered. Massively so."

"I'm aware."

"There could be any number of surprises waiting for us."

I folded my arms, sticking out my hip. "Really, Heidi? Come on. You said yourself: I'm a Brand. You don't think I won't have one of my own?"

Her eyebrows came down low over her eyes. "Borrick has a horde of orcs, Mira."

"So?"

"So?" Heidi threw up her hands. "Unless you've got a plan for us to get past them alive, I don't think whatever little surprise you have up your sleeve really matters."

"My surprise," I said, "is *how* we get through that horde

alive."

She waited. Then: "Not gonna tell me, huh?"

I shook my head. "It'll be my little secret—just like your little flashbang thing back there. So. Are you in, or aren't you?"

She weighed it up for a moment. Then, finally, sagging, she loosed a long, agonized breath.

"*Yes*, I'm in."

I clenched my fist, pumped it. "Thank you."

"When are we doing this?" she asked tiredly.

"Now."

"Right this moment?"

"Of course," I said, stooping and opening the fridge, retrieving my can of liquid caffeine and stuffing it back into my jeans pocket. "There's no time to waste."

I stepped through the doorway and back into the library—no, *strode*. I was on a mission, carried by pure fire and determination, fatigue all but a distant memory as I marched down the central aisle for the wall leading to London.

"And the Chalice Gloria?" Heidi asked, keeping pace beside me. "Where's that?"

"The Tower of London," I responded. "But we're not going there just yet."

"We're not?"

"No." I shook my head. "There's someplace else I need to go first."

# 28

"Salutations!"

We were in Kensington, illuminated from behind by coppery sodium lights, a shaft of glowing white coming from the partially opened door in front of us. Lady Angelica's ground-floor butler greeted us, peering around the wood's edge with its eternally cheerful face.

"All right, G?" I said.

Heidi's eyebrows knitted. "Who's G?" she mouthed.

"Regrettably I am neither 'G', nor do I know such a person," the butler chirped. "It appears you have stumbled upon the wrong property, visitors!"

"I was here literally today," I said.

"Oh, but of course! Have you come to visit Lady Hauk? It is rather a late hour, but she remains wakeful. Please wait while I confirm that she is entertaining visitors!"

We waited awkwardly on the doorstep as the butler silenced. He did not move, remaining perfectly still, gears turning over and over in his body, whirring away.

I bet he and his buddies would feel right at home with my fridge.

"Err," I said. "Why isn't he going to see if she's around?"

"Remote link, isn't it?" Heidi muttered. "They've probably got, like, mobile phones embedded in their brains or something."

"Not quite!" the butler chirped again, then quieted.

I glanced behind us, up and down the street. The butler was only three-quarters in view, but with night descended and a great big bar of light cast around him, his otherworldly appearance was pretty obvious.

Then again, I shouldn't really say Heidi, Carson or I had been doing the greatest job of laying low. How many hours ago had it been that I swung a spear around my head in the middle of Russell Square? How long since we'd ridden the train, drenched to high heaven when there had been not a drop of rain in days?

"Who's G?" Heidi asked after a moment.

"Yes!" the butler joined in. "Who is—oh, pardon; it appears Lady Hauk *is* available for visitors. She is on the third floor as we speak. Please! Come in!"

He wheeled back, the door opening wide for us. I took a quick glance back along the street to check no one saw, then hurried in alongside Heidi.

We trundled down the hall. At this hour it was lit by candlesticks. But they were too bright—more like miniature suns—and they were not held in sconces; instead they floated quite serenely. Wax trickled down their sides, but when it reached the bottom the drips vanished before spattering on the floor.

We were escorted onto the third floor by the usual string of robotic butlers. Mostly they hummed, although the butler on the second floor, whose faceplate was tinged blue, asked, "So who is this 'G'?"

"Geoffrey, the butler from *The Fresh Prince of Bel Air*. That's what Will called him. Seen it?"

"I have not, visitor!"

"You should check it out sometime."

"Alas," he said, a melancholy note in his electronic voice, "I am rather devoid of eyes." And then he went along humming, cheerful as you like.

I exchanged a look with Heidi. The expression she shot back was just as baffled as mine as she mouthed, "How does he *see*?" I decided not to ask.

Lady Angelica stepped out to meet us as the last in our line of mechanical escorts concluded the journey's leg.

"Young Mira," she said. "And Miss Luo. I see you've made each other's acquaintance."

She looked much the same as when last I'd laid eyes on her, late this morning: all proper, dark hair still pinned up and adorned with the fat-petaled rose holding it together, her wide-skirted dress so much like something I might expect to see in a Victorian painting, or a period piece on TV. But there was something in her face—her composure was not quite as complete as it had been this morning. A modicum of worry had crept into the crow's feet around her eyes, the tight lines radiating from her lips.

"Lady Angelica," I greeted.

"Lady Hauk," said Heidi.

"Your visitors, Lady Hauk," the butler said. "I shall pass them into your capable hands. Do call when you wish them retrieved, ma'am." And he wheeled back a couple of feet, as though giving us privacy, and stilled beside the wall.

"When I said your spell would be complete tonight, I did not anticipate you actually returning so soon to collect it," Lady Angelica told me.

"I need it. Is it finished?"

"Of course. This way." She began for the stairs. Despite her age, she took rapid steps that both Heidi and I struggled to keep pace with.

Even more impressively, she took the stairs two at a time.

"I hear it has been quite the day," she said as we strode past a butler who she waved off.

"It has?"

"The Order of Apdau mounted another attack in Russell Square." She glanced over her shoulder at me. "News travels fast." Flicking her gaze to Heidi, she added, "I shan't enquire as to how you made your getaway."

"It's been kind of hectic," I admitted.

"And it's not over yet," Heidi added in a low mutter.

"I can imagine." Looking over her shoulder at me again, Lady Angelica asked, "Would your late visit also happen to correlate to the absence of the young man in your company earlier?"

"Unfortunately, yes. We're conducting a rescue operation."

"Idiot got himself captured by orcs," Heidi grumbled. "Luckily their arse of a leader was kind enough to offer a trade."

"Oh?"

"Decidian's Spear, and Feruiduin's Cutlass—essentially, the Chalice Gloria—for his safe return," I told her.

"And you plan on taking him up on his offer?"

"Apparently," Heidi said.

We reached Lady Angelica's brewing room. She ushered us inside, where candlesticks burst into light of their own volition, hovering on the walls just as they had been in the many corridors we'd passed through to arrive here. The bright light threw the room into sharp relief, like the entire thing existed beneath a giant desk lamp.

Lady Angelica stepped to her brewing station. The spell, started this morning, was now housed in a round-bottomed vial held around the neck in a metal stand. A cork stoppered the little bottle. Wax sealed it.

Even before Lady Angelica retrieved it, the silvery liquid in the bottom seemed to swirl, like tiny clouds eddying around and around.

She clasped it delicately around the neck and passed it to me.

I took it, looking past my bulbous pale reflection into the softly churning fluid.

Such plans I'd had for this.

I still did, I reminded myself. The end goal had just changed.

"Thank you," I said.

I had everything I needed now. Spear, cutlass, and Lady Angelica's spell.

She escorted us right the way down to the front door, just as she had this morning.

"This fellow and his army who have your friend," she said as we stepped back out into Kensington night. "What do you intend to do about them?"

"Simple," I said. "Kick some arse, beat his orcs—and get Carson back."

# 29

The Tower of London closed its doors at four-thirty.

With nine p.m. fast approaching, getting inside, as was necessary to reach the temple where the Chalice Gloria was now held, became slightly problematic. Fortunately, I'd prepared for that in the course of my research, and with just a handful of back-and-forth gateway passes, first via Madame Tussauds and second at the edge of a jute field in Bangladesh, we found ourselves right where I wanted to be.

The lights were off. As soon as we stepped through, Heidi clanged into something.

"Ow!"

"Careful!" I pulled the flashlight from my pocket, where it nestled against the umbrella, and flicked it on.

The armory came dimly into view.

The walls were loaded with racks, and in them were dozens—hundreds—of guns. Rifles, mostly, side by side, surfaces polished and gleaming. Some of them sported bayonets.

Much of the floor was taken up too, by long, sleek, dark cylinders. Cannons, I realized as my flashlight sailed across the one Heidi had slammed her knee into.

"Careful with that," I warned, nodding to the Bluetooth speaker in her hand. "Don't want to lose it."

"Thanks for your sympathy." She massaged her knee.

"You think they're loaded?" she asked of the rifles.

"I very much doubt it."

"Shame. Could've helped us along a bit."

"Decidian's Spear and Feruiduin's Cutlass not enough for you?"

"Against an army of orcs? Not even close. Even with that little concoction of yours from Lady Hauk."

I'd filled her in on the train. The vial was nestled in my back pocket now. I'd been careful all the way here; it was a kind of Get Out of Jail Free card, and the last thing I needed was to smash it before the right moment.

"Come on," I said, beginning to pick my way over the cannons spread across the floor. "The temple's just on the other side."

Heidi followed. The cannons were close, but just tall and wide enough to be awkward, even for her frame— although that was perhaps more a function of my jeans coming up so baggy on her legs than any ungainliness on Heidi's part.

"Know what I don't get?" she asked.

"What's that?"

"These objects were lost for years. *Centuries.* The best and brightest minds searched for them for their entire lives, and still came up empty-handed."

"You better be leading into a pretty solid compliment, Luo. Thus far it doesn't sound too promising."

"What I don't get," she continued, "is how all the gateways are contained throughout London. Strikes me as awfully convenient, that's all."

"Well, convenience is our friend, then."

"Don't you think it's strange, though? How they're all here?"

I shrugged. "This gateway isn't accessible to the public, never has been. And the gateway to the elves' temple, that was underground; until the station was built, that space was all dirt and rock, or whatever. Doesn't seem so strange to me."

"I guess." But Heidi didn't look convinced, going by the illuminated side of her face. "Makes you wonder what other gateways are buried and inaccessible to us. Or in the sky, just waiting for some tower block to be erected." She clunked against another cannon, and bit off a curse. "These stupid things. Why did they need so many?"

"Carson would've loved this," I said.

"Carson would've tripped on every single one of these things on the way across the room, and probably knocked half his teeth out."

Mm. I couldn't really disagree with that.

At the opposite wall, I eyed my compass in the torchlight.

"Right here," I said.

Heidi made it to my side. "Another temple?" She peered down at the image on the compass face. "Of course."

"You sound disappointed."

"The last time I was in one, the walkways broke away and we only escaped thanks to the sort of ridiculous luck you see in action movies. You can see why I'm less than thrilled to be going back." She added, glancing at me sidelong with pursed lips, "Especially after you told me what we're in for."

"Chin up, Heidi. You're spry; way more cut out for this than I am."

She snorted with disbelief. "Just open the gate and let's get this over with."

I affixed the compass to my belt again. Taking my talisman in hand, fingertips caressing the spiraling pattern etched into it, I steeled myself against the soft warmth it radiated. Eyes closed, I inhaled, long and deep—and swiped.

The gateway split apart, edges shimmering. Cheerful color bloomed and danced its frenetic twists. Pulses of red and blue and green and yellow sailed up and down and across the cannons' sleek surfaces.

Then we were through, weightless for a few long

moments, breath held—

Out the other side.

There was no time to prepare. No sooner had I stepped into the rocky room from the gateway's invisible antipode did something lumbering and far, far larger than me sweep me into its clutches.

"GET OFF!"

Heidi came through, and cried out a moment later as she too was snatched up.

I fought, kicking. My arms were clamped to me from behind, so I couldn't grab for the umbrella on my belt—

And then it *wasn't* on my belt. A hand slipped it off.

A *human* hand.

I ceased my wriggling, and set eyes on Alain Borrick.

He held the umbrella balanced between his forefingers, appraising.

A cold smile lifted his features.

"Decidian's Spear. You brought it."

"Put me down!"

"And Feruiduin's Cutlass?" he asked. His eyebrows rose on his forehead and stayed there, like a teacher awaiting an answer from an unprepared student.

"Here, Mr. Borrick, sir," rumbled an orc on my left. "The small girl has it."

"I have a name," Heidi retorted.

Borrick made his way over.

Although clamped in much the same fashion I was, Heidi swung up her legs, kicking madly through the air. Borrick was not quite in reach, so she did not manage to sail a foot into him. But he did pause.

"Let's not make this difficult, now," he said. The victorious lilt had left his voice now; his words were clipped, terse.

"You want it, come and get it," Heidi snapped back.

Borrick's lip curled. "Fine." Glancing to the orc clasping her tight, he gave a nod. "If you'll please." And before Heidi had even opened her mouth to yell, a vast hand twice the size of her head reached down, ripped away the material of her bulging left pocket, and removed the Bluetooth speaker.

"HEY! GIVE THAT BACK!"

"Here, Mr. Borrick." The orc threw it in a low arc.

"GIVE ME THAT—LET ME *GO*, DAMN YOU!!"

Borrick ignored Heidi's frantic kicks. He had eyes for only these two things: one in each hand, atop an open, flat palm as if each of those were pedestals too, he took them in with fiery eyes, devouring each and every millimeter of their surfaces.

"Decidian's Spear and Feruiduin's Cutlass. Home at last."

"You got what you wanted," I grunted. The clamp around my chest was too tight; not enough to suffocate, not even close, but the vast power of the brute grasping me was impressed into my bones. Just one sharp squeeze and my entire body would be broken, chest compressing into my lungs, spine crushed. "Now where's my friend?"

"Your friend? Oh. Yes. The American. Of course." Borrick turned to a corner of the room, blocked by orcs, and snapped his fingers. "Bring him out."

The orcs shuffled, parting like the Red Sea. I was able to glimpse a dark passage leading away which they had obstructed. Torchlight licked the walls, floor and ceiling, coming closer.

Clasped between two ugly, green-skinned orcs was Carson. They had an arm each. He struggled to keep pace. Although close to six feet tall, he had to hold both his arms up at an awkward angle, like a puppet on strings, to prevent the height differential from tearing his limbs from his sockets.

He stumbled into the lighter chamber we were in.

His gaze was on me immediately.

"Mira!" he gasped. "What are you doing here?"

"Rescuing you," Borrick answered for me. "You ought to thank them for accepting my deal."

"Your deal? Mira, what—" He glanced to Borrick, and saw, perched on his hands, the umbrella, as well as the Bluetooth speaker. So out of place that although he hadn't been around to see its glamoured form on our return to London, it was clear that Borrick now possessed both Decidian's Spear and Feruiduin's Cutlass.

"No!" he gasped.

"It's fine, Carson—"

"The Chalice Gloria! What about everything you said?"

I ignored him. "Did they hurt you?" To Borrick, without waiting for Carson's response: "I swear, if you touched so much as a single hair on his head ..."

"I haven't harmed him," Borrick said, sounding irritated. "I even let him keep that ghastly satchel on his person."

Sure enough, he still had it slung over one shoulder.

Looking to Carson and then me in turn, Borrick added, "You ought to be very thankful. That little bag of his sent more than a few of my orcs to their graves. Those remaining were *very* keen to exact a fitting punishment. They're a very honor-driven race, you know."

"Doesn't much seem like it," I muttered, "seeing as they're helping a thief."

"Ironic," rumbled a low voice emanating from the chest pressing into my back, "coming from you."

I flinched. Looked up and around.

The scar-faced orc from the elven temple. He was the one who had me. And although it had been Heidi who'd lopped his fingers off, going by the dark sneer on his face as he looked down at me now, I was the focus of his rage.

In another universe, a better version of me would have asked, "How's the hand?" This me only swallowed.

"You got your toys," Heidi grunted, "now let us go."

"I will, I will," Borrick said dismissively. "I'm a man of my word. But first—let's go for a little journey together, hm? What do you say?"

"A journey *where*?" I asked.

A smile curved his lips. Cruel, I thought—or just the

cheeriness of a man who had won—and who, going by his next words, felt he was offering me a great unrivaled kindness.

"You came so very close to the Chalice Gloria, Miss Brand. An admirable effort, unquestionably so. I feel it's only right that you join me in the final chamber to witness it in the moment of its long overdue acquisition." And without waiting for my answer, he ordered several of the orcs at his elbow: "Move."

They shifted, clearing a path.

Behind him was a passage. Like the one blocking the way to Feruiduin's Cutlass, it was blocked by a sheet of unbroken rock.

"Let's see," he said. "If I just …"

The spear and cutlass extended, shaking off their glamour.

Borrick inched closer to the barricade. "How did it work before? Was it—ah, never mind, here we go."

The rock rearranged. Even from here, in Scarface's clutches, I could feel the static electricity growing in the air. It darted over my skin, causing goosebumps to rise. Stronger here than before, it ratcheted up, and I felt the hair on the back of my neck begin to rise as though I were touching a Van de Graaff generator.

Two openings formed in the rock.

"Oh, really?" Borrick asked in surprise. "The keys are the glamoured forms. How very strange." He shook the weapons, and they accepted his unspoken instruction, once again becoming an umbrella and a thin black speaker. Slotting the umbrella in the higher opening, he muttered, "It's really very peculiar, isn't it? How the keys are so modern. They change according to the times, do you think?" He glanced around at me with a look of genuine curiosity.

"Couldn't tell you," I murmured.

"No. I don't suppose you could. Well then, let's just …"

He pressed the speaker into the bottom slot.

A dim green glow illuminated both.

"It wants me to retrieve them again, does it?"

He was looking at me again. I said flatly, "Yes."

Borrick slipped them out carefully—

The rock face split in two, perfectly down the middle, just as the other had, along an invisible seam. Rumbling filled the air as the halves were retracted by some unknown mechanism—and then the corridor was open.

Borrick was already moving down it, face alight.

The orcs followed. I was ushered in first, still carried by Scarface. Heidi was dragged behind, and going by the gasping noises coming from over my shoulder, Carson was being manhandled along too.

"Can't believe it," Borrick was saying. His muttering came doggedly over the clicking of his boots as he half-jogged down the tunnel. "All my research ... knew it would pay off ... if Father could see ..."

Then he burst out the mouth—and stopped.

The orcs followed, us in hand.

The chamber was staggeringly huge, an enormous cube, and we had entered onto the bottom. At the very top, some three hundred feet above, was a single stone platform. It hung by chains in the middle of the ceiling— and standing upon it, although invisible from here, was the Chalice Gloria.

There were no other platforms whatsoever. No vines, like the first temple. No bridges or walkways or staircases. Just the one ledge at the chamber's apex—and thousands upon thousands of handholds etched into the walls.

"What is this?" Borrick said in disbelief.

I allowed a smirk to curve my lips. "A temple. What ... your *research* didn't tell you there were no platforms?"

Borrick gaped. Then he whirled on me with manic eyes.

"And how did you intend on dealing with this?"

"Simple." And flicking a glance to Carson that I hoped communicated the words *HOLD ON*, I answered, "Like this"—and pushed my body back into Scarface's as hard as I could.

The flask in my back pocket broke.

As it did, a flash of energy swelled out from me in a spherical blast, and the gravity in the room switched off.

Suddenly lifted from the floor, noises of surprise went up from the orcs around us. Scarface released, rumbling in shock—

Heidi was in action first. Kicking off from her captor like a gymnast, she twisted through the air like a missile aimed straight at Borrick.

He gasped, jerking back, still caught off-guard by the fact he was floating through the air—

Then Heidi was past, and in her hand, fully extended, was Feruiduin's Cutlass.

"Catch!" she cried to me.

I slipped out of Scarface's grasp as the umbrella sailed end over end.

"NO!" Borrick shrieked.

I caught it, and brought it round as Scarface grappled for me.

The sharp metal tip, tinged with purple ooze, cut him short.

Then I was darting for Carson.

The two orcs who had been holding him grabbed out. But they were unprepared, and off-balance. As though the air had been replaced with millions of gallons of water, they swum in slow-motion, maladroit and lumbering like dogs still under the effects of a general anesthetic.

I swiped Carson out of there, using the shoulders of a nearby orc to kick the both of us up and toward the wall.

*"How is this happening?"* he asked, sounding like he was two steps below full-on freakout.

*"The spell from Lady Angelica,"* I answered.

"So you knew about this?" Maybe only one step.

"I've been researching it for years. Of course I knew."

Borrick was just springing into motion, as were the orc army. Five or six were swimming toward Heidi already.

She made easy work of them, spinning in a flurry of onyx strikes as she pirouetted away time and again. But yet more of the army were coming toward me and Carson—and these ones were taking notes from us, because they grasped the handholds, pushing themselves higher.

"Get them!" Borrick roared. "Get my keys!"

Carson glared at him, eyes flashing. "Borrick."

He untangled himself from the arm I'd slung around his back—"What are you doing?" I shouted—and then kicked off.

"CARSON!"

Orcs grabbed for him as he shot overhead, miraculously missing—

Borrick's face flashed in panic. He held up his hands, ready to block—

Then Carson slammed into him.

They tumbled in the air, end over end.

"What's he doing?" Heidi shouted.

"Carson!" I yelled—then swung the spear below. An orc's fist had swallowed my foot. I slammed the tip into the fleshy patch between thumb and forefinger. Purple spurted, and he howled, sinking into the writhing mass beneath. Another replaced him, and I swung again, pushing myself higher up the wall.

Carson's hands clawed at Borrick's face. Borrick gripped his neck in return, squeezing as he bared teeth, roaring as Carson pressed thumbs into his closed eyelids—

"Leave my friends alone!" Carson shrieked.

*"Get off—!"*

"Mira is a better Seeker than you'll ever be!"

"I said—"

*"A million times better! You hear me?"*

"I said get—*OFF!*" Borrick swung a punch into Carson's face.

Carson grunted, spinning backward in the air, head jerking back—

"Carson!" I yelled, fighting off another grabbing hand

from below.

Borrick swung again, holding Carson steady around the neck. The blow hit him hard in the cheek, and he groaned, jerking around. His glasses came lopsided, somehow holding to one ear instead of flying off.

"No one is a better Seeker than me!" Borrick threw another punch, the ring on his middle finger glinting as it sailed—

Carson grabbed for him, catching Borrick's hand between his fingers. He gasped—but he held it, grappling—then it came away, and Carson's fingers hooked into claws, sailing down bare fingers and drawing long bloody lines—Borrick screeched in pain—

I swung Decidian's Spear in a wide arc. The orc army had truly sorted itself out now. Climbing up the handholds with untold ease in this field of zero gravity, they no longer reached but swung bony clubs. I met them with the spear, fighting them back—being pushed back myself—

And still Borrick and Carson grappled, floating toward the room's center some fifteen feet from the floor.

Only now Borrick had the upper hand again.

His hands tightened around Carson's neck.

Carson tried to claw at his face—but the motions were weak, ineffective.

"Useless simpering boy!" Borrick's voice was strained, strangled. "You—are—*nothing compared—to—m—*"

He didn't finish. After one last swing of Decidian's Spear, I kicked off the wall, sailing across the space—

And slamming into him, ramming an elbow solidly into the small of his back.

His hold on Carson released immediately. Now tangled in a ball with me, he yelled in confusion as the world spun around us, grappling for anything he could manage to make contact with—then his face met mine from above the spear, horizontal and gripped between us. His eyes bulged, manic.

"You—!"

"Leave my friend alone," I spat—and booted him in the stomach.

He released, ejected, and sailed away.

My arc carried me past Heidi. She spun like a ninja, carving with Feruiduin's Cutlass at the four orcs swinging at her. Their clubs clanged off the blade. She used the momentum to push higher.

"What now?" she called to me.

"I need to get up there!" I jabbed toward the platform holding the Chalice Gloria. The fray had brought us some fifty feet closer—but it was still a long way from being within reach.

"I'll do what I can to hold them off," Heidi said. "What about Carson?"

I looked over to see him swinging his manbag around in a wide arc at one of the orcs snatching for him. It yelled and jerked back, and Carson loosed a victorious hoot—then another orc fist sailed out of nowhere and clapped him hard in the chest.

"Carson!" I cried.

He spun in an endless cartwheel—and clattered to a stop at my side. Upside down, he looked up at me in a daze.

"Hey, Mira," he said. "That was lucky."

"Come on," I told him. "You're coming with me."

"Where?"

"Up."

And snatching his hand, I pulled us toward the ceiling.

Borrick's roar echoed after us. "They're going for the chalice! Stop them, *damn it*!"

"Go, go, go!" Heidi cried.

We leapt up, handhold after handhold.

"I can't believe you came back for me," Carson was saying in my ear.

"Of course I came back for you."

"And—did you mean that? About being a friend?"

"Yes!" I leapt again, casting a look below. Heidi was still managing—but Borrick and his orcs were gaining on us, vastly more of them than I could ever hope to deal with. "Now can we keep the real-talk to a minimum, just until I have this bloody Chalice?"

"Sorry!"

Up we went again. Another leap. Another.

A hundred and fifty feet still in it. Halfway there.

"Mira?" Carson suddenly said.

I shot a frantic look below.

Twenty feet between us and the ascending orc army, if that.

Scarface led it, climbing one-handed. A furious sneer clouded his face, eyes almost black as they stared as down.

"Mira!"

"I know," I said. "I can see."

"No, not that. *That!*"

I looked up to where Carson pointed—

My stomach dropped.

Shooting toward us over the chamber's expanse came the Order of Apdau.

# 30

I released Carson and swung Decidian's Spear around. It clanged as three cinquedeas slammed it all at once. I slung it up and over my head and the force sent the Order of Apdau spinning backward.

"Quick," I ordered, clambering higher one-handed, and sweeping the spear beneath me at the encroaching orc army.

The Order of Apdau shot back in again. Carson gasped as a cinquedea swung over his head. Then I was swinging the spear again, blocking the jab.

*"Leave—my friend—alone!"*

I flung them back again.

"Mira, orcs!"

Scarface was right below. He grabbed for me. I shunted sideways, grunting, my ankle just sailing through his fingers before they closed—

"Piss off!" I shouted, and thrust the wooden end of the spear down at him. It stabbed him in the eye, and he wailed and dropped from the handhold, knocking the orcs below him back too.

Before I had time to enjoy it, the Order of Apdau were sailing in again, as though they had jetpacks hidden under those black robes.

"Oh, *come on!*"

Spear and cinquedeas collided. I thrust with it, sending

them backward—

"Mira," Carson suddenly said. "Where's your compass?"

Before I could answer, he reached across me and snatched it from my belt.

Apdau were back again. I blocked, yelping at the high-pitched whine as steel rang on steel—shoved them back, already swiping at the renewed orcs pushing from my feet—

"What are you doing?" I cried as Carson scrabbled up and away.

"Seeking!" he called back, climbing higher still.

"But you don't have a talisman!"

No answer: he was gone, hand over hand—and I was stuck, Order of Apdau on one side and orc army on the other.

I had no idea what he was thinking, doing—but the orcs were still coming, the Order reorienting themselves for another strike. At least I had a weapon. Carson didn't. Now that he'd broken away from me I couldn't directly keep him safe without following. So I'd do the next best thing instead.

Leaping sideways, I stilled my upward climb, turning it into a horizontal one. I wanted to get to another wall—the opposite one, preferably—and take as much heat off Carson as I possibly could.

The Order came after me in flawless flight. Without Carson to protect, I was freer to move now, so I kicked away, cutting off the corner. Spinning in the air, I whipped Decidian's Spear around.

It sliced black cloak—but there was no flash of red; I had just swiped off a corner.

I landed, lifted the spear above me to absorb the Order's blows—

"Can you just *bugger off*?"

I thrust them away—body aching now—and hurtled down the wall.

"Get her!" cried Borrick.

The orcs leapt off of the wall, swimming across for me.

Damn it! Why did there have to be so many balls to juggle?

Had to get to the next one, the wall opposite Carson.

I dodged another attack from the Order—why were they so acrobatic, able to relaunch attacks so *fast?*—and skittered farther across. When I turned, I cried out as I moved to block another attack. I wished I could see what Carson was doing, how Heidi fared. All I could do was trust they were safe.

I leapt to cut off the next corner. Opposite wall now; the heat was as far from Carson as I could take it.

I gripped the handhold as I sailed into it—

A cinquedea slammed the wall just above me. Sparks flew.

I yelped, retracting my hand, turning—

They were right on me, swinging—

I lifted the spear—

The impact sent it spinning out of my grip.

I gasped.

The cinquedeas were coming around now, to slice again—

They sailed, metal gleaming—

In my moment of panic, I did the only thing I could do. I reached into my pocket and pulled out a well and truly shaken can of energy drink. I lifted it, eyes tight, fingers on the ring pull as I popped it and hoped—

Stinging fizz erupted in a fountain.

It was the first noise I'd ever heard any of these Apdau guys make—a sudden hiss of pain. Acidic spray found its way into their cowls. Blinded, they flailed, cinquedea swings cut short as hands grappled for their eyes.

I had just short seconds to savor the victory. Leaping sideways again, I grabbed Decidian's Spear where it turned a slow cartwheel—

And then an orc's fist enclosed around my ankle.

# 31

Not Scarface, this one, but another. He looked up at me with bulbous yellow eyes. In his other hand, he held a club. His fingers tightened, the knuckles paling. Then he was lifting, ready to swing—

"Mira!" Carson cried from across the chamber.

I ducked the first blow. Tried to bring Decidian's Spear around. But it was too late; the orc clambered higher, dragging me down like an ape with its hand on a toy. I tried to grip a handhold, keep myself up—but he was too strong, his hand wrapping my thigh now, like I was a rope he could climb, end over end.

"Leave her alone!"

I tried to swing with the spear again—

The club sailed down, pinning it against the wall between the barbs, the shaft of the spear anchoring me against the wall. My eyes widened.

The orc lifted himself fully ahead of me now, face to face. Hot, acrid breath blew against me.

"Your journey has concluded, thief."

He opened his hand, reaching for me, my face, to take me by the head—to *crush it*, exterminate me as I was trapped here—

"I said to *get off of her*!"

So very far over the orc's shoulder, Carson gripped something in his hand. Balancing on two handholds underfoot, he held up a hand in a manner I was so familiar with, having done it so many times before—

And I realized now, suddenly: in his fracas with Borrick. One moment Borrick had worn a ring; the next it was gone.

That was Borrick's talisman.

And *Carson had it*.

He swiped.

The wall between us ripped open.

Where my gateway looked like a more imprecise version of Heidi's, Carson's was something else. Dim at the edges, the hole it opened in the chamber wall looked torn. And it was *gargantuan*. It did not open from a tear, but instead ballooned in spasmodic, jerky moments, edges contorting as it grew. A burst of dull color erupted in it, forking in lazy stop-start jags, dimming—

And then it split apart.

My eyes bulged.

"What the—?!"

Instead of every gateway I had ever known, which dumped you into a kind of ethereal middle-ground filled with fireworks before spewing you out, this one had gone into full-on wormhole territory. There was no space between, no barrier. On one side was the temple—and on the other, visible as the great gateway only shuddered and kept growing, was a busy intersection. I didn't know if it was London, New York, or snatched from another other city in our world. But it was there, with us, all lights and streaking traffic and horns and the belch of fumes.

The orcs caught sight of it.

The terror that took hold of them was absolute. They screamed, a cacophony of high-pitched wails that were completely unlike what you would ever think orcs were capable of. They released their handholds, their weapons—and although not drawn earthward by gravity, they swam for the floor.

Heidi gripped the cutlass tight, poised to strike, but

frozen in shock.

The orcs swam past.

"WHAT ARE YOU DOING?" Borrick cried. *"WHERE ARE YOU GOING?"*

A taxi sailed by the tear, narrowly missing entering the gateway. Its horn blared as it passed, as though the driver were simply angry at another car rather than the sudden appearance of an inter-dimensional gate in his path. The sound was amplified to a near-deafening level—

The orcs scurried faster. Half of them were at the floor now, and they dragged themselves along by the handholds for the exit.

"Come back!" Borrick shrieked at their disappearing backs.

Another horn blared from the tear—and then it collapsed, like a sheet of paper wadded up, then simply blinked out of existence.

*"Get back here!"*

But it was too late. The army had dissipated almost entirely. Aside from Borrick himself, the only orc remaining was—

I gritted my teeth.

Scarface.

He'd been jostled down the wall by the flood of orcs making their way past. But his eyes were on me.

I got to meet them for just a second before the Order of Apdau arced back into view.

I raised the spear—

But Carson had me covered.

"And you can leave her alone, too!" he cried.

He gripped Borrick's ring. Holding himself steady with his feet only, he released his handhold, swiping his hand—

Another gateway opened, on the opposite side now. Like the other, it was more like a tear—and instead of the dancing show of lights that should have been there, the other side faded through instead.

A windswept beach. And just out to sea—
"HURRICANE!"

A gale howled. The air was sucked out of the room—

And I was being pulled with it.

The Order of Apdau flailed. Closer to the tear than I was, they were drawn to it first. Their cloaks whipped. Arms jerked, and legs kicked, as though swimming against a tide intent on dragging them out—

The tear's edges widened jerkily.

The vacuuming power of the hurricane roaring through the waters grew.

The Order of Apdau were whipped through the gap—

I was flying for it too—

Carson's cry was almost lost to the sheer force of the gale. "Mira!"

I tumbled, yelling—

My only hope was—

I grabbed the spear, bringing it around, angling as best I could in the fraction of an instant I had before—

Then I was out. My legs hung in the air, horizontal. Water was coming at me, traveling almost sideways as I clung to Decidian's Spear. It had lodged at the edge of Carson's tear, an anchor, ends resting on either side of the chamber wall where the gateway's shuddering edge had not yet reached. It, and my grip, was the only thing keeping me from being sucked out into oblivion.

Carson shouted from beyond the tear. Braced on the opposite wall, his manbag was dragged horizontally too.

I could not hear his words, but I could read them on his lips.

"I don't know how long it'll hold!"

This was it. All I had to do was drag myself back through.

I tensed.

A pull-up. That's what this was. Just one pull-up.

I could do that, hurricane bearing down on me or not.

Teeth gritted, I bent my forearms. The gateway came

closer and closer, inch by inch, as wind howled in my ear
… as my jeans whipped around my ankles …

Just as my face was an inch away, Decidian's Spear
shifted. I gasped, bracing—

The tear had shuddered again. But it held.

Come on! I could do this. I could *do this!*

I pulled, with every fiber of my being, every muscle,
every last bit of energy I had left. I called on the last
surges of adrenaline that had kept me going on this manic
forty-eight-hour journey, willing them to just give me the
strength to *pull—myself—through!*

I was back on the other side. Somehow, the wind was
worse here; the chamber amplified the deafening uproar
as air was whipped about, sucked out around us.

I scrabbled up the spear, using it almost as a plank,
positioning my body over the top and fighting to balance
against the roar, one hand on the nearest handhold—

Then it shifted as the tear's edge shuddered again.
Inward, this time.

I panicked, jolting as the spear's tip was pressed close to
the tear's edge, almost close enough to go in and send me
down with it—

Then, with a last violent roaring spasm, the tear
collapsed.

My ears rung.

I gripped the wall's handholds, eyes closed. Desperate
gasps for breath filled my chest over and over.

Then, through the ringing noise: "Mira!"

I spun just in time to see two things: first, Alain Borrick
was making his way up the handholds on the wall between
me and Carson, jaw set and determined eyes on the
central platform up by the ceiling. Second—and way more
important—the scarred orc was bearing down on me,
sailing through the air in a great leap, bony club raised
overhead.

I threw myself sideways with a yelp. The club slammed
down behind me, smashing my handhold—

"You cut off my fingers, spineless thief!" he roared, swinging for me again. I swam backward to dodge; the club sailed between my legs.

"Actually, that was me!" Heidi called. She was leaping from the ground, handhold to handhold, after Borrick.

And she was never going to make it in time.

"The Chalice!" Carson cried.

"I know, thanks!"

I flung myself back from Scarface, bringing the spear up to meet him. He batted it out of the way, and in the antigravity field I was sent spinning.

My foot found a handhold as I stuck it out. I lurched to a sickening stop—

"Shame!" the orc roared. The club sailed for my head—I yelped, ducked—it crashed into the wall, sending fragments of stone into the air, spraying the back of my head—

"Borrick's going for the Chalice!" Carson yelled.

"So do something!" Heidi cried.

"I'm—I'm stuck!" Carson cried back. He was tugging at his manbag frantically where he'd looped it around an adjacent handhold. Try as he might, it would not come loose.

"It is *mine*!" Borrick shouted back. His cry was desperate, the yell of a man who was making his last ditch attempt—but there was a touch of victory in it too. Because Carson was frozen, Heidi was far too low to ever catch up—and in just a couple of seconds, I would be no more.

Borrick couldn't take it. Not after all this.

I had just one shot at this.

Scarface swung his club again, and I dodged, pirouetting in the air. A barb sailed so close to my face I felt the kiss of air as it soared past, a mere half-inch from tearing me open.

*"Pathetic creature,"* he growled, drawing back for another swing—

NOW!

I drew myself into a crouch on the wall, as low as I could go, pointing at the central platform—and sprung.

I sailed through the zero-gravity, the platform's underside coming closer—the Chalice Gloria coming closer!—I prepared to land, legs ready to jet out and stop me before I sailed right over …

But I had misjudged. I realized, almost too late, that I was going to be too low.

I thrust out my free hand, grabbing for the edge.

I caught it—

Borrick, almost even keel with me on his wall, flashed me a manic look of victory. "Sorry. End of the line, Mira Brand."

I twisted behind me, following his look.

Scarface sailed through the air, an unstoppable mass. Face contorted with rage, his club was raised overhead.

No time to dodge.

"FOR HON—"

There was no more. Just moments before he careened into me, the orc was thrown back like a cricket ball slammed by a bat. The word turned to a wail of pain and surprise—and then he crashed into the floor far below us.

I stared, wide-eyed. What the …?

Carson's cry broke me from my wonder. "Mira, he's on you!"

I twisted.

Borrick braced his feet against the wall, ready to leap. He took aim—

I dragged myself up as he leapt. His arms were extended, and he flew—

Time seemed to slow, and we drifted through the next moment like the pull of time had gone just as powerless as the gravity in the chamber when I'd smashed the flask. The surface against my hands was slick, the sweat of my palms working to dissolve the traction as I pulled myself up again. My stomach complained as I bumped it against the edge while I tugged up.

This was it; Borrick was feet away.

But so was I.

The Chalice Gloria glittered in its resting place, resplendent and bejeweled, light shining down on it from above as rubies and emeralds glittered like Christmas decorations in the gilded handles and surface.

It was right there.

Everything I needed to prove myself to my parents. To my brother.

A second away, and I was on the edge, out of breath, a hundred little pains rolling over me.

And none of that mattered.

I rolled for the platform's middle, where the Chalice Gloria stood, resplendent and bejeweled—and grabbed it, finally—FINALLY—taking glory in my own two hands.

# 32

Borrick landed awkwardly, like he'd missed a step, face twisting in agony. He'd seen me take it, and the twist of emotion that ran across his handsome features in that moment would have scared a less jaded person.

I was getting pretty jaded by now, though.

I spun, arranging the Chalice behind me, jabbing Decidian's Spear toward his neck with my other hand. It had a clear line right to the jugular, and he eyed it warily. "Don't even think about trying something," I growled.

He looked like he might. But then Heidi joined us, landing nimbly behind him. "That goes from me too." She extended Feruiduin's Cutlass. One step backward, and he'd go all Nathan in *Ex Machina*, blade sinking into his back.

He looked across me, down Decidian's Spear, and then to the Chalice Gloria in my other hand.

Gaze stuck there, he stood frozen and let out a low grunt. It didn't sound like a concession.

"To the victor go the spoils," I said.

"That was supposed to be my Chalice," he said.

"Oh, shut up," said Heidi.

"All my work ... all these years ... a whole *army*—and it's bested by a China doll and a dumb, helpless American."

"He's not *dumb*," I retorted, voice hard. "And he's not

helpless either. He dismantled pretty much your entire army single-handedly."

"Not to mention our cloaked friends," Heidi added.

I gave Carson an over-the-shoulder look that was … downright affectionate.

He returned it—then swayed. "Uh, hey, I think the gravity's coming back!" he called.

Heidi nodded. "I'm definitely feeling the pull a little bit."

"Just ride it down," I said. "It'll be like that scene in *Willy Wonka*, with the fizzy lifting drinks." To Carson: "Your bag still stuck? Need me to come over?"

"No, I've got it." Looking somewhat terrified, he released his hold on the wall. Sure enough, he slowly began to descend.

"Come on," I said to Borrick, prodding at him with the spear. "Down we go."

Bracketed by me on one side and Heidi on the other, Borrick begrudgingly stepped off the platform. Slowly, the three of us slid down to earth, weapons pointed at him all the way.

"I came so close," Borrick said, more ashen and regretful than angry. "*So close.* And you had to go and rip it all away from me." On this last part, anger came out. "Do you have any idea—this was supposed to be my chance! My chance to … to show my family … show my father … what I can do."

"Cry me a river," Heidi told him.

"My whole army … just gone." Borrick was still rambling. And now, suddenly, he snapped around to me. "You've ruined everything."

I was sure for a second he was going to come for me, weapons be damned, and try to throttle me the way he had Carson. I hefted the spear, ready. But he didn't move, at least not my way. Only his face shifted, contorted in hate. Hate for me.

For just a moment, his words from before came back to me.

*We're just two sides of the same coin, searching for the same prize.*

Not just that—we were doing it for the same reasons.

Then my feet touched the chamber floor.

Borrick stamped for Carson, who'd landed with approximately the same lack of grace as I had expected.

"You stole my talisman—"

Heidi stopped him with Feruiduin's Cutlass.

"Not one more step toward the geek," she said.

Carson puffed himself up. I had the feeling that even if Heidi had not stepped in, he still would have done so.

"So what if I stole your stupid ring? You took the spear and cutlass. At least I actually got my hands dirty when I took it."

Borrick gritted his teeth. He looked about ready to burst into flame.

"Give it back," he growled.

"No."

Borrick's face darkened. Definitely, definitely about to burst into flames—

Then he sagged.

When he spoke again, his voice was piteous.

"How am I supposed to get home?"

"I'll find you an exit," I answered. "Carson, compass?"

He threw it to me.

We walked back to the tunnel, Borrick slumped ahead of us. He was muttering, but I couldn't make out the words. Probably for the best. If he mentioned his family again, in that same quavering tone, I might just feel sorry for him.

I stopped when the compass showed a snow-capped peak. Skies were blue, a chilled sun glowing just above the horizon, sending sparkles across the ice.

"Here," I said, stopping. "A nice little mountain for you."

Borrick's eyes flashed with panic. "But—you can't just strand me—"

"I'm not." I showed him the compass, held just out of arm's reach in case he decided to snatch it. "See? A cabin.

227

Knock on the door, and see if you can orient yourself from there."

I clutched my talisman, and cut open a gateway. The normal kind, with shimmering edges, and dancing colors illuminating the weightless in-between space.

When it was wide enough, I nodded toward it, eyes on Borrick. "On your way, now."

He pressed his lips into a line, eyes burning in barely held fury. "This isn't over, Brand."

But even so, he stepped through after a moment and was gone.

# 33

To the victor goes the … burrito?

Well, at least it wasn't spoiled.

I made my way into Tortilla, taking a well-justified break from my new compatriots. I hadn't been around people for this long since before I'd run away, and while I was strangely pleased to find myself in the constant company of Heidi and Carson—well, now anyways—there was something of a wearing effect.

To wit: I felt tired, mentally, in a way I didn't normally feel.

Of course, that could just be the lack of calories. Hence, the burrito.

You can almost picture it—big wooden sign with white letters under a series of red awnings. Store front with windows that look straight in off the Strand. Tables scattered on the main floor, a serving counter where you get your food, and a staircase in the back that leads up to the second story.

The tables on the main floor were half-filled, this being an off hour, and the long bar that lined the lefthand wall was dotted with people. I wasn't in the mood for people, so I took my chance and took the staircase up.

The second floor was near empty, a couple talking in hushed voices overlooking the windows and the street. They stopped talking when they saw me, and piled all their rubbish on their trays and left in a rush. That didn't bother me, and I replaced them at one of the circular tables that gave a choice view of the foot traffic passing below.

It was rush hour in London, but then ... it's always a bit of rush here, isn't it?

My burrito was meaty deliciousness, a feast for a starving girl. Carson had given me the money for the meal, and in return, I was going to pick up something for both him and Heidi. But on my way back.

Because for now ... I cherished the silence, the sweet enjoyment of victory—glory, really—in a crowd of all my admirers.

Yeah, it was pretty quiet up there alone, but hey, I liked it. Fame doesn't come in a day, after all.

"Why aren't you celebrating with your new friends?" The voice was playful, and cool, and with a hint of sweetness.

I turned to find the man who'd passed me in the underground just before I'd met Carson. He was smiling, his jaw the very definition of a lantern, blond hair swept back nicely. There was no denying he was *fit*, as the girls at school used to say, and I tried to keep my jaw from unhinging downward to land in my burrito.

"You," I said, gawping. "You warned me about those Order of Apdau fellows, didn't you? I didn't even catch it at the time."

"I tried," he said, sidling over. "You were ... thinking about other things, I'm sure." He nodded at my belt, where Decidian's Spear hung. "Your newly acquired toy. Glories yet to come." He grinned wide. "Or that have come, now. I heard you landed the Chalice. Congratulations."

"Thank you," I said, a little more guarded that I might have been otherwise. This mystery man had come out of nowhere, after all. "And you are?"

He stepped over and extended a hand, gingerly.

"Clayton Price, at your service."

I regarded him with the care I might give a snake about to bite. A very handsome snake. Gorgeous, almost. "And why are you following me about, Clayton Price?"

He got a very shy look on his face just then. "Just trying to offer a little bit of help. Warn you about the Order before they came your way, that sort of thing."

I stared at him. "You could have done a better job of it. I wasn't exactly left with the impression I was about to be chased by crazy men with knives from the little you said, now, was I?"

He almost laughed. "I'll try to do better in the future."

I started to say something else, but stopped myself, catching the inference there. "The future? Does that mean—what, I'm going to hear from you again?"

He bowed, blond locks swishing forward as he did so, making a slow retreat toward the stairs again. "If you keep this up, Mira Brand? I can pretty well guarantee it."

And then he was gone.

# 34

Back in my hideaway just off the Strand, Carson and I sat together in one of the side rooms, filled out with plush chairs and beautifully stained surfaces. An endless stretch of maps adorned the walls, looking like no place I had ever seen, all hand-painted in black against deep crimson.

One bulb illuminated us from the ceiling. Somehow, without instruction, it seemed to detect the late hour; it was much softer than the ones in the library when Carson and I first stepped in here. Like candlelight, almost.

Reclined in an overstuffed chair, I admired the Chalice Gloria. Its jeweled surface winked back at me.

"All of that, for this," I mused in a whisper.

From the chair opposite, Carson asked, "Was it worth it?"

I chose my words carefully.

"I wanted to show my parents that ..." I paused, changed tack. "My dad did well in this work, obviously—I mean, you've heard people saying ..."

"Your famous name."

I nodded. "But really it's my—my older brother." Anger flashed across me, a dark flush of it. Not at him—but at *them.*

"He's the heir," I spat, "and I'm the spare. That's how it always was. *The chosen one.* Nothing he ever did was wrong, and nothing I ever did was right."

Carson asked, "What's his name?"

"Emmanuel." And now, like when Carson started his panicked babbling, and much the same as when Borrick's irritation and self-pity was unbottled, I couldn't stop myself. "The day he finished sixth form, he was off, with my dad's blessing. Started making a name for himself in months—another *famous* Brand." The words were venomous, sarcastic. "But then when I came close, when I wanted to follow him, they said, 'Mira, you can't follow your brother. You're meant to go to university, see? You're not supposed to be a Seeker!'"

I shook my head. The words still stung. So did the looks on their faces, falsely kind, like they were talking to a girl steeped in fantastical delusions that needed to be broken.

"It's all I ever wanted though. To be a Seeker. Ever since I was a kid. And they never—not *once*—supported me, told me that I could do it, that they believed in me. Not *once*." This last, a whisper. "Everything for him ... nothing for me.

"But now ..."

I raised the Chalice Gloria.

The jewels embedded in its surface glinted.

"You showed them," said Carson.

Had I?

"I guess," I admitted, to myself more than him. I scrutinized it. "I mean, it's a good find. Solid. And when word gets around ..."

When I didn't go on, Carson prompted, "But?"

"But it's only a start," I said. "It'll get attention—a lot of it, you know? But ... I don't just retire after this; I don't go home and toss this at them and say, 'There you go, Mum and Dad. You said I couldn't, and now look what I did.' Being a Seeker—it's a *life*, not a moment. A career. And you don't build a career out of one success."

"You could," Carson said earnestly. "Harper Lee did, with *To Kill a Mockingbird.*"

I tamped down a smile. "Fair point. But that's not what

I want. I want to be known for more than one thing. More than this."

"You want to beat your brother."

"No," I said, too hastily. After a hesitation, I corrected: "Okay, yes, I do—but not just that. I want my parents to say that they were wrong. I want them to tell me that I'm right. That I *can* do this."

"Seems to me like you proved it."

I stared into my ruby-red reflection, bounced back from one of the Chalice's gemstones.

Had I? I was so sure of it … but now, with the Chalice Gloria in hand, I was certain I was wrong. I hadn't proved it—not yet. I felt more like I'd just started—taken the very first step.

"You asked if it was worth it," I said at last. "And … I think so. But I was prepared to lose it, too—to rescue you. And if I had …" I glanced past the Chalice, at him, met eyes I wanted to look away from. "… well, that would have been worth it too."

The ghost of a smile crested his lips, tugged up on one side.

"Thank you."

I nodded and let my eyes drop back to my prize—and away from Carson. Not for the first time tonight, I remembered that he was leaving soon. For all my fighting, up to even just this afternoon, I was acutely aware that suddenly, I didn't want him to go. Didn't want this little hideout to go back to being dead quiet save for the times when I got bored and lonely and started singing or talking to myself.

It came back to me; him talking on the platform with Feruiduin's Cutlass. About his parents being dead.

"Do you have any siblings?" I asked.

"Huh? Oh, err. No."

"Grandparents?"

"Nope."

"Aunts? Uncles?"

Carson shook his head. The smile came back. This time, it was sad.

"Just me, now."

He was alone. And my heart ached for him.

I leaned forward. "So where are you going to—"

But then Heidi stepped in from the main chamber, and I cut myself off. This wasn't a "moment" *per se*, but it was close enough to something Heidi didn't seem to like. I figured I'd spare her—for now.

She seemed to have realized she'd interrupted something, because she looked somewhat awkward. A little like Carson yesterday, outside Piccadilly Circus.

"So, the Order of Apdau, then ..." she said at last, to fill the quiet. "What do you think they showed up for?"

I eased back in my seat, frowned, shook my head. Except for the tiny slice of information Lady Angelica had given me, I still was in the dark, both as to who they were and why they were after me.

"No clue," I said. "And it doesn't matter—at least, for now."

"You think they're still out there?" Carson asked.

"Sunk in the hurricane, I hope," I said. I doubted it, though. They'd gone through worse trying to get to me.

I pushed them out of my thoughts. Today had been a success. I saved my friend—my *friend*, that was right—and hadn't needed to give up on my dreams of claiming the Chalice Gloria either.

Speaking of:

"I was thinking," I said to Heidi, rising to meet her. My hand delved for my back pocket. "You, uh, seemed pretty good with this thing."

I extended the speaker—Feruiduin's Cutlass—to her.

She frowned at it, eyebrow raised. "You're just giving it to me?"

"I only really needed it to get this." I lifted the Chalice. "Plus, I have a spear now. And like I said: you were pretty good with it. Figured you might want to keep it on you,

you know? Just in case, or whatever."

"Um. Okay. Uh. Wow." She took it, looking it over, a little boggled. "Thanks."

"No problem. Thank you for helping."

There was an awkward quiet for a moment.

Then, very slowly, Heidi reached into her pocket. She drew out a piece of paper, folded and ancient, leathery and beaten through years of weathering. I peered at it, wondering for a brief moment if it was something I'd left in the jeans before she'd borrowed them? No, couldn't be. This was something Heidi had moved there herself.

"I have this, um, this one treasure," she said slowly, unfolding it carefully, "that I've been after for a while." She placed it on the circular table the chairs were arranged around. "But I can't ..." She took a deep breath. "I can't do it alone."

I lifted an eyebrow.

Carson bowed forward in his seat. His lips moved, sounding out a name that I knew meant absolutely nothing to him.

I expected him to ask what it was.

Instead, he looked up, eyes bright and alert, not at all the look of a man who'd not slept since the night before last, and said, "So when do we start?"

We looked at each other, all three of us.

*Us.*

A team.

We were going to keep going.

"Well," Heidi began, and we shuffled in close—to hear where the next adventure would take us.

# Epilogue

Mira and Carson fell asleep almost immediately, their breathing regulated and heavy.

Heidi, completely awake, listened for them to sink just a little deeper ...

Carson let out a soft snore and shifted in his sleep.

That was it.

She rose.

Tiptoeing silently from her room and into the library, she slunk beneath the dim glow of the lights overhead to the wall with the scrap of paper on which "LONDON" was written. Then, glancing behind her to check Mira and Carson had not woken, she slipped her bracelet down her wrist so she could squeeze the talisman there in her fingers, and cut open a gateway.

For a moment, she admired its widening edges. It was not like Mira's; hers had a slightly shaky quality, as though drawn by a hand that she could not steady, making the brilliant white glow shimmer. Neither was it like the gateway Carson had opened, ragged and torn and almost half-formed, without any in-between space. Hers was thin and controlled, a perfect gateway from a steady soul who knew exactly what she wanted to accomplish.

Then it was wide enough to step through, and she went.

If London was ever truly deserted, Heidi did not know when that would be. But this was close enough: the street held only a couple of stragglers, couples mostly, making their way to someplace or another.

She would blend in perfectly.

She slunk along the Strand, then past the Duchess Theatre on Catherine Street. It split in a crossroads just past it, Tavistock Street forking left and right.

She crossed over.

Talisman in hand, she checked around to see if anyone was near—no one, at least for the moment—and then cut open a new gateway at the corner. No compass, like Mira's—but then, she knew where this gateway led. She'd followed it plenty of times before.

Before stepping through, she clasped the Bluetooth speaker tight.

A city loomed on the other side, also clad in velvet night. The architecture looked as though London had bled through: Victorian-style buildings with grand spires reared, all elaborate brickwork and magnificent. But they were just a little off from London, as though seen through a fractured lens: they stuck out in obtuse angles, entire wings out of alignment and without a support in sight.

The green glow leaking from the streetlights, orbs mounted on zigzagging steel rods, further reminded her that she had stepped away from London.

Factories, wedge-shaped or rectangular or a whole unnameable series of spastic jags, were nestled between the brick buildings. Dark, reflective metal without windows, they belched smoke into a night sky that was lit by only a handful of stars, and the moon: full and much larger than the one Heidi knew from home, but far more pallid and sickly.

Like the street she had just left behind, these ones were empty.

Heidi set off. The speaker had transformed into Feruiduin's Cutlass automatically on transitioning, and she squeezed its grip.

Two blocks later, and an alley loomed. A familiar one.

She ducked in.

Halfway down, where the alien glow from the streets could not press any farther, something skittered past her.

She tensed, spinning, cutlass drawn. Breath caught in her throat.

The alley's mouth was empty. Just a rat … or the dog-like things that passed for them here, anyway.

"Good evening."

Heidi turned.

A figure emerged from the darkest end of the alley. If not for the voice, it could be anyone, it was so dark.

"I hope I didn't startle you," the figure said.

Heidi lowered the cutlass. "I thought maybe I'd missed you."

"You're late." Without waiting for Heidi's excuse, the shadow launched right in: "Does she know why the Order of Apdau are after her?"

Heidi fired back, "Do you?"

"No." Barely visible, Heidi caught the subtle shift of shadows: the figure shaking their head. "The Order has always been thorny, with their vague holy mission to stop Seekers. But never like this. Not across such distance. And certainly not to our world. Attack, strike, harass, yes—but they never follow a person to Earth and darken their doorstep. Very peculiar indeed."

"Do you think they'll come back?" Heidi asked.

"Hard to say." A pause, and the figure moved on. "You will continue to keep an eye on Mira Brand." It was not a question but a statement, a rehash of the facts as they stood. "In exchange, I will grant you what you want most, Ms. Luo. Are those terms acceptable?"

Heidi swallowed, throat dry. In opposition, her palm had started to sweat on the cutlass's grip, and she rearranged her fingers around it.

"Yes. I'll watch her for you."

"Good." The figure straightened to full height. "Inform me if anything changes, or if the Order appears again. I expect they will."

There it was. Confirmation.

"I also expect," the shadow continued, "she isn't going to give up and go home either, is she?"

"I wouldn't count on it. She's already—*we're* already," Heidi corrected quickly, "planning our next job."

The silhouette tilted its head. A faint shaft of light managed to press far enough to illuminate a faint smile on lips edged by lines.

"Keep her close."

"As you will it." Heidi nodded, the perfect submission of a soul who knew where her true allegiance lay. "As you will it."

Mira Brand Will Return in

# THE TIDE
# OF AGES

**The Mira Brand Adventures,
Book 2**

**Available now!**

# Author's Note

And so begins a new saga—new heroine, new world, new places, new adventures. You may be forgiven if you've never heard of me before—Robert J. Crane, I'm the author here, pleased to make your acquaintance—but I've been at this a while. This is my forty … uh … somethingth book, (you kind of lose count after a while, rather like birthdays—especially, when, like me, you've written more books than you've actually had birthdays), and so this is not my first rodeo. If this is your first adventure in one of my worlds, I hope you've enjoyed it and want to go on. In the pages that follow, you'll find a listing of my other books, including some upcoming volumes. Book 2 of this series is available now, as is book 3, and further ones are currently in the works. If you run out of those … well, I can certainly offer you some other options to keep you busy until the next Mira adventure …

To wrap things up, let me say thanks for reading! If you want to know immediately when future books become available, take sixty seconds and sign up for my NEW RELEASE EMAIL ALERTS by visiting my website. I don't sell your information and I only send out emails when I have a new book out. The reason you should sign up for this is because I don't always set release dates, and even if you're following me on Facebook (robertJcrane (Author)) or Twitter (@robertJcrane), it's easy to miss my book announcements because...well, because social media is an imprecise thing.

Come join the discussion on my website:
http://www.robertjcrane.com!

Cheers,
Robert J. Crane

# ACKNOWLEDGMENTS

Editorial/Literary Janitorial duties performed by Nick Bowman and Sarah Barbour. Final proofing was once more handled by the illustrious Jo Evans. Any errors you see in the text, however, are the result of me rejecting changes.

The cover was once designed by Momir Borocki.

The formatting was provided by nickbowmanediting.com.

Once more, thanks to my parents, my in-laws, my kids and my wife, for helping me keep things together.

# Other Works by Robert J. Crane

## World of Sanctuary
*Epic Fantasy*

Defender: The Sanctuary Series, Volume One
Avenger: The Sanctuary Series, Volume Two
Champion: The Sanctuary Series, Volume Three
Crusader: The Sanctuary Series, Volume Four
Sanctuary Tales, Volume One - A Short Story Collection
Thy Father's Shadow: The Sanctuary Series, Volume 4.5
Master: The Sanctuary Series, Volume Five
Fated in Darkness: The Sanctuary Series, Volume 5.5
Warlord: The Sanctuary Series, Volume Six
Heretic: The Sanctuary Series, Volume Seven
Legend: The Sanctuary Series, Volume Eight
Ghosts of Sanctuary: The Sanctuary Series, Volume Nine*
*(Coming 2018, at earliest.)*

A Haven in Ash: Ashes of Luukessia, Volume One* *(Coming Fall 2017!)*

## The Girl in the Box
*and*
## Out of the Box
*Contemporary Urban Fantasy*

Alone: The Girl in the Box, Book 1
Untouched: The Girl in the Box, Book 2
Soulless: The Girl in the Box, Book 3
Family: The Girl in the Box, Book 4
Omega: The Girl in the Box, Book 5
Broken: The Girl in the Box, Book 6
Enemies: The Girl in the Box, Book 7

Legacy: The Girl in the Box, Book 8
Destiny: The Girl in the Box, Book 9
Power: The Girl in the Box, Book 10

Limitless: Out of the Box, Book 1
In the Wind: Out of the Box, Book 2
Ruthless: Out of the Box, Book 3
Grounded: Out of the Box, Book 4
Tormented: Out of the Box, Book 5
Vengeful: Out of the Box, Book 6
Sea Change: Out of the Box, Book 7
Painkiller: Out of the Box, Book 8
Masks: Out of the Box, Book 9
Prisoners: Out of the Box, Book 10
Unyielding: Out of the Box, Book 11
Hollow: Out of the Box, Book 12
Toxicity: Out of the Box, Book 13
Small Things: Out of the Box, Book 14
Hunters: Out of the Box, Book 15
Badder: Out of the Box, Book 16* *(Coming September 12, 2017!)*

# Southern Watch
*Contemporary Urban Fantasy*

Called: Southern Watch, Book 1
Depths: Southern Watch, Book 2
Corrupted: Southern Watch, Book 3
Unearthed: Southern Watch, Book 4
Legion: Southern Watch, Book 5
Starling: Southern Watch, Book 6* *(Coming Fall 2017!)*

# The Shattered Dome Series
*(with Nicholas J. Ambrose)*
*Sci-Fi*

Voiceless: The Shattered Dome, Book 1
Unspeakable: The Shattered Dome, Book 2* *(Coming 2017 –*
*Tentatively)*

# The Mira Brand Adventures
*Contemporary Urban Fantasy*

The World Beneath: The Mira Brand Adventures, Book 1
The Tide of Ages: The Mira Brand Adventures, Book 2
The City of Lies: The Mira Brand Adventures, Book 3
The King of the Skies: The Mira Brand Adventures, Book 4*
*(Coming Late 2017!)*

# Liars and Vampires
*(with Lauren Harper)*
*Contemporary Urban Fantasy*

No One Will Believe You: Liars and Vampires, Book 1*
*(Coming Fall 2017!)*

*Forthcoming, Subject to Change

Made in the USA
Middletown, DE
22 December 2020